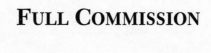

FULL COMMISSION

Also by Carol Brennan

Headhunt

FULL COMMISSION

A Liz Wareham Mystery

Carol Brennan

Carroll & Graf Publishers, Inc.
New York

Copyright © 1993 by Carol Brennan

First Carroll & Graf edition 1993

Carroll & Graf Publishers, Inc.
260 Fifth Avenue
New York, N.Y. 10001

Library of Congress Cataloging-in-Publication Data is available.

ISBN:0-88184-911-1

Manufactured in the United States of America

To Eamon
for all the reasons he knows, and for the things that go without
saying—but too often go unsaid.

Acknowledgments

To the Carroll & Graf team—especially Margaret Norton,
for continuing to teach me, and Laura Langlie, for being such a
joy to work with.

To Anita Diamant, for her expertise and generosity of spirit.

To my buddies at The Corcoran Group, with admiration for
their indomitable optimism and thanks for the great broker
talk.

Chapter 1

I stood on the corner of Charles and Bleecker, shifting from one foot to another and waving my frozen right hand at a cab that was yet to appear. It was well after midnight. Sunday. The kind of hard-bitten, too-cold-for-snow February weather that keeps anybody with any sense off the street. A laughing gay couple hurried along past me, their arms around each other, heading downtown toward the warmth of a Christopher Street bar or their apartment. I wished I were one of them, with someone's arm around me, and that *he* were hailing the cab. Maybe he'd have better luck. I put my left hand on duty and burrowed my right into the pocket of my fur-lined raincoat.

"It be okay, baby, he see you," said a tall black man wrapped in a khaki army coat three sizes too big for his skinny frame. He tipped a flat bottle to his lips and shambled past, not even bothering to panhandle. For the moment he had everything he needed.

He was right, though. I'd been so absorbed in the frustration of not finding a cab that I'd failed to notice one had appeared.

"Central Park West and Eighty-fourth," I told the driver as I flexed my toes to see if they were still with me.

"You got it." I recognized the accent as Israeli. The upbeat tone in his deep voice matched the jazz coming at me from the rear speakers of his toasty cab. "No night to be out alone," he tossed over his shoulder as he pulled away from the curb and headed west on Charles, "wadjoo have a fight with the boyfriend?" The white smile might have been winning had I been in any mood to be won.

As it happened, he was precisely right. "No," I said. The edge I heard in my own voice made it clear to Elie Halevi that a conversation with me wouldn't be a lot of fun. He pursued one no further. Elie Halevi. His driver photo smiled the same confident smile he'd given me a second ago. Thirty? Maybe a little older. Did he own the taxi or was he driving for some other, more entrepreneurial Israeli? I closed my eyes. Why was my brain nattering on about the goddamned cab driver? Just to keep it off Ike and how furious I was at him—and at myself.

Maybe I'd been unreasonable, a frequent accusation by husbands one and two. After all, the call had been from his broker. It was *business.* Only it had been past midnight. Only his broker looked like a *Vogue* cover. Only the conversation had gone on a hell of a long time with more chatting and chuckling than I'd felt like listening to from a man who'd just made love to me, and on whose chest I'd been dozing when the phone rang.

That bastard! I could feel my face burn as I reprised the scene. After fifteen, twenty minutes I'd reached across his chest and pressed the phone button down in mid-chuckle.

"What the hell do you think you're doing?" Ike had roared as he sat up and fixed me with the frigid blue look that probably chilled murder suspects all over Manhattan into babbling submission.

"If you think I'm just going to lie here," I responded, upping the decibel ante—I've known Ike O'Hanlon far too long to be afraid of him—"while you play midnight phone footsie with some—"

"Jeannie's my *broker,* for chrissake. We were planning an important strategy . . ." Maybe such nocturnal confabs were the reason he'd made it into the seven figures, and could live in a restored nineteenth-century firehouse in Greenwich Village rather than a postwar two-bedroom apartment in Bensonhurst like other homicide lieutenants, but I was too mad to care.

"Bull*shit.*" I couldn't see my panty hose, so I pulled my jeans on over a bare butt and my boots onto bare feet. "Your strategy"—I put mocking quotes around the word—"took a whole five minutes. I'm talking about the rest of it, you thick Mick son of a bitch." I hooked my bra and put my sweater on.

"I am deeply offended by your ethnic slur," he said solemnly. Maybe he could tease me out of it. A glance at my face told him he couldn't. "Besides," he continued, giving it another try, "in the eyes of organized Jewry, I'm a thick *Jew*—Jewish mother, after all, and—"

"Just shove it, O'Hanlon, okay?" I snapped.

"Come on, Lizzie, you're acting like a spoiled teenager. Just like—"

"Oh, you want to talk about *that,* do you?" I shrieked. "That" had happened twenty-six years and three marriages—two for me and one for Ike—ago. But I was still capable of feeling sore at the recollection of Ike ejecting me from his father's Nash at three in the morning after my high school senior prom, following a heated difference of opinion: I'd thought that he'd danced too many times with Jeanette Albano; he'd disagreed.

"Oh, cool down, will you? Look, Liz, if we're going to live together, you can't—"

"We're *not* going to live together," I shot out, my anger of the moment eclipsing all other feelings. I grabbed my big black shoulder bag and ran out of the room while I still had the last word.

The cab made the slight jog that put us on Central Park West. It's amazing how fast you can get around the city at—what was it, I looked at my watch—1:15 A.M. Suddenly my eye caught a flash of action in the deserted street. A tall, overcoated man was grabbing the arm of a frail-looking woman in a pink bathrobe, who didn't look as though she was enjoying it a bit.

"Stop the cab."

"Huh?"

"He's hurting her. Halevi, stop the cab." Maybe it was the unexpected sound of his name on my lips, or maybe the command summoned up memories of some army captain who'd made his life miserable, but he turned west on Sixty-first and lurched to a stop with no New York protestations about the dangers of getting involved in other people's hassles.

We both jumped out of the cab, surprising the combatants into a second of silent stillness, as though posed for an eccentric snapshot. He was in his middle forties. Six feet, give or take, with dark straight hair that grew in an upside-down *W.* The hair was mussed, and dark red blood ran from the left side of his high, sloped forehead down his furious, fox face, just missing a small, deep-set dark eye. She was smaller than my own five four by a good two inches and wouldn't have weighed in at more than 102 even after a steak dinner. Her wispy hair was a mercurochrome red, which made no bow toward subtlety. At seventy-five—which is where I put her age—I figure you can be as unsubtle as you want. The pink chenille bathrobe and carpet slippers reminded me of a similar outfit my grandmother used to wear. She must have been freezing.

"Get your hands off her," I said, "and let me take her inside. She'll catch pneumonia." Was he a burglar? A nut? Her son? I was too angry to be scared.

"Ahhh no! This crazy, old bitch tried to kill me." The hand that wasn't gripping the woman gestured up toward his wounded forehead. "You see that? She assaulted me. I called 911. Until the cops get here, she doesn't move." He yanked her arm for emphasis, and she tried uselessly to break free.

"Hey, buddy, let the lady take her into the lobby to get warm," Halevi said quietly. I'd forgotten he was there, but was relieved to notice that though he was a good four inches shorter than Chief Bleeding Forehead, he was sufficiently burlier and younger to be a likely winner in a street fight. "Come on, she's an old lady. She's shivering. You want her to get sick? She's not going nowhere—just into the lobby."

The man released her arm. She stepped back and glared at him. "Motherfucker put rats in my apartment," she barked in a contralto that bespoke decades of cigarettes and booze.

Halevi and I exchanged quick "she's nuts" looks.

"Crazy old bitch," the man repeated, taking a menacing step toward her. She squared her thin shoulders and looked up at him with her bony chin stuck out in defiance. For a second I could see the girl she'd once been.

"You don't scare me, Zeibach. And neither does your boss." She turned to me. "Some big man," she said, her watery blue eyes narrowing in scorn. "Rats!" A gust of frigid wind attacked the bottom of her robe, revealing stark-white bird legs. I unbuttoned my coat, slipped out of it, and put it over her shoulders. Then I took her arm.

"Come on, let's go inside," I said, leading her through the

building's front door, which shut behind us with a rusty clank. The building was typical 1920's Upper West Side gone to seed. The marble floor was cracked, the iron grillwork on the front door mostly rusted. The rush of comforting warmth I'd expected was notably absent. I glanced toward the inner door, which was slightly ajar.

"Is there a doorman?" I asked.

"Hah!" she replied with a hoarse snort. "They dumped the doorman eight months ago when he bought the building. Also, they used to give heat. Not much of that now either, thanks to Mr. Alfred Stover and his stooge out there."

Alfred Stover. Of course. This was Sixty-first Street. It hadn't clicked immediately. "Westover," I said. "Your building's part of Westover." Stover was a British developer who'd moved very quietly into New York about six years before. He'd bought and upgraded a few office buildings in the Wall Street area, filled them with high-paying foreign tenants, and promptly sold them for megaprofits—how mega one could only speculate, because Alfie Stover's idea of an answer to any question involving a number was "a grite deal" or "no' a lo'," both uttered in an accent Professor Higgins would not have applauded. I'd gotten to know Alfie Stover pretty well because I'd handled his public relations during those early years. Our parting had not been a happy one.

"Don't give me Westover. There ain't gonna *be* a Westover. Not unless that bastard wants to build around us." The husky voice had an intensity that signaled trouble for Alfie Stover or anybody else who thought he might be dealing with a pushover little old lady.

The controversy between Stover's grand plan for a mammoth residential and office condo and the narrow twelve-story apartment building it would displace had been all over the media at least once a week since Stover had closed his deal on the corner. I suddenly remembered that quote, minus the "bastard," from last week's *Times.* It had been attributed to "the feisty eighty-one-year-old head of the tenants' committee."

"You're Ada Fauer, aren't you?" I asked with a sincerely admiring smile.

"That's right, honey. Who're you?"

"I'm Liz Wareham. I—" Just then a blue-and-white jerked to a stop a foot and a half wide of the curb and two uniformed cops rushed out of it. "Wait here for a minute, okay? I'm going to talk to the cops and see if we can't—"

"Oh, no! I'm only too glad they're here. I'll tell 'em a thing or two. I'll tell 'em about the rats and—"

"Ms. Fauer—"

"Ada, honey. Everybody calls me Ada."

"Ada, let me be straight with you; we don't have a lot of time. It'll be better to cool it with the cops, if we can. He . . . Zeibach is going to claim that you . . . uh, imagined about the rats and—"

"And I'm a crazy old bitch like he said. Well, I got all my marbles, honey. *He* should only have the marbles I got."

"I believe you, Ada." I did for some reason, maybe just because Zeibach looked like the kind of guy who'd put rats in your apartment if he thought it would get him what he wanted. "But the problem is, the police may not. And they could take you to a hospital or something." A look of horror crossed her face at the thought of being dragged off to Bellevue for observation. I pushed my advantage. "Look, public relations is what I do. Let me do it for you with the cops. We'll get this settled, and then you can—"

"Go to the papers about the rats later."

"I'm going to offer you a PR job if you don't watch out." I squeezed her shoulder, which felt nonexistent under my heavy coat. "Now, when I bring the cops in, just follow my lead and don't say one word more than you have to to answer their questions. Got it?"

"Got it," she said with a smile that crinkled her small eyes and made her upper lip almost disappear.

I swung the rusty door open and walked over to where the group was standing.

"And out of the blue this crazy old b—woman just—" Zeibach, still holding his handkerchief to his head, though the blood seemed to have congealed, was an upstanding, outraged citizen appealing to New York's Finest to protect him. The Finest, in the present instance, were represented by a chunky jet-black man of about thirty who looked as though he had a good sense of humor, and a tall, thin, rabbity, blond woman, maybe five years older, who looked as though she didn't. The ID tags on their parkas said that he was Jessup and she, Christiansen.

"Excuse me," I said, "my name is Liz Wareham. This gentleman and I"—I gestured toward Halevi—"happened to be driving by and stopped to help. There's a whole nother side to this story and—" Jessup smiled and made a football "T for time" sign with his heavily gloved hands.

"I bet there's a coupla other sides," he said. "Anyplace a little warmer we can go to hear 'em, like inside?"

"Suits me," I said, realizing that I'd become so absorbed that I'd forgotten to feel cold. "But I don't think you'll find it much warmer in the lobby," I added with a dirty look at Zeibach. I took two tens out of my wallet and reached out to Halevi. "Look, I'm sorry you're getting held up like this. Officers, can Mr. Halevi go? He can't tell you any more than I can, and this is costing him money."

He handed one of the tens back to me. "Ten's enough. And I will stay. I want to be sure the old lady's okay. He grinned. "Reminds me of my bubby back in Tel Aviv—tough, you know?"

As the two cops led us into the building, I hung back for a moment and buttonholed Zeibach. "You know, Mr. Zeibach, if you press charges here, you could wind up hurting yourself and Mr. Stover a lot more than Ms. Fauer."

"What do you mean?" he asked sharply, turning suspicious beady blacks on me.

"Well, public relations is what I do for a living," I responded, feeling a little foolish at volunteering my credentials yet again. "My advice, though I know you didn't ask me," I added quickly, "is not to put yourself and Mr. Stover in a position of seeming to mistreat a poor old woman who's just trying to hang on to her home."

"Who the hell are you to"—his face flushed to a dull red—"Think how it'll look if you insist on having her arrested. The papers. The TV crews. She'll say you sneaked into her apartment and let rats loose to force her to move. Then there'll be the questions about what were you doing in her hall at two in the morning. And about the doorman who's not here anymore. And the inner door that doesn't shut. And no heat in February. Where do you think the sympathy'll be?"

He took it in for a couple of seconds without replying, and I could see his high dudgeon lower as resignation moved in. "Hmm," he grunted irritably, "you may have a point."

Now all I had to do was get rid of the cops while everyone was still reasonable. As Zeibach and I entered the vestibule, I saw that I might be a little late.

". . . and I was on my way to take a . . . to use the bathroom when I heard someone trying to open the door. So I go and get Jack's Louisville Slugger. My Jack—passed away two years now—he always kept the Slugger handy backstage and in the boardinghouses. We played some pretty rough towns, you know, specially when the coffin nails got to the old pipes and the Warbling Fauers couldn't get the top bookings anymore. You know what I started to do then?" Without waiting for an answer, Ada cupped her hands near her mouth and emitted a sound that was a dead ringer for a prize canary.

"Mrs. Fauer," Christiansen cut in with an edge to her voice slightly colder than the temperature inside the vestibule, "please keep to the point." She glanced at the notes she'd been taking in her spiral book. "So you took this baseball bat and went to the door, right?"

"Right. And who should it be but this bastard, and he's openin' a box with—" I scooted around in back of the cops and wigwagged frantically at Ada, shaking my head no.

"She's imagining all this," Zeibach said with a we-understand-each-other smile. "There *was* no box. You know, when they get to be that age . . ." He twirled his finger next to his ear.

"I'm not nuts, you lowlife," Ada rasped.

"At ease, troops," Jessup broke in. His voice was a mellow, calming bass. "What were you doin' at this lady's door at two in the morning, Mr. Zeibach?" he asked politely.

"I'm in charge of this building for Stover International, Officer. One of the other tenants reported to me that Mrs. Fauer was making funny noises and might be having some kind of attack, so I came to check it out."

"Don't make me laugh, Zeibach. Those walls are two feet thick. Nobody can hear a thing through 'em. Besides, you'd dance in the street if you thought I was sick."

"You have a key to her apartment because you run the building?" Jessup asked skeptically.

"Well, Officer, in case we need to get in to fix something, or—"

"Fix something!" Ada exploded. "When was the last time anything around here got fixed?" She turned to the two cops. "You like the weather in here, folks? That's—" She caught my insistent head shake and stopped.

"Look, Officers," Zeibach said with a pass at graciousness, "I'm not going to press charges here, so why don't we just drop it." I gave Ada a warning look and put my finger to my lips. She compressed her thin mouth and didn't say a word, though it was obvious she was dying to.

"You gonna press charges, Mrs. Fauer?" Jessup asked, fixing his large round eyes on her.

"No," Ada said softly, not meeting his gaze. I silently applauded her self-control.

"Well," Christiansen sniffed, "you two could probably have worked this out on your own." She added self-righteously, "Nine eleven is for emergencies. Let's have everybody's names, addresses, and phones." For her, the whole incident was a variation on a domestic dispute, the police euphemism for anything short of murder that family members do to each other.

Nobody gave her any mouth. We all wanted her and Jessup, nice as he was, to leave as quickly as possible. They did, but not before Jessup had taken Ada's thin hand in his big, gloved one and said, "You get your lock changed, Mrs. Fauer, hear? And don't give the key to anyone, 'cept maybe a neighbor you like."

Chapter 2

"Thank you for your help, Miss Wareham," Zeibach said smoothly. He turned to Halevi. "And yours, Mr.—uh. I'm sure you both want to get home, and we've taken up too much of your time already with this"—he smiled with effort—"unfortunate misunderstanding."

"No misunderstanding," Ada croaked in pretty accurate parody of his nouveau-suave intonation. "You put rats in my apartment. The cops are gone now. You can cut the act. You just trot back and tell Stover he's not gonna win. This is my home and I'm not leaving it till I go feet first!"

"It's okay, Mr. Zeibach," I said, "I think I'll stick around a bit longer. Make sure Ada's all right."

"You want me to take you someplace else to stay, Ada? You got a son, a daughter maybe?" Halevi asked with a concerned look. Before she could answer, Zeibach muscled in.

"Look, you can both butt out now, understand?" So much for civility. It didn't suit him anyway. "It's not a good idea to mix into matters that are none of your business." He fixed first Halevi, then me with hard black eyes, the left one puffy and bloodshot.

Halevi advanced on him a couple of slow steps, his hands at his sides. "You're gonna have one terrific shiner in the morning, champ," he said quietly. "You don't get your ass outa here in about three seconds, I'll arrange a matched set." Now I knew one thing for sure about Elie Halevi. He watched lots of forties movies.

Zeibach's face went almost purple as he decided that Halevi wasn't bluffing. He turned furiously and opened the door, letting in a new gust of icy wind. I couldn't resist a parting shot. "Two Excedrin, Mr. Zeibach, and cold compresses. You can always say you ran into a wall if you think being beaten up by a senior citizen would be bad for your image." The door shut with a rattling slam that threatened to disable it, and he was gone.

The three of us waited a beat. Then Ada started to laugh—a real laugh, free and throaty, that unloaded years from her. It was contagious. Within seconds we were all in tears with laughter.

"Most fun I've had in a year," Ada gasped when she was able to catch her breath. "Boy, didya see his face?" The recollection sent her into new peals.

I wiped my streaming eyes and said, "Seriously, Ada, do you have anyone to stay with for what's left of tonight?"

"I'll go up and sleep on Percy's couch. He's gonna want to know about this rat stuff anyway."

"Oh, a neighbor," I said, "great!" Percy. My mind drew a sketch of a wizened old party walking his poodle.

"Yeah, Percy *is* great. He's the *real* head of the tenants' committee, ya know. We just put me out front 'cause it's more dramatic—an old lady and all. I guess I better give him a call first. Make sure he's alone." Her wink made clear what he might be doing in case he wasn't. My mental sketch underwent a quick revision. A *raunchy* old man.

Chapter 3

It turned out that Percy *was* alone and eager to have Ada come right up. Maybe this crisis would brew a twilight romance. I smiled to myself—a sweet idea. Halevi and I escorted Ada to the elevator, I gave her my card, home number scrawled on the back. "If you have any more trouble with Zeibach, give me a call. I don't know if I can be of any *real* help, but . . ."

She leaned over, face uptilted, and kissed my cheek—a dry bird peck. "You've been a lotta help already."

Halevi put his arms around her, lifted her off the ground, and planted a healthy buss on her cheek. "You're a great girl, bubby. I'm gonna keep an eye on you, so don't you worry."

I climbed into the front seat of Halevi's cab with him. It took us almost no time to cover the fifteen blocks to my apartment at Eighty-fourth and Central Park West. As we pulled up in front of the building, he flashed me one of his dazzling smiles. "So maybe we can see each other, Liz? If you don't have a boy-friend."

I gave him a sisterly kiss. "I'm really flattered, Halevi, but I've got a vicious temper and a lousy track record with men. I think you deserve better." I jumped out of the cab and made for the lobby before I could change my mind.

As my key turned in the lock, the soft thump of padded feet and a two-part harmony of meows announced that Elephi and Three were ready for an early breakfast. I waded through the frenzied furriness wrapped around my legs to the kitchen, where I reached for a can of creamed kidneys. I scooped the food into their bowl with the can lid and gave them fresh water.

With an abrupt thud the euphoria of the Zeibach victory deserted me. I headed down the hall to my bedroom, feeling depleted and alone in an apartment that suddenly seemed huge and peculiarly unfamiliar. Since Scott and Sarah had left for

college in September, I'd been spending so much time with Ike
O'Hanlon that I hadn't been home a whole lot. Maybe that was
it.

Ike. My gut gave a little glitch. He'd been my first love—when
I was nine and he was the big boy around the corner who did
exciting things like play hooky and run away from home. He'd
been my first lover, too, when I was seventeen, and I've never
had a better one. I hadn't seen Ike for twenty-six years—not
since our fight the night of my senior prom. Then, last fall, a
client of mine had been killed and there he was, in charge of the
case.

I plunked myself down on the bed and checked the message
machine next to the phone on the night table. A big zero. Goddamn him! He hadn't even called to see whether I'd gotten
home. But he hadn't *wanted* me to go home. Why did I have to
run off like a snotty . . . ? Well, why did *he* have to be such a
. . . ? The tears started to roll down my cheeks. I rubbed them
away with my fists. Dammit, why couldn't I just find myself an
easier man? I knew the answer to that one. I *had* found easier
men, but I wasn't an easier woman. I knew the prudent thing
would be to crawl into bed and catch a couple of hours sleep.
But I wasn't feeling prudent or sleepy. I pulled off my boots and
padded back down the hall toward the living room.

My apartment is a sprawling 1920's three-bedroom with two
bathrooms, plus a maid's room and another tiny bath off the
kitchen—what real estate agents call a classic seven. It also has
a WBFP, FDR, and hi beamed ceilings. It's worth about a million dollars, and would go for more if it had a full park vu,
instead of the open city vu it does have. The reason I was up on
all this real estate agentalia was that the place had been on the
market for the last three weeks, since the day I told Ike
O'Hanlon I'd come live with him in his firehouse.

As I entered the living room and snapped on a fat blue gin-
ger-jar lamp, the apartment snapped back into focus for me. I
loved this place. I really did, and had since Alan Bernchiller,
husband number one, and I had bought it, with an assist from
my parents, for fifty thousand dollars fifteen years ago. I had
painted and scraped and sanded it into shape, while Alan had

concentrated on building his ob/gyn practice. Scott and Sarah had grown up here.

Suddenly I shivered with a chill that was bone-deep. All that coatless standing around had finally gotten to me. A drink in front of the fire seemed like a swell idea. I stuck a packaged sawdust log onto the grate, with a real one on top, and put a match to it. Then I went to the long harvest table I use for a bar and poured a generous tot of Hennessey into a snifter, which I carried back to one of the squashy red sofas that form an L around the fireplace.

I took the big paisley shawl from the back of the sofa and wrapped myself in it. Then I burrowed into the cushions, legs tucked under me, staring into the flames, while my warring emotions chased one another from head to gut and back again. I sipped my brandy and felt the tears renew themselves. Screw it! I *wouldn't* sell the apartment. This was my home and here I'd stay—just like Ada Fauer, till they carried me out feetfirst.

Chapter 4

I spent the next few hours nipping at the brandy and listening to records—first an old Jacques Brel album, then *Pal Joey,* and finally Roger Miller, singing country home truths that cut close enough to the bone to make me wince. By the time I felt ready to sack out, it was seven A.M., so I settled for a long, hot shower, shampoo, and coffee. The results were middling successful. I was no longer sleepy; instead, I was so revved up that when Gus, the daytime doorman, called out a cheery good morning as I got off the elevator, I jumped like Flo Jo approaching a ten-foot hurdle.

Normally, I walk down Central Park West to 57th Street and hop the crosstown bus to Fifth Avenue, persuading myself that the jaunt is an effective substitute for the gym I don't go to and the Exercycle I don't pedal. However, this morning I had neither the character nor the time for a stroll. It was 7:58, and Monday at The Gentle Group, the public relations agency where I ply my trade, begins with an eight A.M. meeting for senior staff—devised by our leader to keep our collective nose to the new-business-getting grindstone and to make sure no one has a doubt about when the weekend is over. Gus hailed me a cab and within seconds we were on the Eighty-first Street transverse, crossing the park.

It was 8:22 when I slipped into the gray leather swivel next to Seth Frankel, one of my two top aides. The other one, Angela Chappel, was off basking on some island so chic that nobody else had yet heard of it. I put the pearl-gray mug of black coffee I'd picked up in the office kitchen on the polished conference table in front of me. The table is gray too. So is everything in the whole office—decorator's idea of a perfect backdrop for John Gentle's silver hair, slate-gray eyes, and ruddy complexion (usually a bit ruddier after lunch). Funny thing is, it works. John raised an unamused gray eyebrow at me and continued speaking. He does not smile upon lateness to these things.

"So, congratulations, Briggs," John said with the kind of smile that crosses his face only when a chunk of new business comes in, "you sure deserve it." I turned to Seth, who silently mouthed the words "Top Round," the dogfood account that Briggs Drew and his staff had been courting for the past six months. I smiled across the table at Briggs and made a V for victory sign with my fingers. He grinned an acknowledgment. I was sincere, but not entirely.

Briggs Drew is my opposite number at The Gentle Group. We're both executive vice presidents, each handling a little over two million in fee billing. He's got a staff of nine to my eight—an intermittent point of sensitivity that makes me feel petty. We're keenly competitive, Briggs and I, which John encourages. Also, we don't much like each other. He thinks I'm a smart-ass Queens Jew, and I think he's a rod-up-the-ass Greenwich WASP. We're both right. Still, it's hard not to feel an instant flash of good for a colleague who's landed a new account.

"It was the Lovin' Puppy contest that put us over the top," Briggs said, his voice glowing with pride. "All those thousands of kids and dogs coming to Kansas City. *Good Morning America, USA Today*. They just flipped out for it."

My good flash was over, since Briggs had failed to mention that the Lovin' Puppy idea had been born in Seth Frankel's surprisingly inventive mind during an agency-wide brainstorming for the pitch. Briggs hadn't thought much of the idea at the time, but it apparently had grown on him. I gave Seth a surreptitious wink, which he countered with a quick heavenward roll of protuberant brown eyes behind thick hornrims, as if to say, What can you do? These cossacks always win. Seth's world is pretty cossack-heavy—the clients, the media, Briggs, sometimes even me—and twice a week he and his shrink plot defense strategies. If I said anything, it would look as though I were trying to muscle in on Briggs's party—to grab a piece of credit for my group. Retaliation would have to wait.

"Reminds me of the Sun Shun sunglasses race," John broke in. "I ever tell you about that?" The unspoken answer from everyone at that table was "more than once," but to interrupt John here would have been as unthinkable as telling General Washington that, yes, we all know what happened after you crossed the Delaware.

"Pigeons," he began with the practiced tones of a mommy reciting once upon a time. "I came up with the idea of pigeons. After all, who gets more sun in their eyes than birds, right? So we get this flock of carrier pigeons, and Sun Shun makes little pigeon-size sunglasses for half of them. See? Half the little guys would have the glasses and the other half wouldn't and we'd see who won the race. Of course it'd be the ones with the Sun Shuns, because they'd see better. Well"—he smiled craftily here, as he always did when he told this story—"we also made sure that the champs in the flock—the fastest ones—would have the glasses. No harm in making sure.

"Well, day before the race we have a dry run, and every goddamned one of them knocked off the Sun Shuns. Just nudged them off with their little wings. By the time they get to the Astor Hotel—that was the finish point, right there in Times Square, you're too young to remember the Astor . . .

"So we round up the pigeons at the Astor, and the handler puts them in the coop and we drag them back to the Bronx. The question is, what're we going to do? The coverage is all laid on. The *Daily News* is sending a photographer, and so is AP and *Look* magazine." He glanced around the table at our expectant faces. We all knew our lines, and in this scene nobody but John had any. "I'll tell you what we did. I called Sun Shun over in Jersey and rush-ordered new pigeon glasses. Had to holler a little, but we got them. This time we glued 'em on." He nodded and chuckled—customary at this point in the tale. "That's what we did. Glued sunglasses onto sixty fucking pigeons—took us eight hours. Lucky the ASPCA didn't get us. And I gotta tell you those little bastards performed like troupers. We had that account sewed up for the next five years."

And that's where John's heart really is, with the pigeon races, the puppy contests, the biscuit bakeoffs. He's damned good at the corporate stuff too—the kind of thing I do—and he loves the big bucks it makes, but it never really rings his chimes.

The meeting went on for another twenty minutes or so. Mostly, I just nodded when everyone else did and tried to look as though I were paying attention, which I was not. John finally released us at 9:25, but he intercepted me before I could reach the door.

"Liz, damnedest thing. I had a call right before the meeting. Alfie Stover himself. Wants to meet with us. Yeah, he said *us*— meaning you and me. Can you beat that?"

I couldn't. I also have my limits as a believer in coincidence.

"Hey"—he clapped my shoulder, which possibly looked as unenthusiastic as my face—"come on, maybe we've got a chance to win the account back."

"No, John." I shook my head. "I don't think so. Maybe you could take Briggs." Was I really saying that?

"*You*, kid. That's who he asked for. That's who he gets. Look, I know your pride's dented from the way he bounced you, but if I ran this agency on pride, we'd've been out of business years ago. Tomorrow, four-thirty, their offices." He was gone before I could say another word.

Chapter 5

I hurried along the corridor, hoping to reach my office unintercepted so I could shut myself in and decide how to handle the Alfie Stover dilemma. Few professional activities I could think of held less appeal than designing clever strategies to help Alfie throw Ada Fauer out of her home.

So far so good. I rounded the corner—the safety of my office only steps away. I ducked in and closed the door harder, in my eagerness, than I'd intended. Morley, bent over the far side of the huge bamboo palm in the corner, jumped at the sound.

"Starting our week with a bang, are we?" he drawled quizzically as he straightened his tinted aviator glasses.

"Sorry, Morley, I didn't see you back there playing Sheena of the Jungle." Morley Carton is my secretary, and there isn't a better one in New York. He's thirty-three and about the most sartorially elegant man I know—gay or straight. He can thank his Louisiana-planter genes for the great body, and a fashion photographer who admired it for the great clothes. "What's that funny smell—like stale cheese?"

"Fungicide. This dry heat's lousy for him. I put that bowl of water on top of the radiator." He gestured toward a cobalt blue vessel I'd never seen before. "That should help some." He leveled a severe look at me. "Also, you've been dumping coffee in his pot again, and you've got to stop it."

"Guilty as charged." I held my hands up, palms out. "But I'll sin no more, I promise. What makes you so sure it's a he?"

"Well, just look. You think he looks like a she?"

"I'll have to give it serious thought. But not now. I've got work to do, so I'm going to have to ask you to leave me to my smelly office." He bent down and gave the earth in the terracotta pot a final swipe with the miniature rake he kept there for his biweekly ministrations.

"I'm all done anyway," he said, brushing off his hands. "A couple of messages on your desk." My stomach glitched. Ike? "Main one—Margaret Rooney. She wants to know if you're free for lunch. Noon at her office. Said it was kind of important."

"Sure." Just what I was in the mood for—a client lunch. "Would you call and say I'll be there?"

"Already done. I ordered you a turkey on rye with Russian." And he was gone. The door closed quietly behind him.

I slipped into my black leather swivel and leaned my elbows on the old country French table that I use for a desk. In times of stress I find my office comforting—maybe because it's the one place in The Gentle Group that contains not a single gray item. I watched the feeble February morning sun dapple the large Paul Davis poster on the wall facing me and tried to think of some really clever way to squirm out of the Stover meeting. I failed.

I glanced at my watch—9:50 already. Only a couple of hours before my lunch with Margaret Rooney. She wasn't one to use the word *important* lightly. I wondered what was on her mind. Margaret owned the Rooney Property Company, which had in five years become one of the city's top residential brokerages. She'd been my client for three of those years, and I felt very much a part of her success.

Before starting her own company, Margaret—and everyone called her that, never a Maggie, Margie, or Peggy from anyone —had been in a middling successful partnership with a guy named Ray Mentone for seven years, selling mostly low-priced one- and two-bedrooms on the Upper East Side. The reason for their breakup depends on whom you talked to. The popular version was that Margaret was just too smart, too ambitious, too talented for a plodder like Mentone or a life of flogging cheapie apartments. But insistent minorities painted other pictures: a brutal, relentless Margaret who'd connived to get what she could out of Ray, wrung him dry and then discarded him. A sleazy Ray, whose business practices Margaret grew to abhor. Margaret herself wouldn't talk about it at all. She'd just smile her perky, determined smile and say, "That's history. I believe in the future."

Thinking of Margaret reminded me of my resolve to take my apartment off the market. I dialed Norrie Wachsman, the Rooney agent who was handling it, and a friend dating back to college days. She was out, and I left word for her to call me. Suddenly I had an overwhelming urge to talk to Ike. My hand dialed his direct line under no conscious orders from my head. One ring. What the hell would I say? Two rings. He hadn't even called to see whether I got home okay. Three rings. The sandy voice, "O'Hanlon." I hung up.

I gnawed my thumbnail and forced myself to focus on the Alfie Stover problem. John Gentle was far from wrong about my hurt pride. When I'd first met Alfie four years ago he'd been a diamond in the rough, a smart Cockney who'd made his first million in London real estate before he was twenty-three and a decade later was ready to take on New York. Back then I'd had to do a lot of persuading to get Alfie to talk to the press at all. "Let them write about my buildings, not about me," he'd argue. "You start getting in the pipers and on the telly, it's asking for problems." I could still see his plump cheeks filling and jowls wobbling as he chewed "problems" in that peculiarly British way.

But that was before the ship. When they'd broken ground for Alfie's third New York project, an office building over on Water Street, the remains of a seventeenth-century merchant ship had been unearthed and, what with plans for excavating, preserving, and donating it to the Smithsonian, Alfie had been pushed into the limelight. Turned out he liked it. His wife, Doreen, liked it even more. In fact, they couldn't get enough of it. Pretty soon Alfie began to wonder whether The Gentle Group was quite large enough for the Alfred Stover Organization, prestigious enough, expensive enough to be the custodian of his new celebrity and Doreen's social aspirations. So he moved his account to a bigger, fancier competitor at fees that John Gentle has rubbed my nose in often enough to make it raw.

The last service I performed for Alfie should alone have been worth a year's billings. I had talked him out of ASO International as his new corporate name. I confess I'd been tempted to keep quiet, since a corporate identity is supposed to embody the spirit of the company, and by then I was feeling that Asshole International pretty well said it all.

My phone buzzed.

"Yes, Morley."

"Somebody named Ada Fauer, she said you'd know who she is."

"I do. Put her through. Hi, Ada. Everything okay?"

"Just fine, honey. I'm sitting here, waiting for the exterminator."

"That's great," I said, feeling awkward as well as traitorous about my incipient collaboration with the enemy. Most acutely, I wanted to get off the phone. "I—I'm in a meeting now, Ada. Good luck with, uh, everything, and if I can ever help you out just let—"

"Matter of fact, you can."

"Huh?" She'd caught me off guard.

"Yeah. I told Percy—you remember, Percy Tuthill—all about you. How smart you are about PR and how well you handled everything, and he'd really like to meet you. Maybe we could, waddayacallit, pick your brain a little."

"Well, I don't know . . . I mean, I'm kind of tired . . ."

"Oh, honey, I know. I don't mean *tonight.* How about tomorrow. About seven or so at Percy's apartment—that's 12G.

"Come on, Liz. Please. Percy's a pretty special guy." So she *was* sweet on him.

Liz Wareham, Double Agent. For a crazy second the idea appealed to me. Well, what the hell. "Okay, Ada. Seven o'clock tomorrow it is."

Chapter 6

Margaret Rooney's decorator had done her office in French blue and peach, flattering shades for Margaret's fair skin, pale blue eyes, and blond hair. Margaret herself had about zero interest in matters of decor. She just wanted it to look "right," which meant top quality, and be priced "right," which meant wholesale.

She felt the same way about clothes, which her motherly secretary, Selma, chose for her in Seventh Avenue designer showrooms twice a year. Sel stuck pretty much to the same pastels as the decorator—in styles anything but risky. It didn't matter a whole lot. Anything Margaret put on her angular five-foot-six frame somehow became a parochial school uniform. There was a lot of the nun about Margaret—in fact she'd come pretty close to taking the veil after she'd graduated from Our Lady of whatever—and a lot of the cheerleader too.

New York magazine had had some fun in a recent profile piece placing Margaret's smiling face atop a cartoon cheerleader's jumping body. The balloon coming out of her mouth blared, "We're the New York Winners!" her opening battle cry at sales meetings. Seth Frankel, who'd placed the article, had been a little nervous about Margaret's reaction. So had I, actually. Clients can sometimes lose their sense of humor quite abruptly. But Margaret hadn't. She'd showed up at that Tuesday's sales meeting in full cheerleader regalia and done a few proficient whoops and jumps. Everybody'd had a good laugh and loved her for it.

"Hi, Liz. Come on in." Margaret clapped a welcoming aqua Ultrasuede arm around my shoulder and squeezed tight. Her greeting always made you feel that you were the one person in all the world she really wanted to see, and she appreciated your being generous enough to give her your valuable time. I recognized the underlying management strategy, but appreciated the grace note anyway. "Sel," she called over her shoulder before closing the office door, "give us half an hour and then bring lunch."

Margaret motioned me to the peach satin settee and sat in one of the ivory slipper chairs opposite. As she leaned forward, I noticed the strained look on her face, which seemed unusually pale. She got right to the point.

"Someone is trying to sabotage my company," she said. I was startled. High drama was not Margaret's style.

"What do you mean? Stealing customers? Trying to lure away your listings?" I asked.

"No, no," she said quickly. "That kind of thing's par for the course in this business. I wouldn't bother you with nonsense like that." She clenched her fists and rested bone-white knuckles on the rosy marble table between us. "I mean just what I said. Someone's trying to wreck the Rooney Property Company. And unless they're stopped, they may succeed." I said nothing and waited for her to continue.

"Dirty tricks. Those are the weapons they're using. I don't know who's behind it yet." Her pink lips thinned in determination. "But I will."

"You mean someone's playing dirty tricks on your agents? What kind?" I figured maybe bogus no-show appointments, or stolen keys, or defaced appointment books, or . . .

"Not on my agents," she said sharply. That would be manageable. No, on our sellers—our exclusives. Our high-end West Side exclusives."

I could well understand why Margaret was upset. Exclusive listings were the most precious merchandise a real estate brokerage had—money in the bank—and those seven-figure exclusives were the cream. Margaret had spent the last four years and a great deal of money cultivating the high end of the market. First she'd gotten a solid foothold on the East Side gold coast, and last year she'd launched a new initiative on my side of the park. "Rooney Goes West" our release had proclaimed.

She saw my puzzled look. "Maybe I'd better talk you through

it from the beginning," she said, sitting back and clasping her hands.

"Yes, I think so."

"Three weeks ago, at our sales meeting, Bobbie Crawbuck told us that his exclusive at the Beresford wouldn't be available to show for the next couple of weeks because the owner was home recovering from a freak accident. It seems she started to clean the makeup off her face one night, and her cold cream or whatever had been mixed with lye. She was rushed to the hospital with second-degree burns. I gather she'll be okay ultimately, but she'll need some plastic surgery on the scars. By the way, the woman I'm talking about is Bebe Nordenheim—you know, one of the lunching ladies. Anyway, I didn't think too much about it at the time. Maybe her best friend had it in for her, or her maid, or a . . . lover." Margaret knew that "lover" was quite okay to say, but she had trouble actually getting her mouth around the word.

"But the following week I heard that Dr. Shepperton, the owner of Norrie Wachsman's exclusive at the San Remo—great nine-room apartment, he's some kind of fancy dentist, friend of Norrie's ex—had also ended up in the hospital. He drank some scotch and got violently sick. Turned out it'd been laced with ipecac and he couldn't stop throwing up. Now, that seemed like a funny coincidence to me."

"Well, maybe," I cut in, "but I can certainly think of other explanations. How do you know these people didn't move in the same social circles and that one of their mutual friends isn't simply nuts?"

"Exactly what I concluded . . . then."

"But something else happened?" I asked, knowing the question was unnecessary.

"Oh, yes. Kevin Craigie—you know, the actor?" I nodded. Who hadn't heard of Kevin Craigie? And his girls and, as I understood it, boys. It looked as though he'd snag an Academy Award nomination this year.

"Wait a minute," I said, "you're not going to tell me that—"

"That's right. The paint incident." Last Wednesday's tabloids had featured front-page shots of Kevin Craigie arriving at Roosevelt Hospital's emergency room in his bathrobe, his head and face covered with black paint. The story was that he'd been in the shower, preparing for a night's outing and squeezed some shampoo from a plastic bottle onto his golden locks. Only it turned out not to be shampoo. Actually, the incident was less amusing than it seemed. Oil-based paint can blind you—and it almost did Kevin. "His penthouse at the Eldorado was Vi Royal's exclusive."

"Wow," I said softly.

"You're darned right, wow," she replied, looking grim. "Three in three weeks is no coincidence. And I promise you that the Nordenheims and Dr. Shepperton, even if they knew each other, do not have friends in common with Kevin Craigie. No, Liz, these are three high-priced Rooney exclusives—one eight to three million—all in top Central Park West buildings. We pulled out all the stops to get into those buildings, as you well know. You helped us do it. Somebody wants us out. So badly that—"

"Wait a second," I interrupted, "how do you know this isn't some citywide epidemic. Maybe some nut is just out to get rich people and—"

"And what? Just happened on three who have their apartments up for sale with Rooney?" She made a face. "The odds are just too great. We're new on the West Side. We don't *have* more than a dozen exclusives there over a million."

"Margaret, you seriously think that another brokerage would risk burning and blinding people just to damage your reputation? Why, that's cra—"

I was interrupted by Selma's arrival with the sandwiches and coffee, which was just as well. It's wise to avoid words like "crazy" with clients under any circumstances.

"I know it sounds crazy," Margaret said, too concerned to be semantically touchy. She took a sip of the milky coffee that Selma had prepared for her. "But crazy things *do* happen. I can't think that word has spread to our other sellers yet, but it will. No one around here can talk about anything else, and it's going to leak, I know it. Also, every agent with a high-end exclusive is terrified that theirs'll be next. We have to make it stop."

I chewed my thumbnail as my mind raced into some unappealing paths. Who'd have had access to these three apartments, each in a different building? The easiest answer I came up with was a Rooney agent. It seemed absurd, but there it was. Manhattan real estate folkways are a lot more rigid than those of the suburbs. No casual extra keys or lock boxes. An agent from another firm could show a Rooney exclusive only if accompanied by the Rooney agent who represented the property. But a Rooney colleague could, in most cases, show the apartment independently.

Of course, the dirty tricks Margaret had described *could* have been effected by an outsider, even under the watchful eye of the broker, during a quick trip to the bathroom or a lingering couple of seconds at the dressing table.

"Margaret," I asked, hoping for a yes, "has any single outside broker or customer seen all three of the apartments?"

"No. That was the first thing I checked, of course. The Craigie apartment is brand new on the market, and we're not even letting co-brokers show it yet. I went over the showing sheets myself. You know the agents keep lists of everyone they show property to—a matter of self-preservation. You'd be surprised—or maybe by now you wouldn't be—how often buyers and other brokers try to go behind your back directly to the seller. If you have your list, you can defend yourself and protect your commission. If you don't, you can't. I wish it were an outsider, but it isn't." We looked at each other over untouched sandwiches.

"I assume that more than one Rooney agent has shown all three apartments," I said quietly.

"Four," she answered just as quietly. Bobbie Crawbuck, Norrie Wachsman, Vi Royal, and Arlyne Berg." I knew the first three—Norrie, on and off, since college.

"Who's Arlyne Berg?" I asked.

"She's new. 'Broker to the stars,' they call her. I've been meaning to get you two together so you can make some hay out of her. I've just hired her away from Elliman. A real winner—and she lives at the Conquistador, which'll be a big help in getting more good exclusives there. Unless—"

"Unless she turns out to be your traitor." The word sounded
so melodramatic as it echoed back at me. "Isn't that the most
likely explanation, Margaret? I mean, you hardly know her, and
the others are some of your top people. Well, okay, Norrie isn't
exactly a world beater, but . . ." I gestured, hands out. It was
easier than finishing that sentence. Margaret completed it for
me.

"Of *course* it's hard to believe—of *any* of them, Arlyne every
bit as much as the others. Wait till you meet her, you'll agree.
But these are *facts,* Liz, and I must face them."

I took a sip of tepid coffee and thought for a second. "Look,
Margaret, maybe we're both going off the deep end here. Even
if this *is* some sort of plot to get at you—and that's not certain"
—her eyes were suddenly icy—blue-eyed people do that so
much more effectively than the rest of us—"it doesn't have to
be one of those four. Maybe your—uh—enemy smuggled someone into those apartments, posing as a cleaning woman or an
exterminator or something." The eyes thawed slightly. I
plunged ahead. "I hate to say this, but maybe you should go to
the police."

"No!" It was as sharp as a slap.

"But, Margaret, you *can't* check out all the possibilities yourself. You're not equipped to. You can go to the police in confidence. They can be discreet. They—"

"I said no and I meant no." The thaw had frozen over and
her thin lips had all but disappeared. "And I want to underscore
that I am speaking to *you* in confidence, and would not take
kindly to that confidence being broken."

"I don't deserve that from you, Margaret," I said stiffly. For
the first time since we'd known each other, I wanted to let her
have it right in the chops.

She reached across the table and took my hand in two of
hers. "No, you don't. I'm sorry I said it." She squeezed my hand
and I squeezed back.

"Accepted—and thanks." All of our hands returned to their
owners. I used mine to lift the cup for another spot of cold
coffee. "I can understand why you're jumping out of your skin
about this."

"Liz, I need your help. I'd like you to spend some time—one to one—with the four of them. See what you can pick up."

"Why would they level with *me?* They'll see me as just some kind of company spy poking around for information to use against them. And that's what I'd be, only I'm not qualified. I don't—"

"Norrie is your friend—she wouldn't *be* here except for you. You have good relationships with Bobbie and Vi, and Arlyne knows I've been planning to have you spend some time with her about publicity." She looked at me. The eyes weren't icy, but they meant business. "What I'm saying is that they may open up to you. At least three of them may. I think it's worth a try."

I let out a deep breath. Of course I'd do as she asked. I didn't have a lot of choice. But that didn't make it a bit more comfortable.

"I can see only one bright spot in this mess," I said, "and it's a purely personal one."

"Yes?"

"I decided last night to take my apartment off the market. As soon as I reach Norrie, I'll no longer be a Rooney seven-figure West Side exclusive."

Chapter 7

The Rooney sales staff operated out of a huge room divided
into eighty-four work stations arranged in long double rows.
Chocolate carpeting covered not only the floor but shallow ver-
tical dividers between stations—a not entirely successful effort
to afford some privacy for the all-important phone work upon
which the business relied. The place hummed with a constant
sound somewhere between white noise and a crowded restau-
rant.

The office was about a third full—women of various sizes,
shapes, and ages, and a few men. Several agents stood near the
computers, discharging bursts of animated shop talk while they
waited impatiently for printouts of searches they'd done to find
Trudie and Herbie Glotz just the right 3 BR apartment, not a
penny over eight hundred thousand, before some other agent
did.

". . . you get to the open house at 925 Park?"

"What a cave! Gets two minutes of reflected sun at three in
the afternoon. And for that they want . . ."

". . . my new exclusive at the Normandie. Fabulous! The
river from three rooms, and *he's got to sell!*"

". . . aahh, don't waste your time. She broke four appointments with me. She's not real."

". . . and can you imagine? After all that grief, now they're
pushing me to cut the commission."

Most of the agents sat hunched at their desks with phones at
their ears in concentrated conversation. As I made my way
down a center row toward the West Side Group, hoping to find
Norrie Wachsman, I caught bits and pieces. ". . . you won't
believe the views . . ." ". . . just been reduced to seven and a
quarter . . ." ". . . well, look, they've come up seventy-five
and in *this* market . . ." ". . . the kitchen's to die for . . ."

". . . should drop it below two million—I *know* you paid more, but the market's soft . . ." "Look, the owner'll take back paper, and that'll save you a bundle in closing costs alone." "No, no. I told you right up front, the commission is six percent." Selling. Selling. Selling. The business of business, no matter what business. All the corporate suites, the private planes, the lavish lunches. Finally it all comes down to someone with a phone pasted to his ear, selling his heart out.

Norrie was not at her desk. Though I'd already left a phone message, I scribbled a note on her memo pad to give me a call ASAP. Bobbie Crawbuck, two desks over, was into deep phone, his head down for greater privacy despite the fact that all the surrounding desks were empty—habit, I guessed. I turned to leave, but before I'd gotten three steps away, his vibrant voice stopped me.

"So the beautiful but cruel Elisabeta is going to leave without even a hello."

"Well, if you insist," I said, walking back, "you may kiss my sneaker, toad." I raised my booted foot a couple of inches. It was a schtick we did. I was the dominatrix. Bobbie was my slave. "I didn't want to interrupt you. Sounded like you were making a deal."

"Nah. Some asshole. He's been running me around for nine months. Every time I show him something he likes he stops returning my calls. Then I stop calling him. Then he starts calling me to see more apartments, 'Bobbie, haven't heard from you, fella.'" He completed his wickedly accurate Larchmont lockjaw imitation and threw his arms out wide to dramatize the futility. "Couple of years ago I'd've told him to get lost, but hey, he's a live body with the bucks, and in *this* market . . . well, I don't have to tell *you*." He rolled his swivel back. It looked absurdly small under his lanky six five. "What brings you out among the working stiffs?"

"The fact that I'm a working stiff," I answered. "Actually, I was looking for Norrie. I'm taking the apartment off the market."

"Oh, don't do that. Yours'll sell. It's priced right and it shows well. I just showed it this morning. She loved it."

"That's not the reason, Bobbie."

He looked at me sharply, all traces of playfulness gone from his chorus-boy face. "You know about it, huh? And you're scared. Who told you?"

I didn't go through the charade of pretending not to understand what he was talking about. "Margaret told me. But I'd already decided. My plans to move have changed."

"Trouble with the delicious lieutenant?" I'd brought Ike to a Valentine's party that Bobbie and his lover, Art Blyfield, the antiques dealer, had thrown at their loft in TriBeCa. Bobbie was no stranger to love-life problems. He and Art had had more than their share before they'd both stopped drinking.

"That's an understatement. I hate to do this to Norrie after she's worked so hard, but . . ."

"Do I hear my name taken in vain?" I turned. Norrie leaned over and we exchanged cheek pecks. "I've just come from your place, Liz. I was going to call you. I've got someone seriously interested and—"

"Norrie, could we sit down for a minute and talk?" I felt my face flush in discomfort.

"Sure." Her large doe eyes looked concerned. "Excuse us, Monsieur Robert," she said, holding out her flared black skirt and dropping a graceful curtsy, "Madame and I are going into conference."

"Au revoir, mes enfants," Bobbie responded with an airy wave as he picked up the phone and returned to privacy-crouch position.

I followed Norrie back to her desk. "Roll up a chair and come into my office," she said as she swiveled around to me.

I nudged Vi Royal's chair over from across the aisle with my foot and sat.

Norrie's surprised fawn face hadn't changed all that much in twenty years, when it used to get her cast as every tragic heroine from Ophelia to Blanche du Bois. She'd been Lenore Rose back then, commuting to NYU from Brooklyn, as I did from Queens, passing the subway time with dreams of taking Broadway by storm. Somewhere in our freshman year someone had begun calling her Norrie, and it had stuck.

She'd kept her dark hair long, but wore it in a decorous bun now rather than streaming over her shoulders as it had in college. Depending on her mood, she could evoke either Audrey Hepburn or Olive Oyl, but the big surprise about Norrie was that she was funny. She could leave you helpless with laughter, your mouth spewing cafeteria coffee, the zingers all the more effective sneaking up on you from her tragedienne's face.

After graduation she'd put together a comedy act—one-liners, impressions, a song or two—played some little Village clubs. We all showed up, laughing and applauding wildly. She'd even made it onto Johnny Carson once. It had looked as though Norrie was on her way.

The laughing stopped when she met Attila the dentist. That's how she referred to him, and it was apt—heavy-handed, power-tripping, humorless. So it caught everyone off base when she married him and traded her budding career for a white-uniformed job in his office. We'd lost touch after that, Norrie and I. I couldn't stand Attila, and he was equally enthusiastic about me. In short order, he'd whisked her off to some New Jersey exurb with horses. Our lunches became less frequent and finally stopped altogether—until two years ago, when she'd turned up single and almost broke. I'd introduced her to Margaret and suggested—well, maybe pushed—the idea of her selling real estate.

Norrie leaned forward expectantly, bringing me abruptly back to the present. It was my move. "Norrie, I'm taking my place off the market."

Her face clouded over. "You've heard about the . . . crazy stuff. And you're scared." Her voice was quiet.

"I *have* heard. Margaret just told me—and it *is* pretty scary, you have to admit. But that's not the reason. I decided last night. Ike and I had a fight. A bad one this time."

"So you won't be moving."

"No."

She laughed, which startled me. "I'm sorry, Liz," she said, "I'm not laughing at you. I know you must be upset about Ike. I'm laughing at me. The Story of Norrie, otherwise entitled

Mary Clumsy Triumphs Again. Ta-da!" She raised her arm in a mock flourish.

"God, I feel *awful* about this, Norrie. I don't know what to— Look, I've wasted your time. Can I . . . can I pay you for it? I know money's tight and—"

"Don't even think of it," she said quickly. For a split second I thought I saw her eyes flash fury. Then it was gone. She reached over and took my hand. "It's not your fault. Things just . . . happen." She looked down at her watch. "I've got at least twelve calls to make and—"

"I'll get out of your hair, Nor." I gave her hand a parting squeeze. "I'll make this up to you. I promise," I said as I stood, wishing I had even the remotest idea how to do that.

"Thanks. You're a good friend." As I turned to leave, she added, "You and Ike will patch it up, you know."

I didn't respond. Good friend indeed, I thought bitterly as I waited for the elevator. Why the hell had I gotten Norrie into this business that was so wrong for her? What had I been thinking of? Even as I asked the question, I knew the answer. Where except in real estate can a woman over forty with a blank résumé have a shot at making a grown-up living? Attila was rolling in money, but the divorce settlement had been punitive. I gathered that Attila hadn't much liked being dumped and had responded by getting himself a killer lawyer. The bottom line was that Norrie'd come away with very little after almost twenty years of marriage to a very rich man.

I pulled my coat close around me as I started downtown on Madison. My head was feeling unpleasantly light and throbby from too much brandy and no sleep. I felt an overwhelming desire to crawl under my patchwork quilts, a cat at each ear, and escape from all of it. With no conscious signal from my brain, my hand shot up to hail a cab.

As I climbed out in front of my building, I was almost mowed down by a jet-propelled orange mohair coat trailing a wake of turned heads. But then, Vi Royal always turned heads, even when she traveled at normal speed. Slim and broad-shouldered, with an afro halo framing high cheekbones in a face the color of hand-rubbed mahogany, Vi had a bearing and sense of style

that commanded attention. She was not only the most successful *black* broker in Manhattan, but a successful broker according to any lights.

"Whoa!" I called as I grabbed her arm to steady myself.

"Sorry," she said, not smiling. "I—I didn't see you."

"That's okay. Great coat," I said, giving it a once-over. Vi and
I tended to talk clothes a lot, trading triumphant tales of designer prizes captured at sixty percent off.

"Thanks," she replied, eyes darting distractedly, her desire to
get away more than clear.

"Well—uh—see you," I said. And she was off without a good-
bye. I shrugged. A deal on the brink of collapse, maybe. As
Bobbie had once observed, a broker's life is like an airline pilot's. Hours of boredom punctuated by moments of panic.

"The real estate's up there," Gus said as I walked into my
lobby. To him, all the agents were simply "the real estate."
"Want me to buzz and say you're coming up?"

"No, that's okay, Gus."

I turned my key in the lock and was greeted by the usual
feline reception committee.

"Later, kids," I said softly as I glanced around. I spied a few
Rooney business cards lying on the dining table: Norrie, Bobbie, Vi, and Mac Stitt. I didn't see anyone in the front part of
the apartment, or hear any sounds from the bedrooms. Maybe
that's what felt wrong. It was too quiet. A broker trying to sell a
customer is a fairly voluble animal.

I felt a funny prickle at the base of my spine as I started to
move quietly down the hall to the bedrooms. Why hadn't I just
called out "Hi, it's Liz" when I'd first opened the door? That
would have been normal. Why didn't I do it now? What the hell
did I expect to find, someone putting Lysol in my moisturizer? I
mentally slapped my hand for being a fanciful jerk, but I stayed
on tiptoe and kept my mouth shut. No one in Scott's room, or
Sarah's, or mine. But my bathroom door was closed, and I never
leave it that way. I felt my heart pound. I just stood there, too
scared to feel foolish. A sudden sharp sound jolted me. Then
the door swung open to reveal a woman I'd never seen in my
life.

We jumped back like two astonished cats at the sight of each other. It took a second before I realized that the terrifying sound had been only the flush of my toilet.

We stood there for a beat, locked in a mutual suspicious stare. My explosive sneeze, triggered by the waves of Giorgio she exuded, broke the silence.

"I'm Liz Wareham," I said stiffly. "Who're you?"

"Arlyne Berg," she answered in an appealing Bronx contralto, flashing a smile that looked authentic if you stopped at her mouth and ignored the shrewd appraisal in her almost-black eyes. "My customer had to run off to a *Vogue* shoot. Remy O'Hare." She tossed off the famous name with a calculated carelessness, which had the desired effect, even though I was aware of the craft behind it. A movie star was considering *my* apartment. Wow! "I stayed a minute to use your john," she added.

So this was Margaret's new hotshot broker to the stars. She looked like a star herself, in a way. But a star reflected in a funhouse mirror. Her blocky body was zipped into a bright green Italian designer suit that could've looked smashing had she been able to convert four inches of her width into four inches of height. The longish olive face seemed, as the suit did, to belong on a taller frame. Her makeup was heavy but expertly applied, and her glossy straight chin-length black hair well cut. Nevertheless, she managed to look slightly disheveled.

She stuck out a square hand with a diamond knuckle-duster on its purple polished ring finger and a not-much-smaller emerald on its pinky. We shook. "Glad to meet you," I said. "Margaret was just telling me we should. You scared the life out of me, you know, suddenly appearing like that."

A brief cloud of confusion crossed her face. It lifted almost immediately. "Oh, *sure*. You're the PR. I forgot this was your apartment." She cast an evaluative glance around the bedroom. "Nice place. Too bad about the view, though. If it looked at the park, Remy might've gone for it."

Despite myself, I was nettled. My home had been found wanting. "Well, she couldn't've bought it," I said airily. "I've just taken it off the market."

"Ah, you shouldn't do that." Her smile made it to the eyes this time, transforming her face into something surprisingly close to beautiful, though far from pretty. She perched on my Shaker rocker and leaned forward. "Prices are starting to pick up. I can get you good money for this—even with the view. It's got a certain *personality*. You know, with what you realize on this, you could *steal* Raye Starkway's penthouse at the Courtauld. I mean, it's not as big, but you got two bedrooms and a good maid's, which could be an easy third. And the views! Look, I just got the listing. She's *desperate* to sell. The value"— she shook her head in wonder—"un-be-liev-able!"

While she was talking I'd shrugged off my coat and sat on the bed. Despite my resolve, I found myself caught up in the fantasy of trading my old-shoe apartment for a movie star's penthouse, purchased at a larcenous price. Never mind that Remy O'Hare had rejected my place. Arlyne would simply sell it to someone else, and— What was I, nuts? This woman could sell anyone anything!

"I'm afraid my mind's made up," I said, smiling in admiration as I rejected, with some regret, the penthouse and its view.

"No problem." The transfiguring smile vanished, replaced by a troubled frown, which produced a pair of deep lines between her dark brows. "I suppose Margaret told you about those nutty tricks, huh?"

"She did, but that's not why I pulled the apartment off the market. My reason was—uh—personal." I looked at her and wondered what was going on behind those eyes. Could *she* be playing the tricks? But why would she? Why would anyone? Still, she'd been lurking around my bedroom, my bathroom. What if . . . ? Oh, stop it! "Margaret's really thrilled to have you with the company, Arlyne. What persuaded you to make the change from Elliman?"

"Margaret's a pretty persuasive gal when she really wants something. And I am too. Takes one to know one. I guess we both got what we wanted." Translate that cash. My bet was that she'd gotten herself a seventy percent commission split with the brokerage—sixty-five was usually tops. From what I'd just seen, she was well worth it.

Out of nowhere, a yawn crept up on me. I stretched extravagantly and shut my eyes. "Sorry, Arlyne. Late night. I'm not feeling that great, which is why I came home."

She got up and slung her huge green lizard pouch over her shoulder. "I've gotta go anyway." She checked her gold tank watch. "Five minutes late for showing. But we should get together again. Margaret said you were going to do a good job for me." So publicity was part of her package too.

"Sure. Be a pleasure." I started to get up to see her out.

"No, sit. Lie down. You do look beat. I can let myself out. I'm the broker, remember? And when you get ready to put this place back on the market, let's talk."

"Well, if I ever do, Norrie Wachsman's got first dibs. She—"

"Oh, sure—but you never know, do you?" she asked with a grin that was only slightly malicious. And in a cloud of Giorgio, she was gone.

I took off all my clothes and slipped under the quilt. My eyes were heavy, lids lined in fine sandpaper. I reached over and switched off the ring on the bedside phone. Norrie, Bobbie, Vi, Arlyne. All at once I was sliding down a huge cushioned purple spiral. Then I was asleep.

I woke suddenly, the way you do when you know you have an early morning plane to catch. I was on my side, eyeball to eyeball with the digital display on my clock, which read 9:06. It took my gummy mind a full minute to register that it was P.M. not A.M., solving the mystery of why it was dark outside. I gave a major yawn and stretch, mildly surprised that the cats weren't at their accustomed posts: Elephi at my head and Three in the crook of my knee.

Then I realized that Arlyne had closed the bedroom door when she'd left. I leaned over and checked the answering machine—three messages, all from John Gentle, wanting to talk about tomorrow's meeting with Alfie Stover. By the third call his asperity level was decidedly on the high side. Deferred gratification has no place in John's makeup. His last message simply barked out, *"Eight-thirty. My office. Stover."*

Just as I switched the phone back on, it rang.

"Liz Wareham," I answered, my voice still thick with sleep.

"You're home. Fabulous!" said a woman's slightly sandy voice. "Now I want you to get right over here and—"

"Excuse me, I think you have the wrong number." But there was something nigglingly familiar about that voice.

"No, I don't. It's Becky. Becky O'Hanlon. Well, d'Alless-sandro now. But, of course, all our names have changed, haven't they? If we're women, that is." Instantly, I remembered. A party. Ike's older sister, whose marriage had turned her from a Jewish-Irish princess *manqué* into an Italian princess for real, was in town from Rome.

"Some of us have changed names more than once," I said with a shaky attempt at levity. "It's good to hear you after such a long time, Becky." Twenty-six years certainly was that.

"Well, we'll catch up when you get here. Come on, we're all waiting."

"I'd love to see you, Becky. But really, no." The words tumbled out of my mouth on top of one another.

"Really, *yes.*"

"Look, Becky, I *can't.* Ike and I aren't speaking. You must know that already. How can I—"

"Because *I* am asking you, that's how. It's a very large party and Ike is far from the only attractive man here. Why should you huddle in your apartment like a little coward when—"

"I'm *not* a coward," I yelped, "but—"

"I don't want to hear but. The Conquistador, apartment 23C. The name is Leonaides." *The* Leonaides? Probably so. "You're expected, and if you're not here in half an hour, I'll come get you." A click, and Becky was gone. I laughed in spite of myself. From what I remembered of Becky O'Hanlon, she probably *would* come and get me if I didn't show up.

I scratched my head and made for the shower. When I emerged, I was a hell of a lot improved. I sat naked at the dressing table and applied the contents of various tubes and pots on my face. I suddenly felt sexy in a decadent Weimar Republic kind of way and realized I was humming, "Life is a cabaret, old chum. Come to the cabaret." I touched my left breast and shuddered slightly. I peered at my face in the mirror,

fluffed the mop of dark curls around it and smiled. I didn't look half bad. That nap had worked some kind of magic. Cinderella was going to the ball after all. All at once I was eager to get there.

I sprayed lots of Coco on and futzed around with what to wear. I settled on a new short black silk skirt, the cost of which I had calculated at an alarming $400 a yard, and a white crepe shirt with flowing sleeves. I pulled on sheer black panty hose and slipped into red satin high-heeled pumps. As I stood in front of the full-length mirror on the bedroom door, I was pretty damned satisfied—and banished quickly a fleeting subversive thought that I might look like an aging cocktail waitress.

Chapter 8

Uniformed troops three-deep guarded the entrance of the Conquistador against any undesirables or unexpecteds presumptuous enough to attempt entry. A doorman was the first line of defense. If you got past him, one of the two guys behind the high concierge desk in tricolored marble asked your destination, presented the sign-in book, and handed you a plastic elevator pass which you pushed into a slot to get the elevator to move upward. In front of the elevators stood another gatekeeper, who checked your elevator pass just in case you'd somehow bamboozled your way past the front lines.

My friend Barbara Garment, who makes a bundle writing about why men and women will never make it together, lives in the building, and insists it all makes her feel secure. It would have given me hives had I been well-heeled enough to call the Conquistador home. The building is spectacular, though, one of a handful along Central Park West designed by Emery Roth in the twenties with ornate marble and brass lobbies and names that conjured up the romance of Spain: San Remo, Eldorado, Conquistador; or the elegance of Britain: Beresford, Courtauld, Majestic.

As the elevator door closed behind me, I lost my nerve. I wanted to flee the ball in my rancid mice-drawn pumpkin. Ike would probably be there with Jeannie the broker—she of the straight blond hair and the mile-long legs. I'd have no one to talk to except Becky, who'd feel sorry for me. Goddammit, the skirt *was* too short and . . .

The elevator door opened and a liveried butler took my coat. Suddenly I was onstage, none too sure I'd remember my lines— a feeling I well remembered from long-ago summer stock, when there'd never been enough time to learn them. I smiled a thank-you and handed him my black shearling.

Even before I walked through the door I heard the piano. My stomach jumped. I swallowed hard and walked in. I'd recognize Ike's playing anywhere. I should. He played piano just like my father, who'd taught him. Dad could have made his living as a singing piano player, he was that good. However, that's not what his Lower East Side parents had in mind for their youngest son—not after they'd shlepped this far to the land of opportunity. A son a piano player! For this they could have stayed in Russia. A doctor. That was the thing. And that's what Dad had become. The piano, the singing: his therapy and his joy.

My sister, Roo, learned to play passably well from sheet music, and I, who couldn't even do that, knew the words to everything, but neither of us had the talent. Ike O'Hanlon around the corner did, and Dad started teaching him when he was twelve. Ike would show up Sunday mornings and they'd play and sing together—sometimes for an hour or two, sometimes longer. I'd hang around outside the living room, listening, silently mouthing the lyrics they were singing—wanting desperately to be part of it and knowing that I couldn't, really. I was nine and knew for certain what I wanted when I grew up: to be an actress, and to marry Ike O'Hanlon.

" 'I lost the sunshine and roses. I lost the heavens so blue . . .' " The clear tenor managed to make the corny lyric sound fresh. I knew Ike had spotted me. That old song was one Dad had taught him. All at once I missed my father ferociously. So many things we'd never talked about. So much . . . I had to turn it off, or I'd surely cry. I upped the wattage on my smile and turned determinedly in the opposite direction from the piano.

The living room was huge, maybe forty by fifty. Adjoining it was a dining room, a sumptuous-looking buffet laid out on an endless stretch of ivory-clothed table. The two rooms provided magnificent views in three directions. You got the Central Park reservoir to the east and the Empire State Building south. The north view, while less spectacular, was no slouch either. The north wall also housed a king-size fireplace with a carved stone mantel that featured Neptune surrounded by dolphins and tridents, and which looked considerably older than the building.

The room, all ivory and pale green, was flattered by the soft firelight. So were its inhabitants—at least eighty people clustered in groups of various sizes, talking, laughing, clutching elbows, embracing shoulders, sipping, smoking. The cigarette smoke as well as the sleek European cut of their clothes confirmed that this was an international crowd. Americans don't smoke that much anymore.

Ike had moved into Cole Porter. I heard a self-confident soprano harmonizing with him on "Delovely," and wanted to annihilate them both. Princess Becky was chatting with a glamorous couple at the fireplace. If I'd had any worries about recognizing her, I needn't have. Sleek cropped black hair, cheekbones that wouldn't quit, aquiline nose, generous mouth —she was as ravishing as ever. I headed toward her.

"Liz, my love," she said as she took my hand. "Don't you look marvelous! Same little cat face and those big green eyes." As she leaned over to kiss me, she whispered, "You make every other woman in the room look overdressed."

"Nobody with any sense'll stop looking at you long enough to notice," I said—and meant. The deep purple satin shift skimmed her long, slim body, stopping just north of the knees. Its expensive, simple line was a perfect foil for her dramatic beauty, and for an astonishing rope of pearls, which some overachieving oysters must have worked fairly long and hard to produce.

"Come, Liz, meet your host and hostess. Aristides and Françoise Leonaides, this is Liz Herzog. I'm sorry, Wareham." She drew me into the circle with one hand and placed the other on our host's shoulder to recapture his attention from the fire he was stoking with a long, Neptune-headed poker. "Steed," she said to him, "would you believe that I used to be this child's baby-sitter?"

"You look far too young for that, my dear Becky. On the other hand, Liz here," he pronounced it, charmingly, *Lees,* "perhaps still could use one." He grinned at me and enfolded my hand in two large, furry square paws.

I returned the grin. "Perhaps I could." God knew that was true, but not for the flattering reasons that he meant. Steed

Leonaides was a familiar name from the business pages. He owned cruise lines in Europe and the Bahamas, and had expanded into hotels and casinos. His distinctively Greek male magnetism was powerful enough to make traditional good looks seem beside the point.

"Welcome," said Françoise Leonaides, holding out her hand. "I'm so glad you could join us." Her quiet elegance was outshone by her husband's solar power and Becky's dazzle, but when you took another look, there it was—very real, very French. Françoise Leonaides was medium in height and build. Her hair and eyes were medium brown, her makeup understated. But something about the way she held herself, the way she moved in her long chocolate-velvet hostess gown whispered "perfect."

"I'm delighted to be here," I said, extracting my hand from between her husband's and shaking hers, "I'm sure you've heard this at least fifty times tonight, but your apartment is . . . well, wonderful doesn't quite say it."

"You like it?" asked Françoise with a smile. "Maybe you know someone who would like to buy it." Only the French can manage things like that without sounding crass. I think it's because money is such an essential concern for them that they're never embarrassed to talk about it. That's certainly true of my boss, John Gentle, whose grandmother is rumored to have been a Parisian landlady. John can haggle you down to the last quarter while maintaining an aura of expansiveness.

"You're selling it? How can you bear to?" I asked.

"Ah, yes," said Françoise, "it has been, how do you say, on the market since two weeks now. We are moving across the park —closer to Becky and Tano. It is perhaps foolish, but I shall have a small garden—"

"What she means," Becky cut in, "is that they're buying the most drop-dead penthouse you ever saw."

"That is my Becky," said another voice, "she is never one to mince a word." I turned to see the newcomer, who had wrapped an arm around Becky's waist and was giving it a proprietary squeeze. He stood half a head shorter than Becky and his hairline had receded while his waistline had advanced. However, those things have little to do with the elusive quality we call charm. And in that respect, Gaetano d'Allessandro was a true Prince Charming. He released his wife, grabbed two glasses from a passing champagne tray, handed me one, and raised the other in a toast. *"Saluti,* pretty lady, how long have these barbarians left you with nothing to drink?"

"This nut is Tano, Liz—in case you hadn't figured it out."

"Ah," he said, "so *this* is Liz." He turned to Steed Leonaides. "You are out of luck, my friend. Liz belongs to Ike." I felt my cheeks flush.

"Your brother-in-law," Steed responded, continuing the game with an exaggerated, perplexed head shake, "what do all these women see in him? Why is he so fatally attractive?"

"Stop it, you two," Becky said. "Liz belongs to herself. Haven't you ever heard of women's lib?"

"Heard of it?" Tano laughed. "I *live* with it."

"Let's go back to fatally attractive, Steed. I liked the sound of that," said a familiar sandy voice at my elbow. My heart skidded. Ike. We regarded each other silently for a beat.

"I saw you come in," he said, fixing me with narrow eyes that are bluer than anyone else's.

"I know," I said quietly.

"Would you all excuse us for a moment?" Ike said to the four of them as he took my arm.

"I—" I began, wanting to yank it away—but not entirely.

"Behave yourself, little brother," Becky said with a mock severity that was only partly mock. Ike smiled.

"Big sisters never get over being bossy," he said. "Honest, Beck, I've been housebroken for years."

"Not so's you'd notice," I mumbled just loud enough for him to hear.

"Go ahead, take her away," said Steed with tragic resignation. "As soon as he returns to the piano, I shall come and find you, Liz."

"Never fear," I answered in kind, "I'll come and find *you.*"

As Ike led me away, I noticed Steed bend and take a new log from the ornate brass bin and throw it in the fireplace. Appealing, this earthy billionaire in impeccable evening dress tending his own fire.

Ike steered us to a relatively private spot behind a large bronze sculpture that might have been a Henry Moore. He let go of my arm, or I pulled it away, I'm not sure which, and we faced each other. His curly black hair was just a touch silver at the temples now, the way real black hair gets. He's not terribly tall—five ten—and it's not that his body is remarkable, just a good, square-shouldered, flat-bellied male body. But there *is* something remarkable about the fluid way it moves—as at home in a tuxedo as in jeans—a sense of power held in check. His smile built slowly, crinkling the blue eyes and turning his unequivocally Irish mug into mostly forehead and chin. As I looked at him, I wanted him so much it scared the hell out of me.

"Well?" I asked, batting the ball into his court defensively.

"Well?" He hit it back.

"Look." My voice came out hoarse, and I cleared my throat. I had to break this somehow. What was I, some goddamned Victorian heroine to be swept away whenever it suited the master? "You dragged me away from a perfectly enjoyable conversation. You have something to say to me, or what?"

I never got an answer. Suddenly the room exploded and I was facedown on the floor, Ike spread-eagled flat on top of me. Everything froze for a second. I felt the rug, prickly on my cheek. Then people started to scream.

As Ike got up, he whispered sharply to me, "Stay down." Then he said in a louder voice to the room at large, "Stay where you are, everybody. Don't panic. I'm a policeman." The screams stopped and the voices dropped to a low buzz. This was Ike's turf, and if the rest of them were anything like me, they were relieved that someone who knew what he was doing had taken charge.

I rose to my knees as Ike strode over to the fireplace. Steed Leoniades lay sprawled on his back in front of it, the Neptune poker about six inches from his hand. His wife crouched at his head, staring at him in silent, uncomprehending terror. Becky and Tano knelt at his feet. Fragments of splintered wood were scattered all over the carpet, some smoldering. A lemon-haired woman was rubbing her shin, her face screwed up in pain. Ike bent over Steed's body for a moment or two. Then he turned to Françoise, took her two hands, and gently helped her up. He put his arm around her shoulder and spoke to her, softly enough so that no one else could hear. She started to keen—a piercing, primal sound. I knew for sure then that Steed must be dead.

Ike quickly turned Françoise over to his sister and Tano, who between them led her from the room. Then he grabbed the poker, wheeled on the fireplace, and energetically poked and kicked the flames out. He knelt at the hearth for what seemed like a long time. When he rose, he addressed himself to the guests, who stood waiting like well-behaved students for the professor to begin his lecture.

"I'm sorry to have to tell you that Steed Leonaides is dead. I can't tell you much more than that right now, but I can relieve your minds about one thing. You needn't be afraid that a mad shooter is loose among you. It wasn't a gun that killed him."

I stood and moved closer to the fireplace. My legs felt far from steady. I had to concentrate on moving first one then the other. Steed's face was as perfectly composed as a waxwork, except for the fact that he had a deep red hole where his left eye had been. The champagne rose in my throat and burned there. He'd gallantly flattered me. We'd flirted mildly. He was going to buy his wife a drop-dead new penthouse. Funny that Becky had chosen those words. I felt myself starting to laugh at that and realized I was on the edge of hysteria. I clamped my teeth together and concentrated on calming down. The last thing anybody needed at the moment was to have to minister to me. The buzz from the crowd grew substantially louder as they absorbed what he'd said. Couples found each other and movement started toward the front door. Ike held up his hand.

"Sorry, I'll have to ask you all to stay here. I've asked my brother-in-law, Tano, to call my . . . uh, colleagues, and they'll be here shortly. We'll need to take everyone's names and ask you a few questions. Meantime, make yourselves as comfortable as you can. You're free to spread out into the library and the

television room, find a place to sit. It may be a while." He
spotted the butler, who was standing, ashen-faced, in the entrance foyer. "Peters, please make sure no one leaves." His
voice was neutral, but I knew Ike well enough to recognize that
he'd issued his instructions to Peters publicly to serve as an
extra warning to anyone in the crowd arrogant enough to try to
slip out against his orders. Evidently, he'd spent enough time
among the rich and famous to know they didn't always believe
they were governed by the same rules as the rest of us.

"How come you're so sure it wasn't a shot?" I asked.

"Would have to have been fired from inside the fireplace.
Steed was facing it when the explosion happened—poking at it.
Besides, the sound isn't exactly the same. Something in that
damned fireplace exploded. Just a freak that Steed happened to
be standing right over it." His mouth was grim and surrounded
by a white line, the way it gets when he's furious. He held my
arm tighter and then released it. "Go tell the folks in the
kitchen to make lots of coffee and offer it around. Some of
these people could use it."

A thought hit me on the way to the kitchen, and it stopped
me in my tracks for a second. I rolled it around and hoped as
hard as I could that I was wrong. It was easy to tell the Leonaideses' regular staff from the caterers laid on for the party.
They were the ones sitting stunned and tearful at the white
marble table. I told one of the caterers about the coffee and
then approached the two women at the table. They looked like
mother and daughter.

"I—I don't mean to interrupt," I began gingerly, feeling more
than a little sheepish about what I was going to do. "I just
wanted to say how sorry I am about Mr. Leonaides." That
started a new freshet of tears in the older woman. The younger
one leaned across the table, patted her hand, and looked up at
me.

"My aunt," she said with a small apologetic smile, her Greek
accent making it "hant," "she work for them long time. Love
Mr. Leonaides very much." That would be right, I thought. The
help would love him and respect Françoise.

"I understand," I said. "What is your name?"

"Yeleni," she answered. "I come two month for help my hant."

"Yeleni, you know that Mr. and Mrs. Leonaides were selling this apartment, yes?" She nodded. This would be tough with her limited knowledge of English. "The people who bring cus—uh —other other people to look at it—you know, maybe to buy it?" She nodded again, but more uncertainly. "Do you know any of them?"

She thought a second and shook her head no. "I—I sorry." Well, it'd been a slim chance that I'd get my answer that easily. Then her aunt raised her moist face and dabbed at her eyes with a paper napkin.

"Mees Ahleenberg. She the only one who come all the time. Mees Ahleenberg."

Chapter 9

I patted Yeleni's shoulder, murmured some condolences, and got out of the kitchen as fast as I could without running. I headed down the corridor till I found a bathroom. I turned the lock with relief, ran the cold water, and splashed some on my face. *Arlyne Berg.* Suddenly Margaret's outlandish idea about a dirty-tricks plot seemed very real, and my head pounded with conflict about what to do. On the one hand, I should tell Ike immediately. A man was dead. That was nothing to play around with. On the other, Margaret and I had had a privileged conversation. Maybe PR client confidentiality isn't protected by law the way it is for priests or lawyers, but we take it pretty seriously. If we didn't, we wouldn't have many clients.

I couldn't tell Ike—not until I'd spoken to Margaret and tried my damnedest to make *her* tell him. That wouldn't be easy.

I dampened a towel and held it to my burning forehead. I had to get out of there and call Margaret. I walked back to the living room. Ike's backup troops and Crime Scene Unit had arrived and were doing their stuff—recording the position of the body and putting fragments of the exploded firewood into plastic bags.

I spotted Sergeant Joe Libuti, whom I knew, questioning guests one by one on a sofa across the room, and then apparently letting them go home. I could see Peters opening the front door for a departing couple. Ike was in a huddle with a medical examiner near the fireplace. I joined the waiting crowd, careful to mask myself from Ike's possible glance behind some tall types. I don't often like being short, but tonight it was a distinct advantage. However, if I waited my turn, I could be there for hours.

"Oh, God," I said to the man in front of me, putting on a distraught expression, which wasn't too difficult, "I just called

my baby-sitter and my daughter's fever is over 102." Sarah, forgive me, I added silently, suddenly superstitious enough to
know that God would punish my lie by giving my daughter the
flu. "I've got to get home, and there are so many people in front
of me, I—"

The woman next to him came to my rescue. "Wha, honey,
don't you worry." Her concerned southern tones left no doubt
that she'd take care of it. She marched up to the front of the
line, scotching protests from the other guests with a soft but
firm "There's an emergency." For a panicked second I thought
she was going to approach Joe, to whom I'd have a hell of a
hard time explaining my need for a baby-sitter, since he knew
both my children were in college. Instead, she had a quiet word
with the man who was next to be questioned and then motioned
to me to come ahead. She patted my arm reassuringly and told
me she was certain that my baby would be fine, hers had had
higher fevers lots of times and I wasn't to worry. I told her I felt
better already, which wasn't exactly a lie. A moment later I was
sitting on the sofa next to Joe.

"Liz!" The black caterpillars that served as his eyebrows rose
in surprise. "I guess you're here with the lieutenant." He
stubbed his Camel out in a cut-crystal ashtray and shook a fresh
one out of a half-empty pack.

"Uh, yes," I answered, "but I'm sure you need to put my
name on your list anyway."

"Right you are." He asked me a couple of questions about
where I'd been when the blast occurred and whether I'd seen
anything relevant before or after.

"Not a thing," I answered, and got up to leave.

"You sticking around, Liz?"

"I don't think so, Joe," I said, carefully casual. "Ike's busy
and I'd just be in the way." He handed me a scrap of paper with
his name scrawled on it.

"You're gonna need this to get out the door."

"Thanks. Good luck," I added over my shoulder as I wove my
way through the crowd to freedom, feeling like an escaping
felon.

I ran down Central Park West—or as close to running as I

could manage in three-inch heels. It was ten to one when I unlocked my door. I zipped down the hall to my bedroom, ignoring the cats' pleas for sustenance, and dialed Margaret's apartment. She answered on the second ring, not sounding a bit sleepy.

"Margaret, it's Liz. Something terrible's happened." I told her. It took only two sentences.

"No." She said it with a quiet firmness, as though the word could undo the irrevocable.

"Yes," I said just as firmly. "This isn't dirty tricks any longer, it's murder. I need to talk to you, Margaret. Can I come to your apartment now?"

"I think you'd better," she answered. "Have you said anything to the police?" Her voice bordered on hostile. I forestalled what I knew was coming.

"No," I snapped. I was feeling pretty hostile myself. "I'll be there in half an hour or less." I hung up before she had a chance to say anything.

I chewed my thumbnail and noticed that my message machine registered two calls. I pushed Play and heard my son, Scott, ask me how I was doing and could I spare fifty bucks—just till the end of the month. I smiled in spite of myself. Scotty was about as good with money as his ma, but a lot more persuasive about asking for it. He'd be a dynamite lawyer one day. The second made the back of my neck prickle. Just breathing and something that sounded like a hiss. It's not that I've never had a breather before. What New York woman hasn't? But I'd never felt this terrified by one. I shook my head vigorously and told myself to shape up. I had some hard stuff to go through in the next few hours, and I couldn't wimp out.

I slipped out of my party clothes and into a dark green wool jersey shift, matching panty hose, and businesslike black leather pumps. There was at least an outside chance that I'd be at Margaret's a long time and might wind up going directly to the office.

I grabbed my big black bag and headed down the hall for the kitchen, cats at my heels. I opened a double can of liver, dumped it into their dish, and gave them clean water—which made me realize that I was thirsty. I opened the refrigerator to get some ice water . . . and screamed.

There, right next to the bottled water, were two large gray rats. Zeibach! How had he . . . How could he . . . Suddenly, Elephi and Three were next to me making wild leaps at the open fridge, generations of civilization lost in their atavistic frenzy. The rats were alive, but they barely moved. I realized later that the cold had probably made them dopey. I kicked the cats back and slammed the fridge door shut. They kneaded at it, making feral noises. I stood frozen, holding on to the sink for support. My knees wouldn't hold me and I couldn't stop shaking. The sound of my breathing echoed in my ears, vying for place with the pounding of my heart.

Then the phone rang. One. Two. Three. I made no move to answer it, and on the fourth ring the machine picked up. I didn't know who was on the other end, and didn't care. But the call served a purpose. It snapped me out of my trembling helplessness. I pulled on my coat and got the hell out of there.

Chapter 10

"Juan," I asked the night doorman, making my tone as matter-of-fact as I could, "you were on the door when I left earlier. Anyone go up to my apartment while I was gone?" When I'd put the apartment on the market, I'd left a key at the door with a note that it was to be given only to Rooney agents who presented their cards.

"No, Mrs. Wareham. I don't give the key to nobody."

"May I have it back, please. I'm—uh—I'm not selling the apartment after all."

"Good, good, Mrs. Wareham." He smiled. "We miss you, you go away."

"Well, I'd miss you too. Look, Juan, I have a problem. Somebody . . . well, I don't know how, but there seem to be"—I took a breath—"rats in my refrigerator." I felt as sensitive as Ada Fauer at the prospect of my listener translating that as bats in my belfry. "Freddie is coming tomorrow morning to clean. Would you leave word for Hector to come up right after she gets here and—uh—I don't know, do *something,* but get rid of them." I shuddered involuntarily as I said it. I pulled a notebook out of my bag and scribbled a note to Freddie, warning her not to open the fridge until after the porter had slain the dragons. I thought a second and added an instruction to call a locksmith and get the locks changed. "Here, Juan, would you make sure Freddie gets this?"

"Sure, Mrs. Wareham." He asked no questions. There are eight million stories in the naked city—and doormen know enough of them not to be thrown by something as minor as a couple of cold-storage rats. He hailed me a cab and I gave him a five as he helped me in.

Margaret Rooney lived all the way east on Sutton Place in a smallish building about the same vintage as mine and the Conquistador—but more elegant than the former and less showy than the latter. The doorman expected me and handed me over to the elevator man before he even buzzed Margaret to announce my arrival.

She opened the door to the sedate chime. She was wearing a long peach woolen wrap robe and matching leather mules. We checked out each other's worried faces for a second. Then she took my arm and drew me inside.

Her apartment, ten floors up, wasn't large, especially compared to the Leonaides spread, but it had wonderful river views. The furnishings were a clone of those in her office—French blue, peach, ivory in understated satins and brocades. It'd probably taken the decorator just an additional couple of phone calls to do the whole thing. She lived alone. We'd all speculated on the Margaret and Men question, but nobody'd come up with an answer. She always had an escort—a nice-looking one, but seldom the same one twice—for state occasions. Other than that, no visible trace of an involvement. Bobbie Crawbuck kidded that she was gay, but I don't think even he believed it. I'd decided that the whole thing simply didn't interest her, and had more than once envied her on that score.

Neither of us said a word until she'd taken my coat and hung it neatly in the closet. Then she asked me if I wanted anything to drink.

"Just a glass of water, please." I was still thirsty. I walked with her into the kitchen, where she filled a heavy-bottomed glass from the ice water tap on the refrigerator door. Irrationally, I felt relieved that she didn't need to open it. I downed the water in gulps and followed her back into the living room, where we arranged ourselves face-to-face on a pair of small blue satin sofas across a marble coffee table. I waited for her to speak. I'd be in a better position if she'd spent some of her resistance before I launched my artillery.

"Liz, I want you to understand. I am sorry for that poor man and his family. But there is nothing . . . *nothing* I could have done, or can do, to help him." Her cheeks flooded with feverish color. "But if this gets out, it will be the end of my company, and I can't let that happen. I will *not* go to the police. I will . . .

I will handle it my own way." She almost panted with the passion in her words.

"Margaret," I said carefully, "I am speaking, not only as someone who has just watched a man die horribly in an instant, but also as your public relations counselor." She started to interrupt, but I didn't let her. "Please"—I held my hand up—"let me give you the advice you pay me for. These so-called dirty tricks have been going on now for the better part of a month. All of them have been dangerous, and now someone has died. It was a fluke that he did, but he did. You believe this crazy campaign is directed against your company, you even think that one of your own agents is involved.

"Margaret"—I leaned across the table to maybe help it sink in better—"this is *not* going to stop. *You* can't stop it. Your company *is* in danger. *You* are in danger." I hadn't nailed her yet, but I saw the resolve in her eyes flicker. "The police will find out whether you tell them or not. Trust me, I know what I'm talking about. The detective in charge is very smart. I know him. His name is Ike O'Hanlon—he handled the Carter case." Anybody in New York with eyes or ears remembered well the murder last year of my client, King Carter. It had been the top news story of the week. "He will find out who had access to that apartment. Hell, *I* found out from the maid in about three minutes that it was Arlyne Berg's exclusive." I was getting to her now. "Margaret"—I leaned in closer—"he will grill Arlyne and every other agent who showed that apartment until he gets answers. You can't put a gag order on all those people. You know it won't work."

The sobs started deep inside her and came out in loud, racking waves. She just sat there, as if they had nothing to do with her. There were no tears, just the sobs. Something in her face said that she didn't want to be touched or comforted, so I just waited. After a few minutes the storm subsided. Then it was over. But it had left her face drained of all color—closer to white than any I'd ever seen.

"I don't think anyone, even you, realizes how hard I've worked to build the Rooney Property Company—or how much it means to me." This was no cheerleader. Her voice was quiet and almost without inflection. "My company is the only thing I have now. I won't let it die. No matter what, I won't let it!"

The only thing I have now. Had there been a lover? A husband? God, what an unimaginative clod you are, Liz Wareham. The only painful loss you can think of is some guy. "Margaret, your company won't die. Believe me. If you go to O'Hanlon of your own accord, he'll try his damnedest to keep your name out of it. I promise you that. And you'll be taking a step to end this nightmare. You'll come out a hero. You and the criminal will be separate in people's minds. But if you don't speak up now, everyone will blame you when it all comes out. *It will be your fault.*" Her eyes were trained on me, processing my words like a blue-screened computer. For a minute after I'd finished, the screen went blank, and I thought I'd lost her. Then she refocused.

"You win," she said with an almost normal Margaret smile.

"No," I said, smiling back, *"you* win."

"Where do you see us going from here?" Margaret asked. I thought about it for a moment.

"The first thing is to talk to the police. They're going to want Arlyne's list of who else showed the Leonaides apartment. Then you're going to have to speak to your agents. You should let them all know that you've notified the police about the rash of accidents involving Rooney exclusives." Her eyebrows rose slightly. "That's important, Margaret. If it *is* one of your people, she or he might very well panic now, and if it's clear that the police know everything you know, there'd be no point in . . . in . . ."

"Killing me?" she asked quietly. "Yes, I understand." She nodded. "It makes sense."

"Look," I said, "I have to ask you a totally unrelated question. Do you have anything to eat?" I'm not sure what unleashed it, but suddenly I was starved—not altogether strange, I guess, since my diet of the past thirty hours or so had consisted mostly of coffee and alcohol.

"Sure. Wait a sec, I'll be right back." She bounded up—the return of the cheerleader—and disappeared into the kitchen.

I got up and wandered around the determinedly pleasant pastel room. It suited Margaret perfectly, and yet, in a curious way, it didn't feel as though she really lived there. I ruminated on this as I gazed out over the East River at the illuminated Pearl Wick Hamper sign on the Queens shore. I glanced down and noticed that there were a few personal touches here after all. The top of the small carved French writing table held two silver-framed photos. I picked them up to get a better look. A tall blond man stood beaming between two little girls, the older one astride a green two-wheeler and the younger sitting on a red trike. The older girl was unmistakably Margaret. I hadn't known she had a sister. The second photo was a black and white old-fashioned studio shot of Margaret. But of course, I realized after a split second, it couldn't be Margaret. The woman in the picture was Margaret's age now—about forty—and the photo looked to be from the twenties or thirties.

"My grandmother," she said as she put a wicker tray down on the coffee table.

"You certainly look just like her."

"Yes," she said on a note of finality. I replaced the photos and went back to the sofa.

For the next five or ten minutes I stuffed my face with Skippy peanut butter slathered on Ritz crackers, washed down by Lipton tea. Dorm food—and it was sublime. Margaret sipped milky tea. Neither of us talked. Finally, I wiped the cracker crumbs off my mouth. "That saved my life," I said gratefully. "I can help you reach O'Hanlon now. Probably a good idea to get to him right away."

"No, Liz, I'll do it in the morning—first thing when I get to the office." She saw the disappointment on my face. "Don't worry. I told you I'll do it, and I will. But don't push me." She looked at her watch. "It's past four o'clock, and I must get some sleep. A few hours won't matter." She was right, I guessed. In any case, I knew from her tone that the matter wasn't up for negotiation and I'd better quit while I was ahead. She fetched my coat and handed it to me.

Now I had another problem: Where was I going to go for the next few hours, till I could get into my office? I couldn't call Ike. No way was I going home until home was de-ratted and its locks changed. I didn't want to fall in on a friend at this hour—as much out of reluctance to go into the necessary explanations as out of consideration. Where do the fairly affluent, temporarily homeless go in New York? This one headed for the St. Regis Hotel, where she dissolved, fully clothed, on a blue padded bedspread, into three hours of oblivion—at a cost of almost a hundred bucks an hour. I wondered whether I could legitimately bill it to the Rooney account.

Chapter 11

Sharon, the receptionist, was on the phone when I arrived at the office at a little past eight. I waved and started down the hall, but she stopped me with a held-up hand. After a few seconds she hung up.

"Morning, Liz. I was just picking up the messages from service. Two for you." She handed me a pair of pink slips. One said Mr. O'Hanlon, the other, Mrs. Zeibach. Well, they'd gotten the spelling right, if not the gender. Probably calling to see if I'd received the rats. I was certain he'd sent them—I just had no idea how he'd delivered them.

I didn't even make a pit stop at the coffeemaker. I was far too eager to get into my office and go through the newspapers under my arm to want to run the risk of bumping into another early arrival and having to exchange morning pleasantries. I shut the door, installed myself in my swivel, and attacked the *Post* first. Its front page screamed RESORT TYCOON BLOWN UP. The story, adorned with lots of photos of Steed in happier times, simply said that he'd died in a freak explosion while hosting a "fashionable" party at his "palatial" apartment. Homicide Lieutenant Isaac R. O'Hanlon was quoted as saying, "We have no comment at this time," which was just how he'd brushed off the NBC reporter I'd seen thrusting a mike in his face when I'd switched on the *Today* show at the hotel.

The *Daily News* story (GREEK MILLIONAIRE KILLED) was substantively the same, and so was the *Times* (LEONAIDES DEAD). I was enormously relieved that none of the coverage had mentioned the seemingly irrelevant fact that the Leonaides apartment had been for sale.

Just then my phone buzzed.

"Liz," Sharon's agitated voice squeaked, "I'm sorry, a man, he—" My door exploded open, and there stood Ike O'Hanlon.

The narrowed eyes and the white line around his mouth were not a welcome sight.

"It's okay, Sharon," I said, and hung up. He shut the door and glared.

He advanced just a few steps and looked down at me. "Tell me, Ms. Wareham," he asked coolly, "in my place would you kick your ass around the block, or clap you in the slammer?"

"What do you . . . ?" I thought I'd give injured innocence a try.

"Give me that big-eyed 'who, me?' routine, and I'll do both."

"Now, listen . . ." I barked as I stood up and faced him across the desk.

"No, *you* listen"—he cut me off without raising his voice— "and sit down—while you still can. You are going to tell me everything that you know and I don't about what happened last night. *Do . . . you . . . understand . . . me?*" He asked the question slowly with equal emphasis on each word.

I sat. Not that I really thought he'd carry out his threat, but there are times with Ike that it doesn't pay to test assumptions. "How did you know?" I asked.

He lowered himself into one of the Breuer chairs facing the desk. "Elizabeth Gail Herzog Bernchiller Wareham," he said, invoking my hated middle name along with my others in a mock-formal tone, "I have been acquainted with you in various degrees of intimacy since you were two years old. And I have never known you to want to be anywhere except where the action is. Therefore, when you sneaked out last night, it seemed strange to me."

"I did *not* sneak out."

"I trust that you and your baby-sitter were able to effect Sarah's prompt recovery?" He smiled nastily. "When the maid told me about your little investigation, I knew something was up, but I didn't know what. I still don't. Now, talk to me," he snapped, his quiet sarcasm abruptly catching fire. I stood again, suddenly as furious as he, not giving a damn what happened.

"I spent the night, you fucking bully, persuading my client, who, in fact, *does* have some information you need, to go to you with it! Who the hell are you to treat me like some . . . some delinquent kid just because you happen to know me?" I grabbed a chunk of the *Post* and threw it at him.

"It's because I *know* you that I didn't have you picked up and carted off to headquarters, you idiot!" he bellowed back.

I lost it then. I just lost it. I picked up a brass paperweight shaped liked the letter **L** and flung it. He ducked. *"Don't you call me an idiot,"* I screeched, *"and don't you threaten me!"* The door opened. John Gentle, Ike, and I looked at one another dopily.

"I didn't know you were having a meeting," John said quickly. "Come see me when it's over." He closed the door.

"For chrissake, Lizzie, you could have killed me with that!"

"I didn't throw it *at* you, I threw it *past* you."

"The hell you did! You never had any aim worth shit."

"My client's name is Margaret Rooney," I said icily. "She heads the Rooney Property Company. You probably have a message from her at your office. What she has to tell you involves a series of strange household accidents that have happened to her clients, of whom Steed was one. If I'd told you without consulting her, she'd have stonewalled you on it—and she's a pretty tough lady to break down when she doesn't want to do something. I promised her you'd protect her confidence." I paused. "Now, get the hell out of here." My voice broke. It was my first clue that I was on the verge of tears.

Ike looked at me for a second. The white line was gone from around his lips, and I couldn't read his eyes. Then he turned and left. The door clicked sedately shut behind him.

I leaned against the desk, my clenched fists resting on the satiny old fruitwood, and I cried—hard. Steed Leonaides, dead by stupid chance. Margaret Rooney, protecting her precious company at any cost. Norrie Wachsman, gallantly trying to make it in a job she was entirely unsuited for. Ada Fauer, fighting for all she had—her home. And me, a two-time loser, hopelessly nuts about a domineering, hot-tempered womanizer. I cried for all of us. I hoped that God didn't exist. For if he did, he was surely a senile psychotic, with a sense of humor to prove it.

I didn't hear the door open, or notice that anyone was there until Morley put the steaming mug of black coffee down in front of me.

"Come on, sit down and have a sip," he said, his soft New Orleans twang as soothing as the fresh coffee fragrance, "you'll feel beaucoop better."

I sat and sipped, and did. "Thanks," I said with a watery smile. "You are the best secretary in New York, Morley Carton, and not such a bad friend either. How'd you know a cup of coffee would save my life?"

"Bumped into Ike while I was hanging up my coat. He allowed as how you could use one." He held up his hand. "Don't worry, I'm not asking any questions."

"Thanks for that too. I'm not long on answers." I glanced up at the wall clock. "Oh, shit! It's almost nine and I was supposed to have an eight-thirty meeting with John on the Alfie Stover thing." I took another gulp of coffee, fished into my bag for a compact, and effected a makeshift facial repair.

"We getting London Fats back?" Morley drawled. "You said even a gun at your temple wouldn't persuade you to work for him again. Remember?"

"I remember," I answered grimly, grabbing my still-half-full mug and heading down the hall toward John Gentle's office. His door was open, so I marched in with a "sorry-to-be-late" smile, which I hoped was more insouciant than hangdog, shut the door, and sat down.

He looked at me speculatively, but, to my great relief, said not a word about the scene he'd walked in on in my office. "Okay, Liz, so how're we going to put the move on Alfie?" John usually started these strategy meetings by throwing out that kind of question. If you tried to answer, you'd get about three words out before he interrupted with an "I think . . ." If you just waited a beat, the "I think . . ." would come anyway. I waited.

"I think we should have some damage-control strategies ready to offer on this Westover project. I ordered a computer search on media coverage." He picked up a sheaf of clippings and slapped them down in front of me. "Alfie's been getting killed in the press last couple of months."

"I know. He's deserved it."

"Goddamned right. Canning us for those clowns at Seltzer and Moffo. They don't know squat about crisis management. Couldn't wipe your shoes, kid."

"That's not what I meant, John," I said wearily. "Look, I have a pretty good idea why Alfie happened to call you out of the blue yesterday morning." I filled him in on the Zeibach/Ada/ rats confrontation of Sunday night. "Only Alfie would be naive enough to think he could hire a sleaze bucket like Jerry Zeibach to do his dirty work and—" I was stopped by a loud, unfamiliar female voice which, fueled by indignation, reverberated down the corridor and through John's closed door.

"I don't give a *damn* if she's in a meeting. You get her here right now, or I'll open every door in this place till I find her!" John and I looked at each other and shrugged a mutual "beats hell out of me." He got up, strode to the door, opened it, and started toward the reception area. I followed along, as puzzled as he.

"Really, I—I." Sharon's voice squeaked with uncertainty about how to handle things. Neither her job description nor experience as a receptionist had equipped her to cope with insistent fury—much less twice in one morning. "If you'll just sit down, I'm sure she'll—"

"*No!* You get her *now*. Miss Liz Wareham is gonna talk to me face-to-face!" This, just as John and I reached the reception area, stopped me dead in my tracks. John and Sharon stared at me. I stared at the woman. I'd never seen her before in my life.

"I'm Liz Wareham," I said, mystified, "what can I do for you."

"Oh, listen to her!" She whipped off a pair of large harlequin-framed sunglasses, revealing light brown eyes, swollen and pink-rimmed from crying. "Little Miss Goody Two-Shoes! That's my husband you're screwing, get it?" My mouth opened, but no sound came out. Did Ike have a wife stashed away? I took a close look. Orangy lipstick bleeding off generous lips, contorted with anger. Eyebrows overplucked, giving the round face a curiously naked, vulnerable look. Bottled sunstreaks in

dark brown hair, which could have profited from more comb
and less spray. She didn't look like Ike's type.

"Excuse me," I managed to get out, acutely aware of John's
eyes on me. "Who are you?"

"Who are you?" she mimicked in a la-di-dah voice, striking a
mock-affected pose that showed her honey-colored mink to
sweeping advantage. "As if you didn't know. You sleeping with
that many married guys?" She snorted a derisive laugh. "I'm
Mrs. Jerry Zeibach, bitch, what do you say to that?"

I didn't say anything. I laughed. Relief? Tension? Just the
total off-the-wall surprise of it? Probably all of the above. Her
skimpy brows knit in rage, and she advanced on me. "Don't you
dare laugh at me, you goddamned rotten man-stealing tramp,
I'll—" I lifted my arms to ward her off. By now we had a sizable
audience—most of the agency had been drawn from their offices by this unexpected Tuesday morning drama.

"Mrs. Zeibach," I said, my face flushed with embarrassment
for both of us, "I am really sorry that I laughed. But I wasn't
laughing at you." She hesitated, her orange-lacquered nails
about nine inches from my face. Was she really going to try to
scratch my eyes out? Did people *do* that? I took hold of her
wrists, one in each of my hands, and looked into her miserable
brown eyes. She didn't struggle. "I have met your husband exactly once. I am not having an affair with him, and I have no
idea why you think I might be."

"'Cause you were all over his book, that's why." Her voice
broke. Tears were not far off.

"What book?"

"His appointment book," she wailed. "I saw. I'm not so
dumb. So why didn't he come home last night?" She was sob-
bing now. "He *always* comes home. He—" She pulled her hands
away from mine and scrubbed at the tears with them, like a
miserable child.

"Look, I was at a party last night—with at least eighty other
people, and your husband wasn't one of them."

"Expect me to believe that?" she shrieked. She ran to the
elevator and punched the button, wishing, I'm sure, it were my
face. "I'll fix you. There are lawyers, ya know, and . . . and

other ways!" The elevator door opened. She flung herself into it and was gone.

I let out a deep breath and turned to my assembled colleagues. "Okay, show's over," I said, "we can all get back to work."

Chapter 12

"Hey, kid," John said as we headed back to his office, "your private life is your own, but is something going on I should know about?" That, I thought, is a matter of opinion. John *was* my boss. Some might think that he ought to be told about Rooney's lethal trickster, not to mention the fact that I'd be rushing from our meeting with Alfie Stover to one with Percy Tuthill and Ada Fauer. I decided that no good would come of sharing either of those tidbits at the moment.

"No, John. The scene you walked in on in my office earlier was purely personal. I'm sorry that it happened here. This last thing"—I held my hands out in bewilderment—"I honestly don't know. I met Jerry Zeibach for the first time over this crazy rats thing, just like I told you. I guess he must have jotted my name down and gotten to Alfie right away—which is, I'm sure, why Alfie called you so bright and early Monday morning." I shook my head. "That poor woman, sneaking peeks at his note-book, frantic about who he's screwing—stuck with the bastard."

"Looks to me like she's pretty interested in *staying* stuck with him." The phone beeped. It was Morley. John handed me the receiver.

"What's up?" I asked Morley. "Nothing flamboyant, I hope. I don't think I could stand act three."

"Margaret Rooney. She needs you over there ASAP."

"Let her know I'm on my way." I hung up. "John, Margaret Rooney wants me over there right away. About Alfie, let's just play it straight and hear him out before we suggest anything. He can surprise you sometimes." John looked dubious. "Look, I promise I'll behave and do my damnedest to woo him back here. Deal?" I held out my right hand.

"Deal," he agreed. We shook hands gravely and agreed to

meet in Alfie Stover's lobby at four-fifteen. I got out of there
before John could change his mind.

When I popped back to my own office to get my coat and
bag, I found a pink message slip from Freddie Mae Riggins, the
young dancer who once a week cleans my apartment. I'd forgotten to check in and see how she was coping with the rat situation. I leaned over and dialed my home number.

"'Lo," Freddie's musical voice sounded reassuringly unfazed.
No great surprise—six-foot, ebony Freddie, with her easy, lop-
ing walk and dancer's tensile strength, was possibly the least
fazable person I knew.

"Hi, it's me. Look, Freddie, I'm sorry to leave you with this—
uh—mess, but . . ."

"No problem, Liz. The little buggers are gone, and the lock
man's on his way. I'm gonna put it on my Visa. That's why I
called. I'll leave you a note how much."

"Great. God, I was in such a state, I totally forgot to leave
money. Thanks, Fred, you're the best."

"No problem," she repeated. "But, Liz, what's going on
here? I know it's not my business, but since Sarah left for college, well, I don't know, I worry about you." Me too, I thought.

"I'm okay . . . really. I don't have the time to go into the
whole thing right now—I'm late for a meeting—but I think everything's kind of under control now." A major lie. "By the way,
I've changed my mind about moving."

"I heard," she said, "but you better tell those brokers. One of
them showed up this morning—sore as a boil when Gus
wouldn't let her come up, and then she started to hassle me on
the intercom. I just hung up on her."

"I'll straighten it out. And thanks for everything—including
worrying about me."

When I arrived at Margaret Rooney's office at just shy of
eleven, her door was closed. "Hi, Selma," I said to her secretary
as I took off my coat and hung it up, "I got here as soon as I
could." I gestured toward the closed door. "Am I supposed to
be in that meeting?"

"No, I don't think so," she answered, removing the half

glasses from her eyes and allowing them to hang free from the silver chain around her neck. She rubbed the bridge of her nose between thumb and forefinger. "I believe Margaret wanted to see you as soon as it was over." She shook her head slowly. "Oh, Liz, how terrible!"

"It is that, Selma." I glanced at Margaret's door. "Who's in there?"

"Lieutenant O'Hanlon. Also three of the agents." Three? That was odd. Margaret had talked about suspecting four agents: Arlyne Berg, Vi Royal, Bobbie Crawbuck, and Norrie Wachsman. I felt a chill as I ticked off their names in my mind, especially Norrie's. I couldn't see any of those people—even flamboyant, name-dropping Arlyne, whom I'd just met—as the trickster. There *had* to be another explanation.

Just then the door opened and Bobbie, Arlyne, and Norrie filed out. I managed a "hi," wishing devoutly that I were somewhere else. All three looked devastated. Arlyne's complexion had taken on a greenish tinge, which seemed slightly surreal in contrast with her electric-blue dress. Bobbie's good looks, stripped of their accustomed jauntiness, appeared stagy—unreal. And Norrie was a waxwork. The sadness in her white face looked as though it would be there forever.

Margaret appeared in the doorway and motioned me inside. Her face was wan, but her step had a purposeful spring to it. "I'm glad you're here, Liz. As soon as the lieutenant's finished with us, I'll start the Tuesday sales meeting." She gave my shoulder a Margaret-style squeeze. "I'm going to have to calm the troops down about all this, and I'll welcome your help."

"You've got it," I replied. I gave Ike a cool nod, which he returned in kind, and chose one of the two ivory slipper chairs rather than sit next to him on the sofa. Margaret perched on the other one and leaned forward, looking expectantly at him. "Well, what do you think, Lieutenant?"

"I don't know yet, Ms. Rooney. You've got three pretty tense people there, but that doesn't mean much. I'd be tense in their place too. I'll have a better fix after we've had a chance to do some checking and talk to each of them separately." He gave first Margaret, then me, a speculative blue gaze. "You both know these people well. What do *you* think?"

"As far as I'm concerned," Margaret said with an unaccustomed hard edge to her voice, "any one of them could have done it." Ike saw surprise widen my eyes, and held his hand up in a gesture that clearly meant "shhh." Margaret continued. "Arlyne's new with our company, so I *don't* really know her very well. Bobbie Crawbuck is a . . . a homosexual"—she found the word almost as uncomfortable as the concept—"and who knows what actually goes on in their lives? And Norrie Wachsman is—I'm sorry, Liz, I know she's your friend—but she's a loser, and maybe it's—"

"Oh, come on, Margaret," I cut in before I could stop myself and weathered Ike's dirty look, "do you really think that Norrie would do these terrible things because she's not a worldbeater at selling apartments, or that Bobbie would because he's gay? That's—"

Margaret's face stiffened. "I don't know, Liz. That's all I'm saying." Her pale eyes took on a look I'd never seen in them before—one of desolation. "I've learned to stop being surprised at what people will do and why. It makes life less disappointing."

Ike focused on me. "Well, Liz," he asked with careful casualness, "you apparently take exception to Ms. Rooney's assessments. What're yours?"

What *were* mine? As I thought about it, I realized I didn't have any. "Margaret," I said, "when we first spoke, you said you suspected *four* agents. Has Vi Royal been cleared?"

"Seems so," said Margaret, "Vi hasn't shown the Leonaides apartment for more than a month—since just after Christmas, and the lieutenant says that exonerates her."

"The Leonaideses ran out of firewood a week ago Sunday and got a fresh delivery the next day," Ike explained. "Somebody planted a hollow log stuffed with gunpowder among the new wood, and that had to be within the last week."

"And Bobbie, Norrie, and Arlyne all showed the apartment last week?" I asked. "Were they the only ones who did?"

"No," Ike answered, "but according to Ms. Rooney here,

they were the only ones who showed the Leonaides apartment last week *and* the other three apartments where these so-called tricks were played."

"For God's sake, Ike"—I could hear a growing frustration color my voice—"that doesn't mean there's no other explanation. Maybe it's—"

"A coincidence?" he supplied the word neutrally. "Maybe it is. But we have to start somewhere, and at the moment, this is the only lead we've got." I ground my teeth in annoyance at his lofty putdown.

Ike rose from the sofa. "Thanks for your help, Ms. Rooney. I can't guarantee I'll be able to keep your name out of this, but you have my word that I'll try." He nodded in my direction and added with an almost straight face, "And thanks for *your* help too."

My main goal was to get out of Margaret's office before I blew up. I was still outraged at her depictions of Norrie and Bobbie—a loser and a fag—and I knew I couldn't vouch for the control of my tongue if I had to listen to more of the same. I glanced at my watch. It was almost eleven-thirty. The meeting was half an hour late, and the agents would be restless as hell.

"Margaret, I think you should be circumspect at the meeting. Tell them that the police have been called in and will be talking to some of them, but don't even hint that any of them are under suspicion."

"I disagree. I've got eighty-seven agents. Why shouldn't eighty-four of them know they're in the clear?"

"Because you don't know for sure that they are!" My face flushed to match my angry tone. I forced the volume down. "Look, you can't publicly damage three people when you have no proof. If I were any one of them, I'd sue you—and win." I was bluffing, but it gave her pause. "Please, Margaret, the most reassuring thing you can say is that the police are on the case—period."

She looked at me curiously. "Why are you so resistant to the idea that it likely narrows down to those three people?"

"Because of the word *likely*. Even if you're right, two of those people are innocent. One thing that *is* likely, though, is that the tricks are over," I said as I got up and started toward the door. "Anybody'd have to be nuts to try it again with Ike O'Hanlon ready to pounce."

Chapter 13

The salesroom buzz dropped to an almost hush as Margaret walked in and stepped up on the small platform at the front of the room. I stood against the wall near the doorway, a good vantage point to survey the scene without calling attention to myself. Most of the agents' faces carried a worried look, at odds with their spandy suits and smart dresses.

Margaret kept the meeting short and took my advice about not speculating about possibilities for blame. Her tone struck just the right note between matter-of-fact and comforting—a skillful commanding officer sending scared troops into battle, or a recovery room nurse assuring the patient that everything was under control. When called upon, I stressed the importance of not blabbing to outsiders about the situation. The nods around the salesroom indicated that the point had been taken.

I tried to make eye contact with Norrie, but her expression was so blank that it was hard to tell whether she was avoiding me or just didn't notice. I also scanned the room for Bobbie Crawbuck, but couldn't find him. Arlyne Berg, at whom everyone kept stealing glances—it *had* been, after all, her exclusive client who'd died—seemed to have regained her equilibrium. She reported that the Leonaides apartment would be unavailable for showing for the next few weeks, and went on to describe her new "dynamite" exclusive on the floor directly above it in the Conquistador. "More English-country-house look, and seven hundred thou cheaper."

As the meeting ended, I made for Norrie's desk. She was on the phone. "Laura," I heard her say, "I'm terribly sorry, I'm going to have to cancel this afternoon's appointments. I think I'm getting the flu and I've got to get my bones to bed." She laughed at something on the other end. "You better believe alone. The way I'm feeling, I wouldn't even be tempted. Okay, thanks. I'll call you to reschedule."

She hung up and finally met my eyes, the forced jollity of her phone conversation abruptly gone. "Diplomatic flu," she said wryly.

"Norrie." I bit my lip. Now that we were face-to-face, I didn't quite know what I wanted to say. Besides, the setting was hardly private.

Arlyne Berg, exuding her potent cloud of Giorgio, was no more than five feet away at the desk cattycorner to Norrie's. She turned and smiled, her dark eyes glinting with a wanna-make-something-out-of-it? defiance. "Visiting the suspects' corner, Liz?" she asked. "Seems like one of us has flown the coop. Where'd Bobbie-boy go, Norrie?"

"Maybe out for some air that doesn't smell like Giorgio, Arlyne," Norrie replied with an edge, "which sounds like a good idea, actually." She picked up her large wine-colored satchel and stood.

"Just wait a second while I get my coat, Norrie," I said, "I'll walk out with you." Then I took a closer look at Arlyne. The tension underlying her bravado wasn't hard to spot. She looked ready to crack. Without thinking about it, I put my hand on her shoulder. "Take it easy, Arlyne, I know it's tough—on all of you."

She looked at me for a beat. "What do you know about tough?" she asked quietly with a smile that sat crookedly on her scarlet lips. Then she turned away and picked up the phone.

Norrie and I didn't speak until we hit the street. I think we both welcomed the blast of clear, icy February air. I know I did. "Come have a sandwich with me?" I asked.

"I don't think so, Liz, but thanks."

"Norrie, I feel awful for you, you must know that."

"I *do* know it."

"Well then, maybe I can . . . I don't know, at least be an ear."

She shook her head slowly. "I don't need an ear. I need to be alone." She struck a Garbo pose, head thrown back at an angle. "I vant to be alone." She managed a grin.

"Going home, then?"

"No, to the movies."

"The movies?"

"Yeah. Complete escape. Doesn't matter what's playing. I'll just wrap myself up in it for a few hours—maybe longer."

"Uh-huh." I nodded. It made sense, kind of.

"You know, back in the Far Hills days with Attila, I used to use the mall that way. The rougher things got, the more I'd go —just wander from store to store." She smiled dreamily. "It didn't matter if I bought or not. It was just being there—so safe, so away, so *pleasant*. I'd pretend I was my mother—the original entitled lady. Remember my mother, Liz?"

Oh, yeah. Mrs. Rose had had "a little man" who rewired wall sconces and "a little woman" who restuffed pillows with fresh down. And she'd provide chapter and verse to us budding Bernhardts in a tone of implacable authority. *These* were the truly *important* things to know. And she was so sure of it, you almost believed—for a second. "Yes, I remember her."

"Life was so easy for her, wasn't it? She just *knew.*"

I shivered despite the fur-lined raincoat. "Norrie, I—I don't think you should be alone."

She touched my arm lightly. "You miss the point. It only *works* if I'm alone." She smiled at me once more, turned, and walked away.

I let out a long breath, which froze in a wispy cloud. I was scared for Norrie. This thing had hit her hard, but why wouldn't it? *The movies.* All of a sudden it seemed irresistibly appealing. My watch said twelve-thirty. I didn't have to be at Alfie Stover's till four-fifteen.

Without further consideration I headed briskly for Cinemas I and II, across from Bloomingdale's on Third Avenue. Fifteen minutes later I was unwrapping a Milky Way and watching coming attractions. I'd always had a special fondness for coming attractions.

The movie itself was a romantic adventure/comedy. The two stars met cute, then had a major row. As I crumpled the wrapper of my second Milky Way, they were trading barbed wisecracks while fleeing together from some scowling types with large guns. I trusted that in the end they'd wind up healthy, happy, and together. I felt far less sanguine about how things might work out for Ike O'Hanlon and me.

After the movie I popped across the street to Bloomingdale's and headed for the mezzanine phones. I checked in with Morley and picked up messages—none of which was I dying to return, but did anyway.

It was three-thirty. I killed half an hour at the cosmetics counter, where I ended up dropping fifty bucks for a moisturizer, whose microbubbles would make sure that my face was bathed in perpetual dew, and a lipstick to add to the fourteen others I already owned. Normally, these purchases lift my spirits for at least twenty minutes. This time the glow was gone before I'd signed the charge slip.

I headed for Eastover, the tower-topped glass box that Alfie Stover had built on the corner of Madison and Fifty-sixth. I arrived on the dot of four-fifteen to find John Gentle pacing the lobby in the brisk measured strides of a G.I. on guard duty.

"There you are," he said unsmilingly with a look at his Rolex.

"We said four-fifteen, no?" I responded. This was par for the course. I knew from experience that he'd been there, pacing, for at least fifteen minutes, which was why I'd been careful not to arrive earlier. Immediately before a client pitch meeting, John's like an actor waiting backstage to make his first entrance on opening night. His stage fright tends to be contagious. My problem is that John is a better actor than I. Once he steps out onstage he's instantly relaxed and proficient, whereas I, if I allow myself to get caught up in his frenzy, bump into the scenery.

"Yeah," he mumbled. "Look, Liz, we're talking *upbeat* here —can do. Whatever Stover says, whatever he wants done, I want you to be positive about it. Don't commit to a strategy, but don't be negative even if Zeibach is there eyeballing you across the table."

I looked at him glumly. Stupidly, I hadn't even considered having to face Zeibach. The idea was unappealing enough to make me wish I were behind a Bloomingdale's counter selling microbubble moisturizer. "John," I said, trying for diplomacy— never my strong suit, "I appreciate what you're saying, but Alfie and I know each other pretty well. He knows I don't bullshit him. Maybe that's why—"

"Maybe that's why he canned us." He fired the shot across my bow, knowing it would hit home.

"Maybe," I said coldly, "he's figured out that he was wrong. Otherwise, why ask for me?"

"To buy your silence. To make sure you won't go to the media with your charming story of one of his people menacing an old lady with rats."

"Well," I said pointedly, "my silence is certainly for sale. We can even make it fairly expensive." I reflected uncomfortably on the implications of committing myself to Alfie Stover and then promptly running off to scheme against him with Ada and Percy. If I got caught—even if I *didn't* get caught . . . My two-Milky-Way lunch flipflopped in my gut. I guessed I wasn't cut out to be a double agent after all.

"Okay, Liz, four-thirty on the nose," John said, leading the way to the elevator. "Let's go up."

Chapter 14

The executive offices of Stover International—the corporate
name Alfie had chosen after I'd shot down ASO International
—were located on the top floor of Eastover's thirty-six-story
tower. That he'd chosen to occupy this prime space rather than
realize the whopping rent it would have commanded was a
mark of how our boy had changed. The Alfie I used to know
would have parked his desk on a single-digit floor facing the
back, and gotten his kicks out of raking in the cash. But now
money alone was no longer his issue. As I mulled that over, I
thought it might present, if manipulated properly, a ray of hope
for Ada Fauer and her neighbors.

The reception area was circular, white, and windowless with
cream-colored ultrasuede banquettes lining half the space. The
sleek receptionist was seated at a round module made of glass
blocks and brushed steel. The effect was reminiscent of the
starship *Enterprise.*

"Mr. Stover will see you now," the smart-looking receptionist
informed us in a British accent more than several rungs up the
ladder from Alfie's own. John and I rose and exchanged
glances. We'd been there about ten minutes, during which time
we'd sat in silence—not unusual in a client's waiting room,
where you can't talk about what's really on your mind and don't
much feel like making small talk.

"Through that door, turn left," the receptionist instructed us
with a perky chin-in-the-air smile, "then right."

John and I made our way down a glossy white corridor decorated with steel sculptures which looked to my untutored eyes
like plumbing parts. When we took a right turn the space age
gave way with unsettling abruptness to the Edwardian—all dark
wood paneling and thick wine carpets. Seated at a square mahogany kneehole desk, improbably topped by a word processor,

was one person I *did* remember from my Alfie days, Elvira
Treemor.

"Well, Miss Liz. If you're not a sight for sore eyes!"

"And you, Ms. Elvira." It was the first time that day I'd really
felt like smiling, and I did.

She tipped her head to one side, which made her resemble all
the more a small, plump cockney sparrow. "Still callin' me those
women's lib names. I'm too old for all that." Elvira was seventy-
ish with round brown eyes and gray-brown hair which framed
her round face in a Buster Brown cut. She hadn't changed a bit
in the couple of years since I'd seen her, nor, I guessed, in the
twenty years before that. She'd been Alfie's secretary from the
beginning—had come over from England with him. The fact
that she hadn't been supplanted made me feel a tad more opti-
mistic.

"You'll never be too old for anything, Elvira. I've got great
faith in you," I said. "Do you remember John Gentle, the head
of our agency? John, Elvira Treemor," I added quickly, knowing
that John probably wouldn't remember her name.

"I never forget an 'andsome man, do I? 'Ow've you been
keeping, Mr. Gentle?"

"Very well, Miss Treemor," John replied, his faintly formal,
slight bow reflecting an instant adjustment to the British accent
of his surroundings, "and you?"

"Tryin' to keep me 'ead on straight." She motioned toward a
closed walnut paneled door to the left of her desk. "Right in
there. 'E's expectin' you."

John opened the door and we entered a large square room
with two walls of windows framing spectacular views south and
east, partly obscured, unfortunately, by heavy wine velvet drap-
eries tied back with gold cords. The green carpeting was
overlaid with pinkish Chinese rugs. All in all, it was the sort of
room Alfie Stover must have aspired to as a cockney kid, but off
somehow—a little too much of everything.

Alfie himself was seated in a massive carved walnut throne at
the head of a massive carved walnut table. He was rounder than
when I'd seen him last, but the bulgy, wide-set brown eyes were
as bright as ever.

He was flanked by a woman I knew and a man I didn't. I let out a breath of relief—no Zeibach. The woman, recognizable even with certain recent strategic alterations, was Alfie's wife, Doreen.

"Liz, John, glad you're 'ere," Alfie greeted us without rising, in a tone that indicated that we'd all seen one another yesterday rather than two years ago. "Liz Wareham, John Gentle, my wife Dolores," *Dolores?* "Ray Mentone." If my jaw dropped the way it felt like it did, I hoped nobody noticed. Ray Mentone was a name I certainly recognized—Margaret Rooney's former partner. Coincidences, I told myself, *do* happen, whether you believe in them or not.

"Oh, I remember Liz," the newly named Dolores said, evincing about as much warmth as I felt for her. I'd always believed that her social aspirations had had more than a little to do with our losing the account. Her presence was not great news. "But," she continued, beaming in John's direction, "I have not had the pleasure of meeting her boss." The elocution had, like her name and nose, been altered. She smiled, parting crimson lips to reveal a row of teeth that looked too perfect to be real, because they weren't. Besides the dentist and plastic surgeon, she'd visited a hairdresser who'd gilded her dark hair and eyebrows. If I'd liked her better, I'd've scored it all a big improvement—well, all except the hair, which was unfortunate with her sallow skin.

"Delighted to see you again, Dolores," I said with almost no pause before her name. I took the mini-throne next to Ray Mentone and shook his hand. John performed the same minuet on the other side of the table and sat next to Dolores.

"I won't beat about the bush," Alfie said, fixing his frog eyes on me, "we've got problems." His jowls wobbled as he chewed the word, just the way I remembered. I nodded acknowledgment and waited for him to continue. "Frankly, at this point I wish I'd never begun the Westover project. But that's no matter now. It must go forward. I've a grite deal of money tied up there." I smiled to myself. Alfie still referred to money as either "a grite deal" or "no' a lo'." I felt somehow pleased that he'd decided not to join his spouse in elocution lessons.

"Would you fill us in on what's been happening," I asked neutrally, "aside from what we've seen in the papers and on the tube."

"It's ghastly what those people've been saying," Dolores broke in, "so unfair." Alfie held up his hand to stop her, but it didn't quite work. "I really don't know what they expect. Alfred's been so generous. Why, he—"

"Doreen!" Alfie roared.

"Dolores," she countered with chilled dignity.

"Sorry, luv. My temper's frayed these days." Alfie checked his Rolex, a diamond-studded oyster that made John Gentle's look monastic. "Where the devil is Zeibach? 'E was meant to be at this meeting."

"He knows that," Ray Mentone said. He was a slim, dark-haired man in his mid-forties with a sensual mouth and deep-set hazel eyes surrounded by shadowed skin that made him look a bit like a sexy raccoon. "I talked with him yesterday. Of course he's gonna be here. After all—" He glanced at me and shut up.

"All right," Alfie said, holding up his hands, "let's put it all out on the tible. As you've probably figured out, I decided to arrange this meeting after hearing about the bloody awful incident Sunday night. But"—he leaned in toward me—"I'd probably've called you anyway—sooner or later, because this is all getting quite out of 'and." His jowls twitched indignation. "Just turn on your telly, you'd think I was Ebenezer Scrooge."

"Well, you're talking to the right people," John replied, beaming with a confidence unshared by his colleague.

"I 'ope so. The PR people I 'ave now can't seem to do anything except get Doreen . . . I mean Dolores . . . on charity committees." This earned him a filthy look from Doreen-I-mean-Dolores, which he ignored. His blunt fingers drummed nervously on the heavy carved table for a second. Then he continued. "This is the situation. I was able to pick up that property for no' a lo' of money. Ray 'ere put the deal together last year and then joined my company. We 'ad every reason to believe we could buy those tenants out and proceed to build Westover." He saw my eyebrows rise. "What's the matter, Liz?" he asked defiantly.

"Uh—nothing. Please go on," I said, telling my fractious eyebrows to mind their business. This was no time for a confrontation.

"This is my first experience with residential property," he continued, "and my last, I can tell you—but I understood this kind of thing is fairly common 'ere in New York. You buy a piece of property. You settle up with the tenants and Bob's your uncle." He glanced at Ray Mentone, who offered a confirming nod. "Couldn't do that in London, of course. Take a stick o' dynamite to dislodge a sitting tenant there, but 'ere—why, people like Jerry Zeibach 'ave an entire business doing nothing else!"

"And how did you happen to come upon Mr. Zeibach," I asked.

"Ray set it up. Jerry's 'is brother-in-law, actually."

"I see," I said as neutrally as I could manage.

"Look," Ray Mentone cut in, "I know Jerry's sometimes kind of unrefined, but you have to understand that what he does— relocations—is no easy business."

"I'm sure it isn't," I said dryly, images of Sunday night's sidewalk scene still vivid in my mind.

"What Liz means," John jumped in, setting my teeth on edge by volunteering to translate me as though I were speaking an arcane foreign language, "is that certainly we understand that you and Mr. Zeibach are dealing with a delicate balance of interests here." He gave me a meaningful you-promised-to-behave-remember? look.

"You know, Alfie," I began, trying to choose my words carefully, "you said when you began this meeting that Sunday night's incident—the fact that I happened to stumble into it— triggered your call to John." Alfie nodded. "Well, let me tell you two things. One, if you're concerned about my going to the media with it, don't be. You have my word on that, and I think you know me well enough to trust it. And two, if I *hadn't* happened along and been able to help cool things down, you'd've been all over the front pages and TV with the thing." John beamed me his approval. It was premature. "It's number two that worries me for you, Alfie. How much do you know first-hand about Mr. Zeibach's tactics?"

"Let me answer that," Ray interjected. "Alf pays me to run the Westover project, and I like to earn my keep." A small, disarming smile. "You know, Liz, you can't ride a guy's tail while he's doing his job—not if you expect results. I've known Jerry Zeibach a long time. He's been married to my sister for fifteen years. He's emptied out lotsa buildings in this city for projects just like ours, and never once—never once"—he emphasized the point by slapping the back of his right hand into the palm of his left—"has he been nailed for doing anything illegal." He eyed me triumphantly.

"That's good to know, Ray," John said, preemptively making nice. "Makes our job a lot easier."

"People have been known to do illegal things and *not* get nailed, if they're practiced enough at it," I said, "also *immoral* things, which—"

"Wait a minute." Ray held up his hands. "I gotta interrupt you. Immoral, says who? Your morality, my morality, maybe they're different." Even on brief acquaintance that seemed likely. "This isn't a tea party we're dealing with. This is *business.* Lotta money at stake."

"I don't deal with tea parties, Mr. Mentone," I replied. I knew as I spoke that the sarcasm was imprudent. I just couldn't seem to stop my mouth. "My clients often have a lot of money at stake, and leaving themselves open to public charges of immoral, if not illegal, behavior can be a pretty fast way of losing it." If it had been within John's power, an unseen hand would have swooped down and yanked me from the scene at that moment. I'd broken a cardinal rule: Thou shalt not be snotty to clients—ever.

"So he fired the doorman, so what?" Ray's face flushed as his voice heated up. "That's immoral? God says there's gotta be a doorman?"

"Fair enough, but what about playing games with basic services like heat in February? And a front door that won't lock? And planting rats in people's apartments?"

"Rats?" Alfie shot out, his eyes popping.

"That's ridiculous!" Ray responded, his voice thick with scorn. "I just wish Jerry was here to—"

"Well, where *is* 'e, for chrissike?" Alfie's tone was more than irritated.

"I honestly don't know, Alf," Ray said, "he'd never miss—"

"All right, all right," Alfie cut in, "I don't know whether any of these things Liz is talking about are true." He fixed Ray with his froggy eyes. "But the real point is *you don't either.* I want you to step in and tike charge, Ray. You understand? You talked about earning your keep. Well, that's 'ow you earn it. Up to now I've listened to you tellin' me Zeibach was doin' 'is job—trying to buy those tenants out and keep up the building with minimum service. In my books, fair's fair, and I'm no bleedin' 'eart. But this is the first I 'eard about rats, and if that's true—"

"It isn't," Ray interrupted grimly.

"If it is," Alfie continued, his stare at Ray unwavering, "it's not only Zeibach's arse that's out of 'ere, it's yours." I'd gotten the response I wanted from Alfie, but at a price. Ray Mentone would be an enemy for life, and I'd better watch my back. Alfie then turned his attention to me. "You got pretty cozy with that old woman—the one that 'eads the tenant committee—didn't you?"

"Yes," I said in the most noncommittal tone I could manage. He was on a rampage now. Would I be the next casualty? If it turned out I'd blown the account, John would blister my skin off —at best.

"Good," he continued with a decisive nod, "you go to 'er and you tell 'er that I've got things in 'and. The door will be repaired and the 'eat will be restored. And no rats." He gazed meaningfully at Ray Mentone.

"Great," I said, breathing again, "I'm sure—"

"In return for which," he plowed through, "no more blubbing to the papers or the telly. We'll just negotiate terms—private, like civilized people." Sure. Like Sherman negotiated with the Georgians. Besides, Ada Fauer was hardly civilized where her home was concerned.

"Alfie, you have to understand—" I started to protest.

"I understand that that's what I'll be *paying* you for!" he decreed with an emphatic thump of hand on table, "But no doorman. Definitely no doorman." He rose, strode over to John, and shook his hand warmly. "John, a pleasure to be working with your organization again. Six months to start. Eight thousand a month. Write me a letter to that effect. I'll sign it."

"Great, Alfie," John responded, pumping hands enthusiastically, "twelve thousand's more like it for a project this crucial."

"Ten. You drive a 'ard bargain. Always did." He made his way around the table to me and placed a chunky arm on my shoulder. "Good to 'ave you back, Liz. Counting on you." With those unreassuring words he marched out of the room, Dolores at his heels.

Ray gave me a hostile glance and followed suit, leaving John and me alone in the conference room. "We pulled it off by the skin of our teeth, kid," John said to me with a look that was far from loving, "but I feel like kicking your butt." It was the second time in a single day that a key man in my life had expressed that sentiment. I couldn't toss a paperweight at this one. "You didn't have to alienate Mentone to make your point," he continued, pointing a stern finger. "That was dumb and it's going to come back to haunt you. Maybe it'll teach you a lesson."

I gritted my teeth as we walked out together. He was right and I knew it—and he *knew* I knew it. But as soon as we crossed the threshold, my eye caught something that bumped John's reprimand abruptly to a back burner. Ray Mentone was ushering a tall blond man through a door about thirty feet down the hall. *Bobbie Crawbuck.*

Chapter 15

Bobbie Crawbuck. Ray Mentone. Margaret Rooney. I took my leave of John in a semi-daze as these three people chased each other around my head. It was too early for my meeting with Ada Fauer and Percy Tuthill. Even if it hadn't been, I needed some time to get my brain unscrambled. I crossed Fifty-sixth Street and ducked into a coffee shop—the kind that's jammed at lunch and, luckily, almost empty at an off hour like six P.M. While I waited for my black coffee and grilled cheese, I tried to put some pieces together.

Margaret had said from the first that the dirty tricks were a tactic to wreck her company. I'd thought that was paranoid nonsense. But what if Ray Mentone were starting a competing brokerage? He and Margaret, by all accounts, had ended their association less than happily—not surprising from what I'd seen of Mentone. It was hard to imagine a less likely pair of partners.

But Bobbie. What could have been the hook to get Bobbie involved in such a crazy scheme? *Money,* dummy, what else. Though Bobbie had had a pretty good year, the antiques business had produced far less well for his lover, Art Blyfield. And they lived up to and beyond each dollar, much as I did. Bobbie and I had commiserated about that over dinner only a few weeks ago. A few weeks ago—just before the tricks had started. Oh, my God, Bobbie had inadvertently killed Steed Leonaides! He'd never get over it—never. He'd start drinking again and . . .

The sandwich arrived and, against all odds, I attacked it like a wild animal, as my mother used to say when I was eight. If any of what I was thinking was right, did Alfie Stover know about it? I bet myself not. Alfie would start a brokerage business if someone convinced him it was a profitable idea. And he'd lure top producers away from Margaret, or anybody else, but dirty tricks

were simply not his style. So Mentone was playing his own game
—at least partly out of revenge against Margaret Rooney.

I sipped some tarry, reheated coffee. Should I tell Margaret?
Or Ike? I massaged the question and admitted to myself that
the plot I'd just concocted could be just so much fanciful story
spinning—pretty thin stuff to ruin a friend's livelihood and reputation on. Ray Mentone and Bobbie could simply be old buddies, though they hardly seemed each other's type. Maybe Ray
was a client or a customer, someone Bobbie was trying to sell an
apartment for or to. What if Ray *were* starting a brokerage—
either for Alfie or on his own—and interviewing Bobbie about a
job? That would be Bobbie's private business. I couldn't blow
the whistle on him with Margaret.

What if I finally got sick enough of John Gentle—a real possibility after today—and Bobbie bumped into *me* meeting with
Hill and Knowlton or Burson Marsteller? How would I like it if
he stuck his big foot in and went to John? I'd break his neck is
what I'd do. I took a gulp of the coffee. It tasted worse as it
cooled. I'd talk to Bobbie. That made the most sense. Margaret
had asked me herself to speak with the agents she suspected—
see if I could find out anything. For once I'd just be following
orders.

I walked over to Fifth Avenue and then north to Central Park
South. As I turned west I realized I wasn't minding the chill
February night one bit. I had the illusion that the wind was
clearing my head, sweeping away piles of old papers and debris.
Ike O'Hanlon. It would never work for the two of us, and that
was that. We just couldn't get along—might as well accept it.
Let him find some compliant tootsie, and let me . . .

I arrived at Ada's building to find a note with my name taped
to the front door. I opened it. "Can't buzz you in—broken.
Ring 12C and Percy will come down and let you in. XXX Ada."
Not more than three minutes later the door opened and I was
facing a tall, bearded redhead in a dark brown turtleneck and
well-worn tweed pants, the kind of face you see on ads with a
little placard off to the side saying that his hobbies are scuba
diving and Chinese cooking and his scotch is Dewar's.

He took my hand in his two large tapered ones and said, "Hi,

Liz, ah'm Percy?" with a questionlike southern uptick at the end.

"You're Percy?" I heard astonishment shrill my voice. "But I thought . . . I . . ." It was too much. A giggle bubbled somewhere in my gut, where it expanded until it exploded in a full-scale belly laugh—followed by another, and a third.

He looked on in puzzled good humor until my fit had subsided and I was dabbing my streaming eyes with a crumpled Kleenex. "Well, ah like to think ah'm an amusing fella, but—"

"No—no, really. I'm sorry for being so rude, but Ada said . . . well, she didn't actually *say,* but I got the idea that you were kind of a"—I suppressed a new attack of giggles with some effort—"little, old guy—with a poodle."

"Used to have a Doberman, as a matter of fact. But ah guess ma name sounds that way. Percy Tuthill—now, ah ask you!" He smiled engagingly. Ma mama was distressed when ah took a different name—for ma writing?" That curly up-note again. Cute.

"Writing? What kind?"

"Thrillers—mysteries."

"Oh, I eat that stuff like candy. Maybe I've come across them."

"Maybe you have. Mark Christmas?"

"Mark Christmas! My astonishment hit a new high. His detective was a sexy black PI named Trask, who sheltered the weak, blew away the bad, and screwed the beautiful, all with a grace and pace that made for some of the world's best airplane reading. "Are you kidding? I'm a fan."

"Well, Trask thanks you, ma'am—and so do I," he said with a mock bow. "Come on inside." He threw his arms wide, gesturing at the dumpy lobby. "Welcome to Crestfallen Manor. Ah hope you're ready for a little hike—elevator's out." My face said what I thought about climbing twelve flights. He put his hand on my arm. "Fear not, we're only going up to four—to Ada's. She's a feisty old gal, but ah figure trekkin' the eight floors to my place would be tough on her."

He swung open the fire door at the back of the lobby and loped up the stairs with me trudging along behind him, hitch-

ing up my long coat so I wouldn't trip on it. Percy Tuthill
was charming-and-handsome-and-bright-and-amusing-and-suc-
cessful, the very man you dream of meeting as you paint on
your smile and fasten your bracelets for yet another cocktail
party. The Leonaides party flashed unbidden into my mind and
stimulated an involuntary shudder.

Percy led the way down a shabby tan corridor scarred with
chips and gouges which provided peeks at decades of previous
color schemes. He pressed Ada's doorbell, producing a rusty
beep, followed by the quick tapping of shoes and turning of
heavy bolts. The door swung open to reveal a mini vaudeville
museum. The 1930's green walls were almost obscured. Posters,
handbills, and framed, yellowing photos, press clippings and
programs hung in a chaotic jumble, interspersed with hats—
toppers and derbies, straw boaters and flowered bonnets. A
door that looked like it led to a closet was decorated with a
rakish assortment of canes, and another, partly open to the
bedroom, was festooned with lacy reticules and beaded evening
bags. The heyday of the Warbling Fauers: America's Lovebirds
surrounded us.

Ada watched me take it all in and grinned impishly. "We had
a good time, Jack and me, before the diabetes finally took him."
She drew me inside with a hug. She was wearing a mauve crepe
dress with a large navy flower print and some shirring along one
side. I remember my mother having such a dress when I was a
couple of years old. She wore it with similar open-toed platform
shoes too. A man's navy cardigan was draped over her thin
shoulders, the top two buttons fastened.

"Ada, you look great," I said, "bummer about the elevator,
but I think I have some good news for you on that score."

"See, Percy," she said, taking my hand and leading me to the
faded green velvet sofa. "I told you she was terrific. We haven't
even started to talk yet and she has good news! Here, let me
take your coat, honey. You got a warm sweater on. Good. It's a
little chilly here." She laughed her throaty laugh. "So what else
is new? Let's have a little something to take the chill off. Bourbon, brandy?"

"C'mon, Ada darlin'," Percy said, depositing her in an armchair whose antimacassar lay, useless, a good six inches above her rusty head. "Ah'll get the drinks. Ada's a brandy girl. What'll you have, Liz?"

"Brandy for me too, thanks. Straight up, no ice."

"You got it. And bourbon for me, like any self-respectin' good ol' boy."

"It *is* kind of chilly," I said. "You guys ever try to get the Buildings Department to crack down on them for that and all the other stuff?"

"Not that easy," Ada said, shaking her head. "Believe me, we tried. They got their stooges in the Buildings Department. We call and complain. An inspector comes around, and on that day abracadabra, everything's different. The elevator's running. It's toasty warm. The light bulb in the hall gets replaced, and Zeibach swears the front door just broke yesterday and the repairman's on his way."

Percy passed out the drinks, sat next to me on the sofa, and raised his glass. "To Liz, who's gonna help us beat this thing."

"Whoa," I said, holding up a palm instead of my glass. "I don't think that's exactly the way it's going to go."

"But you said you had good news," Ada said, leaning forward.

"And I think I do. You know, it was a pretty smart guy who first said 'If you can't beat 'em, join 'em.' I'm suggesting you consider that, and I'll tell you why."

"Hold it, honey," Ada broke in, "Percy and me, we put up a good fight so far. No way we're caving in, not even—"

"Wait a second, darlin'," Percy said with a smile so small that it barely moved his mustache and beard. "Let's hear what Liz has in mind. Who knows, maybe it's an offer we can't refuse." He performed the godfather catch phrase in a suitable gravelly voice. "Actually, ah wouldn't put Mafia techniques past them. That Zeibach's a real thug."

"I agree with you there," I said. "What if I told you you wouldn't have to deal with him anymore?"

"What'd you do, have him knocked off for us?" Percy asked with real smile. *"Ah'm* the thriller writer. Ah should've thought of that."

"It's an appealing idea, but I'm afraid I don't have quite your flair for drama—or Trask's," I said. "Seriously, I met with Stover this afternoon. You remember, Ada, I used to handle his PR." She nodded. "Well, he didn't know anything about the extent of the games Zeibach has been playing with you."

"I don't believe that for a—" Ada blasted in disgust.

"No, it's true. He knew the doorman had been dispensed with and he authorized the buyout offers, but the rest of it—the stingy heat, the broken door and elevator, the rats—that was all news to him."

"Doesn't he read the papers, or watch TV?" Ada asked, her chin thrust forward.

"The one message you've pushed in your publicity has been 'he wants to throw us out of our homes'—which has been very effective," I added. "That farewell party for the doorman was a great touch." The glimmer of satisfaction that crossed Percy Tuthill's face told me whose idea that had been. "But the few times specifics like broken doors were mentioned in the coverage, Zeibach just told Stover that you were making a big fuss over nothing to get media attention, and that the problem had been taken care of. And the rats—well, that's new stuff, isn't it? Hasn't been in the papers, at least not that I've read."

"That's true," Percy admitted, "that stunt he pulled with Ada Sunday night was a first. Lucky, though, it brought us you."

"Well, now Alfie Stover knows all about it," I continued, "and he doesn't like it one bit. Zeibach's not going to be running things anymore, and the building's going to be put back into working order—all except the doorman," I added quickly.

"And what does Santa Claus Stover want in return?" Percy asked. "A photo of us all packing our suitcases to leave?"

"A media blackout," I said.

"Oh, honey, not on your life!" Ada croaked. "That's the only weapon we got!"

"No, it isn't," I began. But I never got a chance to finish the thought. Ada's doorbell beeped. She and Percy looked at each other.

"Expectin' anyone, darlin'?" Percy asked.

"Not a soul," she answered. The beep sounded again, followed by a heavy rapping. Percy got up and walked to the door.

"Who's there?" he asked, his fluid southern voice suddenly tense.

"Police. This Ms. Fauer's apartment?" This time the three of us exchanged bewildered glances. But I had a slight edge on them—I recognized that voice. Percy released the locks and opened the door.

I've rarely seen Ike O'Hanlon caught totally off guard, but he was this time. It took him a long few seconds to regroup, during which time he gave me a blue look cold enough to skate on.

"What *is* this," Ada said heatedly, her eyes fixed on the uniformed cop at Ike's side, "that bastard Zeibach call the cops on me again?"

"Are you Ms. Fauer?" Ike asked neutrally.

"I sure am, and let me tell you something. That lowlife's supposed to spend his time keeping this building running, not complaining to the cops about tenants. You see that elevator? Not working since Monday. And where's Zeibach? Is he taking care of it, I ask you?" She struck an indignant pose, hands on hips, chin thrust up to confront Ike.

She stayed frozen just like that when Ike answered calmly, "Mr. Zeibach is in the apartment next door, Ms. Fauer. And no, he isn't taking care of the elevator. He's dead."

Chapter 16

Ada, Percy, and I exchanged mute stares while Ike watched. Then Ada laughed—not the free, rolling laughter of the night we'd first met, but a harsh bark.

"Boy! Can you beat that? First time I ever asked God for something, and he did it, just like that. I can't believe it was a heart attack, 'cause I never saw any sign of a—"

"Ada," I said, taking her arm and easing her down onto the green couch, "this is Lieutenant O'Hanlon of Homicide. I think we can assume that someone other than God is responsible for Mr. Zeibach's death."

As her eyes darted back and forth between Percy and me, they seemed to sink deeper into their sockets, like desperate little fish diving for safety. She began to say something—to Percy, I thought—but clamped her jaws shut after the first sound.

"Lieutenant, ah'm Percy Tuthill?" Percy's voice with its inflection was calm. "Ah live upstairs? Would you mind telling us what happened exactly?" Ike's presence plus the sounds of activity I was starting to hear outside Ada's door were providing some possible answers to Percy's question—all of which were bad news.

"That's what we're going to find out, Mr. Tuthill." There was a businesslike knock at the door, and Ike strode over and opened it to Sergeant Joe Libuti, who raised a surprised furry eyebrow when he saw me. "Sergeant Libuti," Ike said, making introductory gestures, "Ms. Fauer, Mr. Tuthill. I believe you already know Ms. Wareham," he added with a slight formal incline of his head. "Joe, would you begin with these people while I have a private word outside with Liz?"

He steered me out into the hall, where police, some in uniform, some in plainclothes, scurried purposefully. Jessup, the nice precinct cop of Sunday night's episode, was stationed at a door ten feet or so from where we stood. Shit! Zeibach had been killed here in the building—in the apartment right next door to Ada's.

I caught Jessup's eye and started to walk toward him, but Ike clamped a hand on my shoulder and walked me the other way around a corner near the fire stairs. "May I ask what the hell you're doing here?" His hand still held my shoulder. I shook it off.

"As you probably already know from Jessup, I met Ada Fauer *and* Jerry Zeibach in the wee hours of Monday morning, courtesy, actually, of Lieutenant I. R. O'Hanlon and his nocturnal phone flirtations, so—"

"Time!" He held his hand up. "Let's have it, minus the recriminations, deserved as they may be."

I filled him in on the Sunday night incident. "Also, as of"—I looked at my watch—"two hours and forty-five minutes ago, I'm in charge of PR for the Westover project. Look, Ike, I'll level with you, but you'll have to—"

"You'll level with me, but nothing," he snapped.

"Goddammit, why are you so—"

"Because I am a police officer investigating a murder, and I'm not going to make little tit-for-tat bargains with you to get the information I need. I know what you want." I started to interrupt, but he wouldn't have it, "You want to call your client, Stover, to tell him about Zeibach, and you want to keep the old lady's rat allegation out of the papers. Right?" He was—and I wanted to smack him. "Why do you act as though I were some kind of storm trooper, Lizzie?"

"Then stop acting like one!" I shot back through gritted teeth. We traded glares.

He compressed his lips and shook his head slowly. "You can phone Stover as soon as we're finished talking, and the press will hear of no rats from me—not even a mouse. Now, I don't want to hear the word 'but' from you again. Please proceed."

I did, feeling humiliatingly like a reprimanded kid. I told him that Ada'd invited me to meet with her and Percy Tuthill for some pro bono PR help, and that in the meantime, Alfie Stover had decided to take Zeibach off the Westover project and had authorized me to mend some fences. "Zeibach was a really terrible guy. I can imagine lots of people wanting to kill him."

"Maybe, but whoever *did* it did it here, in this building."

"Oh, Ike, get real! Ada wouldn't . . . she *couldn't*, no matter what she says about praying for him to die. That's just, well . . . Besides, I mean, my God, she's eighty-one and he was a six-foot hunk! How was he killed?"

"Not certain yet, but it wasn't by brute strength. And I'm sure your friend Ada's not the only person in this building to wish Zeibach dead. You have any other dealings with him?"

"No. Well, not exactly. But the bastard pulled his rat trick on me too."

"He did?" Ike focused in with a cop's heightened alertness. "When?"

"Well"—I gnawed my thumbnail as I mulled that question seriously for the first time—"I found them in my fridge late Monday night, after I got home from the Leonaides apartment. They weren't there Monday morning when I left for the office."

"What time was that?"

"A little before eight."

"Uh-huh. So sometime between eight in the morning and when?"

"Well, I got home at three or so and went off to the party at about nine-thirty."

"And got home again sometime after midnight, right?"

"Yeah." Just then, Christiansen, Jessup's sourpuss female partner, briskly rounded the corner.

"Lieutenant, the M.E. needs you." She looked at me for a beat before she placed me, and nodded grudgingly.

"Liz, I need to talk to you some more, but I'm going to be tied up for a while. I want you to go to my place and wait till—"

"*No way,*" I said with stony emphasis on each word. Christiansen's eyes widened while her mouth formed a small circle of surprise.

Ike didn't try to fight me on it. "Have you had your locks changed?" he asked.

"This morning."

"Good. Christiansen, take Ms. Wareham home. See that she gets into her apartment all right and have a look-see that nobody's hiding under the beds except cats. Then come back here."

"Come on, Ike, she doesn't have to. I can get home just fine. Besides, Ada—"

"Ada will be okay. I left my truncheon in my desk." He looked at me severely. "I want you to stay in your apartment till I get there, understand? It may be on the late side."

"Now, look, you can't—"

"Oh, yes, I can. Of course, if you'd rather, Officer Christiansen could just as easily escort you downtown to Police Plaza." The look on Christiansen's face said that that would suit her just fine.

Home was where I wanted to go. Why was I making a fuss about it? Why could I never keep my big mouth shut with Ike? Well, for that matter, why couldn't he . . . ? "Okay, gang," I said, manufacturing a wide smile, "I know when I'm outvoted."

When I went back into Ada's apartment to get my coat and bag, Percy sat alone in the living room. The door to the bedroom was shut. "The sergeant's talking to Ada in there," he said. "Ah guess ah'm next. They lettin' you go?"

"Under armed guard," I said.

"Can ah call you later?"

"Sure." I gave him my number.

"Ms. Wareham"—Christiansen and I would never become great and good friends—"this is not a social occasion. Let's move it."

"Coming, Ilse."

"My first name happens to be Karen, but I'm Officer Christiansen to you."

"Funny, you looked like an Ilse," I replied meekly.

It was actually kind of reassuring to be accompanied by an armed police officer on my first post-rat entry into my apartment. Christiansen cased the place as Ike had told her to. There was nobody under the beds, not even the cats, who had bounded into the foyer to greet us. "I'm allergic," Christiansen

said accusingly, certain that I'd discovered this fact and produced the cats specifically to torment her. She did not stick
around.

The moment the door shut behind Christiansen, I ran to the
kitchen phone and tried to reach Alfie Stover, who was neither
at home nor at his office. I left word with his butler to try to
reach him and have him call me immediately. I gave the felines
a snack to get them off my ankles. Then I called John Gentle.

"Jesus Christ, Liz, just our luck! Right after you bad-
mouthed the guy to Stover. Well, maybe it's a blessing in disguise—remind Alfie how effective we are in a crisis."

"A real heavy disguise, John. Look, I got the police to promise not to mention the rats to the media. We don't need all of
New York thinking that Alfie gave the nod to those tactics. Now
I'll have to convince Ada and Percy that it's in their interest to
keep quiet about that too."

"Ada and Percy? Oh, right, the tenants committee folk. Hey,
I know I was hard on you after the meeting—not apologizing,
you damned well deserved it—but I want you to know I'm im-
pressed that you went right over there to work on those people
for Alfie. Hit the ground running—makes us look great."

"Oh"—I breathed a relieved sigh—"thanks." At least John
would never know that I'd arranged to meet Ada and Percy
before we'd talked with Alfie, and that the original agenda was
one that would not have earned his compliment.

"I hope that crazy wife doesn't go popping off to the press."

"What?" For an instant I didn't get what he meant. Then I
did. "Oh, God!" I'd forgotten all about Mrs. Zeibach's visit to
my office. It seemed months ago. Had it been only this morning? "I'd better brief Seth about all this. We may need an official press spokesman who isn't me."

"Kid, about the Zeibach wife, you *are* sure that there's nothing in it?" At least he had the grace to sound sheepish.

Chapter 17

I got hold of my aide, Seth Frankel, on whom I had to pull rank to tear him away from a PBS special on persecuted peoples in the twentieth century. "Seth, you want persecution, I'll give you persecution. You've got exactly twenty seconds to turn the goddamned thing off." When he got back on the line, I filled him in on the Stover story, which by now I'd recounted enough times to consider turning it into a recitation piece for parties.

"Zeibach," he said, "isn't that the name of the mink coat that came to the office this morning and hollered that you were balling her husband?" Seth has a reporter's memory—one of the reasons he's so good dealing with them.

"Yeah, I'm afraid so—which is why I'm going to make you primary media contact on this, okay?"

"Sure." His tone was decidedly more upbeat. Seth had been our media spokesman last year when our client, King Carter, had met an untimely sensational death. He had quite enjoyed his brief stint on camera—preserved on videotape by relatives throughout the borough of Brooklyn.

"I hope to reach Alfie tonight and work out a strategy. I'll catch you at the office first thing tomorrow."

I looked at the phone, trying to decide who else I ought to call, and realized that there wasn't a hell of a lot I could do till I heard from Alfie Stover and Percy Tuthill. Suddenly the Bobbie Crawbuck problem jumped back into my head. It had nothing to do with Zeibach, but it was something I needed to deal with promptly. If I *was* going to put the blocks to Bobbie, why not do it right away—tonight? The prospect tweaked my stomach, and I realized I needed reinforcement to work my way up to the phone call. I opened the freezer, where Ben and Jerry were waiting and scooped myself an extravagant ball of Heath Bar

Crunch—original vanilla, not the arriviste coffee—and licked
another big dollop off the spoon.

I trundled down the hall to my bedroom, sat, legs folded
Indian-style, on the bed and started to eat while I pressed the
Play button on my answering machine. My mother in Florida,
hoping everything was all right, since she hadn't heard from me
for a week. My daughter, Sarah, at Stanford, assuring me that
everything *was* all right, even though I hadn't heard from *her* in
a week. My ever-vigilant friend, Barbara Garment, with a warning about the pitfalls of moving in with Ike O'Hanlon and a
reminder that such situations were covered in Chapter Eight of
her latest book, *Combat Zone: Men Against Us.*

At the risk of being a bad daughter, mother, and friend, I
decided return calls could wait. I flipped through my Rolodex
for Bobbie's home number. I'd ask him to come over—now.
And I could let him know that Ike would be coming too, so I'd
be safe. Safe? From *Bobbie?* Well, if he were the trickster,
maybe he'd . . . no, I could handle it. I could bluff and say I'd
already *told* Ike. But . . . no buts. Just *do* it. You've had your
ice cream. Now just pick up the phone.

"Bobbie. It's Liz."

"Ah, the beauteous Elisabeta. I am at your feet." Now I was
supposed to pick up the "kiss my sneaker" line, but I didn't.

"Listen, Bobbie. I need to talk with you. I wonder if you
could—uh—come over."

"Sure, babe. Dinner? How about Thursday?"

"No, I meant—uh—now, actually."

"Now?"

"It's kind of important, Bobbie."

"Hey, you sound really strange. Oh, my God, don't tell me
there's been another of those . . . *things!*" Innocence or an
artful touch?

"No," I said quickly, "but I *do* need to see you."

"Okay. Just let me change into some jeans and take Pucci for
a pee. Be there in three-quarters of an hour or so."

I checked my watch. It was nine-fifteen. Too early for local
TV news, so I snapped on the radio to WCBS—all news. ". . .
in charge of tenant relocation for British developer Alfred Sto-

ver's embattled Westover project. According to Police Lieutenant Ike O'Hanlon, in charge of the case, police were led to
Zeibach's body by an anonymous phone caller. Preliminary re-
ports indicate that he had been dead at least twenty-four hours.
Lieutenant O'Hanlon said that the cause of death was still un-
certain, and that the police have no suspects at this time. For
WCBS news this is—"

I turned off the radio and just sat for a moment, eyes fixed on
the last melt of ice cream in the dish on my lap, while I did a bit
of quick arithmetic. Twenty-four hours—maybe longer. That
meant Zeibach was dead by, say, seven P.M. Monday. I'd left
that morning around eight and come home by three. A bunch of
brokers had been in and out while I was gone. How could a six-
foot bozo sporting a black eye and carrying a bag of rats have
gotten past a very reliable doorman and into my locked apartment with all those people unpredictably coming and going? He
couldn't. *And he didn't.* Ike, with his cop sense, had seen that
instantly, but I'd assumed that rats equaled Zeibach and—

The shrill of the phone made me jump. "Stover 'ere."

"Alfie, glad you got my message. I don't know if—"

"I've 'eard. I've 'eard. What a balls-up! This could be a *disas-
ter.* 'Tenants persecuted by Stover driven to murder!' I can see
the bloody 'eadlines now."

"I agree it's pretty bad," I began, "but we've got a couple of
things going for us, number one being that none of those tenants is going to want to behave like someone who was driven to
murder. That means we can look for some restraint on their
part—at least until the killer's caught. I think I can get them to
see that hollering about rats and such isn't a smart thing to do
just now. And I've gotten the police to agree not to mention
Sunday night's incident to the press."

"That was quick work."

"Oh, I guess I forgot to mention that I happened to be in the
building, meeting with some of the tenants, when the police
discovered the body. Ironically, I was in the middle of telling
them they wouldn't be dealing with Jerry Zeibach anymore."

"You mean you left our meeting and went right over there?"
Alfie asked. "Oh, Liz, you *are* a wonder. 'Ow did I ever let you

go? What?" This last to someone other than me. Probably Elvira Treemor. If I knew my Alfie, he'd gone right to the office
once he'd heard the news, and summoned Elvira to join him.
"Put 'im on the line." Back to me. "Putting Ray on the line with
us."

Mentone. Just what I needed. "Hello, Ray," I said carefully,
"my—uh—condolences about your brother-in-law."

"Thanks. I'm out here in Cedarhust with my sister." And
here you are on the phone with the putative scarlet woman. I
wondered if Mrs. Zeibach had shared her suspicions with her
brother.

"You know, Alfie," I said, "it's by no means certain that the
killer *is* one of those tenants. Forgive me, Ray, but your
brother-in-law wasn't the most universally loved guy. Anybody
who wanted to kill him would have a perfect cover in the Westover controversy. But that's for the police to find out. Has either of you talked to them yet?"

"Two of them are out here now talking to Ann Marie," Ray
said. So Mrs. Zeibach's name was Ann Marie. It made her seem
even more vulnerable, somehow, that prim Catholic name. "I
just got here."

"Lieutenant O'Hanlon left a message that 'ed be at my office
at ten tomorrow morning," Alfie said. "Should I 'ave a solicitor
there, or you?"

"Neither, I'd say. I know O'Hanlon from the Carter case last
year. You can talk to him. He'll be discreet as long as you're
straight with him. Having lawyers or PR people around will just
get his back up. By the way, the news said Zeibach had been
dead at least twenty-four hours. When did you last see him?"

"I 'aven't seen 'im since last—oh, when was it—Thursday.
Thursday afternoon," Alfie said, "but I spoke with 'im on the
phone early Monday morning, four o'clock to be precise, when
'e called to tell me about the . . . problem with the old lady—
the one you 'appened into. As you know, Liz, anything important comes up, I tell my people to call—day or night."

"He called me from his car," Mentone chimed in, "Monday
morning on his way into the city—about ten or so. I told him

Alf had set up this meeting with you and your boss and we wanted him to show up for it."

"Well," I said, "just tell the police that. They'll ask you both your own whereabouts for the times the murder could have happened, but don't be thrown, it's just routine. Answer straight, and remember, most people don't have twenty-four-hour-a-day alibis, so—"

"Alibis!" Alfie was shocked. I realized the word had been a poor choice. Comes of sleeping with a cop.

"Sorry," I said, "it's what they call it. Doesn't mean they suspect you. Look, let's talk about the media for a second. They're going to be all over you. Duck them for the moment, and refer all calls to Seth Frankel in my office. You remember Seth, don't you, Alfie?"

"Yes. Ugly little fellow—glasses? But why 'im, Liz? Why not you?"

"Because Seth can get away with saying less. I was there when the body was found, after all, and I'm dealing with the tenants. Also"—better lay it on the line—"Ray, your sister descended on my office this morning, accusing me of having an affair with her husband. If she goes to the press with it, I'm certainly not the best spokesperson for the moment."

"Oh, Christ!" Ray blasted. "She always thinks he's banging the whole world. Not far wrong! But what gave her the idea about you?"

"She was awfully upset, but I think she saw my name jotted down in his pocket diary and assumed . . ."

"Ah, Jesus. Don't worry. I'll straighten her out. Oops, gotta go now. Seems the cops are ready for me. Talk to you later, Alf." Ray hung up and Alfie and I agreed to speak again early in the morning, before his interview with Ike.

I went into the kitchen and put on some coffee. Just as it started to drip through, the intercom bell rang. "Meester Crawbuck," Juan announced. I opened the front door and stood waiting in the doorway for Bobbie to make his way up in the elevator. All at once I felt horribly awkward—not scared, but acutely uncomfortable—at the prospect of confronting him.

Then he was there, turning the carpeted hallway corner and

striding on his mile-long legs toward my door. "Hi, babe." He greeted me with a hug and a kiss, which landed on my forehead. "Made pretty good time, didn't I? Pucci did his business like a little trooper. What's up?"

"Come on in and sit down, Bobbie," I said, busying myself with hanging up his buttery leather jacket so I wouldn't have to meet his eyes. "Coffee or designer water?"

"The water's great," he said, making for the kitchen. "No, go sit. I can get it. What about for you? Want a real drink? I don't mind, you know."

"I know, but I think I'll skip it." I went into the living room and sat nervously on the edge of one of the sofas. A minute or two later Bobbie joined me, carrying a tall glass filled with ice and San Pellegrino, or whatever mineral water it was that I had in the fridge. He parked himself on the Eames chair, took a long, thirsty sip, and looked over at me expectantly.

"Bobbie, look, I guess the only way to say it is to say it. I saw you at the Stover office." His pale blue eyes widened in surprise, while his lips parted slightly. "And I don't know what to do about it," I added miserably.

"What do you mean, do about it?" he snapped. "I can meet with anyone I want. What does Margaret have, company spies now?"

"Hardly," I replied, my own annoyance at being in this stupid position showing through. "Let me spell it out, okay? Sure you can meet with anyone you want—to look for a better job, or for any other goddamn reason. Ordinarily. But two nights ago a man was killed, and a few others have been badly hurt—all because someone is trying to sabotage Rooney—"

"Hey—" he cut in indignantly, but I didn't let him finish.

"At least that's what Margaret thinks. And the police don't seem to disagree. Then, all of a sudden, you turn up meeting with Margaret's ex-partner, who might just be starting a competing brokerage."

He looked at me without speaking, eyes almost as wide as when I'd first said I'd seen him with Mentone. "How'd you know?" he asked after a moment, trying for casual and not making it.

"That Mentone was starting up a new brokerage?" He nodded. "Good guess—given the circumstances. The same good guess anyone else who knew the players might make."

"Well, so what, Liz?" he asked, his voice unfamiliarly rough-edged with anger. "Free enterprise system, haven't you heard of it? Man wants to start a business, he—" He cut himself off. "Okay," he continued, sounding more like his normal self, but with a new, guarded cast to his face. "I'm not saying that Ray Mentone wouldn't like to zap Margaret if he could. She's not exactly on his ten nicest persons list. But he wouldn't pull something like those crazy tricks. Besides, how could he?"

"He couldn't." I looked at him hard as I continued. "But *you* could." As if on some perverse cue, the phone rang.

"Me?! What are you, nuts? Why—"

"Bobbie, I didn't mean you *did,* but . . . Shit, I have to go answer that. Might be Ike." I ran to the kitchen and caught the fifth ring.

"Hi"—the soft southern tones of Percy Tuthill—"ah was just about to hang up. Did ah get you at a bad time?"

To put it mildly. "Well, kind of. I really want to talk with you though. Can I call you back?"

"Ah wondered if ah might come over to your place, since it seems the police are finished with us for the moment."

"But they're not finished with *me,"* I sighed, "O'Hanlon's going to be coming here sometime later, and I don't think—"

"Probably not. Tomorrow night better?"

"Much. I'll call you back later." I jotted his number down on the yellow pad on top of the washing machine and hung up.

When I returned to the living room, I found Bobbie still in place, but looking a lot more relaxed. "Sorry to leave you hanging on that terrible note, Bobbie, but you can see how it looks. The police are in on this thing. It's only a matter of time till they—"

"Find out that I've—shall we say—been exploring other opportunities?"

"Exactly."

"I committed a crime. I looked for a better job. Lock me up, guys! How 'bout you, Liz, do *you* think I've been running around burning people's faces with acid?" He stood and threw his arms out in mock drama, sloshing some of the water in the glass he clutched onto the rug. "Wrenching their guts with ipecac? Blowing 'em up with exploding logs?" He laughed with no mirth at all, took a long sip, and sat back down. His face was flushed.

"Jesus, no. Of course I don't think so, but . . ." I didn't know how to finish that sentence.

"But what?"

I took a long breath and let it out slowly. "But I don't think it about Norrie either—or even Arlyne. And you three are—"

"I know, top of the list." He took another gulp of his drink. "Let me tell you shom—something. Money is the root of all good. Makes it *all* happen." A knowing laugh and rubbed his thumb against his fingers. "Trinkle, trinkle." I'm a bit slow, but it came through to me then that while I was on the kitchen phone, Bobbie had switched his beverage from water to one just as clear and colorless, but a lot stronger. I'd screwed this up royally. All I'd accomplished with my clumsiness was to push Bobbie off the wagon.

I got up, walked over, and put my hand awkwardly on his shoulder. "Let me . . . let me get you some coffee." He pulled away, shielding his glass with both hands. "Bobbie, don't do this to yourself."

"To *myself*? That's a fucking laugh! *You're* the one trying to pin this on me, my beauteous Elisabeta." He took another swig from the tall glass. "You and my other pal, Arlyne," he added bitterly.

"Arlyne? What's she got to do with this? Are you saying—"

His face closed down. "I'm not saying another word. I didn't do a goddamn thing except talk to a guy about a job and—"

The downstairs buzzer shrilled. Ike? I hadn't expected him so soon. If I let him just march in, Bobbie would think . . .

"Bobbie, look, Ike's downstairs and I have to let him up, so—"

"You called the *cops*?! I don't *believe* you could—"

"No, no, I didn't. It's not about—"

"The *hell* it's not! I—" The buzzer again.

I ran to pick up its receiver. "Lootenant O'Hanlon comin' up," Juan said.

"Okay," I replaced the receiver in time to hear the door shut with a slam behind Bobbie. I ran to it, turned the lock to the open position, and ran down the hall after him. As I rounded the corner, I caught a glimpse of the staircase door closing behind him. No way I could chase him down seven flights. I stood there, feeling defeated—and deserving of it.

"I appreciate the reception, but frankly I'm surprised," Ike began. Then he took a closer look at me and abruptly stopped the banter. "What's wrong?" he asked sharply.

"Nothing," I replied, a ridiculous response considering how well he knew me. "Everything. But I don't want to talk about it. Come on, let's go in," I said as I started back toward the apartment, "I'll even give you a cup of coffee as a good-will gesture." I tried on a smile, but it didn't fit.

"I see you remembered to flip the door button," Ike said with a grin—referring to a Saturday-night incident a couple of months ago when I'd inadvertently locked us both out, with a pot of rice simmering away on the stove and guests expected. He'd had to hightail it up to the Bronx and tear the superintendent away from a family party to let us in. Happier times. My smile came easier with the rush of nostalgia—if nostalgia was even the right word for something that recent.

When I hung up Ike's Burberry, I noticed Bobbie's leather jacket right next to it. He'd been too eager to get out—and maybe too drunk—to bother about retrieving it. Well, he'd just be running out of the lobby into a cab. I'd call him after Ike left and try to . . . try to what? What if Bobbie actually had *done* those things? Every instinct told me no, he couldn't have. But *somebody* had.

I felt a sudden chill. Ike saw me shudder and gave my shoulder a quick squeeze. "I'm going to make a fire. Why don't you get the coffee?"

In the kitchen I glanced up at the round black clock over the fridge. Quarter of eleven. I quickly dialed Bobbie's number. He wouldn't've had time to get back down to TriBeCa yet, even presuming no traffic, but I left a message on his phone to call me as soon as he got in. Then I filled two chunky blue mugs with coffee and went in to join Ike. Fortunately, we both took our coffee black, since I had no milk in the house and can't bring myself to buy those evil, powdered white chemicals.

Ike was coaxing the logs into optimum position with a poker, which made me feel the opposite of cozy, since it summoned up too-vivid pictures of Steed Leonaides doing the same thing. I put the mugs down on the glass table and sat, legs curled under me, in the corner of the short sofa farthest from the fireplace.

After a few minutes Ike put the poker down and settled himself on the long sofa. He sipped the coffee and then leveled speculative blues at me. "The widow Zeibach has the idea you were getting it on with her late husband."

"Yeah, I know. She expressed that idea, kind of loud, right in front of the reception desk at my office this morning—shortly after you left, as a matter of fact."

"Sounds like a pretty eventful morning."

"You might say. John Gentle kept looking at me meaningfully and asking whether there was Something I Wanted to Tell Him."

"Is there something you want to tell *me?*" Ike asked casually.

"No." Tomorrow, after I'd talked to Bobbie again, like it or not, I might *have* to tell Ike something. But not yet—it would be too unfair.

"Ann Marie said that your name was all over her husband's appointment book."

"I don't get it," I said. I reached over and took a slug of coffee. "I know that he wrote it down Sunday night, but that was the first time I'd ever laid eyes, or, if I have to assure you, anything else on the man. Did you actually *see* his notebook?"

"Nope. Didn't turn up. Ann Marie says he always carried it. Whoever did him probably took it."

"Well, according to her brother, she's hypersensitive—especially on the subject of Jerry's screwing around. By the way, how did Zeibach die?"

"Not for discussion right now," he said, dismissing the subject. Knowing Ike, I hadn't really expected an answer. No harm in trying though. He stared at the now-blazing fire, his mind in transit. "Liz, about the rats. According to your friend Ada, Blitz Exterminators did find a pair in her apartment. We'll check that in the morning, of course. Who could've put them in yours? Unlikely that it was Zeibach."

"Even *I* figured that out once I did the arithmetic. I honestly don't know, Ike. The only people in and out of here that day, as far as I know, were brokers and their customers. Arlyne Berg was here when I got home. I found her in my bathroom, as a matter of fact, and I kind of wondered . . ." I ran my fingers through my hair. "Ah, that's not fair, I have no real reason to suspect her—except that I hardly know her."

He pulled out his pocket notebook and pen and slid them down to my end of the coffee table. "Names, please. All the brokers." As I thought back and began jotting them down, I realized with a glitch in my gut that Bobbie, Arlyne, and Norrie had all been here Monday—along with Vi Royal and Mac Stitt. "Only the Rooney brokers would've left cards, so I don't know which brokers from other firms might've come—or customers' names."

"Why didn't the other brokers leave cards too?"

"Because they weren't allowed in without Norrie. The doormen gave keys only to Rooney brokers, who showed cards. But Norrie'll have a list of everyone who was in and out."

"Mmm-hmm. I don't like the coincidence, Liz."

"I'm not crazy about it myself. But the apartment is off the market now and the locks've been changed, so . . ." I put my hands out, palms up, to finish the thought.

"I'm glad about the latter, and not glad at all about the former. I'm a sonofabitch sometimes. My track record with women —except maybe my broker—is nothing to brag about." He smiled with the self-deprecating irony that I think of as uniquely Irish. "I'm not much of a bargain. But you're no Twinkie yourself and—"

"Then why not move in with your broker?" I shot out, forcing an anger I no longer felt to avoid the danger of being charmed.

"Because I like my broker, but I do not love her," he said quietly.

I shut my eyes. Why couldn't I just go with it? "I can't. I don't know. It's like I always have to keep my dukes up with you, or . . ."

"Or what," he asked after a few seconds.

"Or I'll lose—and you'll win. It sounds so childish, even hearing myself say it. But you know what I mean. I *know* you do."

"Yeah, I do," he said. "Guess that means there's more than one of us who can be childish." He looked at me for a second, his blue eyes darker somehow than usual. "Okay," he said abruptly, "back to business. What about this trio of brokers? The same three seem to surface every time I turn around. Know of a connection between any of them and Zeibach?"

Bobbie to Zeibach via Mentone? "No." Forgive me, Ike, I added silently. I *can't.*

"You're lying," he said flatly.

"No, I—"

"Yes, you are. I know you, Lizzie. There's something. What do I have to do to get it out of you?" Sudden anger colored his voice.

"Beat me, perhaps? Take me downtown and have the boys work me over, or—"

"Knock it off. It's been a long fucking day."

"For me too. Why don't you finish your coffee and get the hell out of here?"

"You got it." He strode out of the room, and a few seconds later was gone with a door slam that made me jump.

I sat, chewing my thumbnail and wondering whether the time would come when I'd do anything right again.

Chapter 18

I was startled out of my funk by the phone. Bobbie. I ran to the kitchen to catch it.

"Hello, Liz?" Not Bobbie. "This is Art. Art Blyfield." Bobbie's lover. "Have . . . have you heard from Bobbie?" Uh-oh.

"No, Art, I thought . . . I hoped he was home."

"Well, he's not. I just got in. I've been in Washington the past few days doing an antiques show, and I got your message on the machine. What's wrong?" His voice was deeply worried, as though he knew what would come next.

"Lots. But most urgent, I don't know where Bobbie is, but I *do* know he's drunk."

"Oh, Jesus," he said in the quiet tones of someone who's just been told about an unexpected death. "He was fine when I left for Washington. What . . . what happened?"

I gave him a quick summary, taking the chance of leveling with him. He was going to need all the help he could get when he found Bobbie.

"Shit," he said softly when I'd finished, "shit."

"Amen to that."

"He's worked so hard. We both have. Never missed a meeting—not once in ten months, no matter where we were." I knew that from Bobbie. They'd gone into A.A. together, with Art leading the way, after booze and coke had poked sizable holes in their professional and personal lives. It'd given them the proverbial new deck of cards, and now . . . "Liz"—Art's voice thinned with tension—"this is worse than you know. Bobbie has a record, and the cops are going to find out about it—if they haven't already."

"A . . . a *record?*" My God, no wonder he'd bent out of shape.

"Back in L.A. Dealing coke. They locked him up for two

years." He spoke so softly, I had to strain to hear. After he'd said it, we let the dead air just sit there. "Look," he said finally, "I can't stay on the phone. I've got to go find him. Let me tell you this though. It may sound funny to say about a convicted dope dealer, but I know my boy pretty well, and no way would he ever, *ever* do . . . those things."

I asked Art to please call me when he found Bobbie. He promised he would. It was past midnight. My body was asking to go to sleep, and my mind was answering, "Fat chance." I went to my bathroom, turned on the tub taps with the accent on hot, and threw in some Coco bath oil. Just as I was about to step into my soporific Valium alternative, the phone rang. I mentally crossed fingers that it was Art with the news that Bobbie was home.

"Hi, sorry to call again so late, but ah didn't hear from you and ah was worried." Percy. I *had* promised to call him back.

"Oh, God, things got kind of . . . hectic here and I just forgot. See your 'sorry' and raise you one."

"Call," he responded, "but you're probably a better poker player than ah am."

"I doubt that. Ada okay?"

"Ah tucked her up with a nip of brandy couple of hours ago. She's fine. Said the police were real gents—her words—to her. Specially liked O'Hanlon." I squashed the pang before it fully surfaced.

"So when should we get together to talk?" I asked.

"How's tomorrow night? A drink here at mah place and then we can go round the corner for some dinner. You like Japanese?"

"Love it. Seven-thirty?"

"See you then."

"Percy, just one thing I wanted to say before then. I don't want to sound presumptuous, but I think it would be a good idea for you and Ada to duck the media for the time being, especially be careful to—uh—not speak ill of the dead." He didn't answer for a second, and I was afraid he might be going to tell me to take my advice and shove it.

"Right . . . yeah, ah think that's right. Seven-thirty it is, and ah look forward to it." The last sentence was delivered with a warm intimacy that somehow did wonders for my mood.

I gave the bath another blast of hot water and stepped in. Ten minutes later my mind capitulated and voted pro-sleep, along with the rest of me. As I slipped naked under the covers and fell off the edge of consciousness, my final thought was of Percy Tuthill—a pretty pleasant one.

Chapter 19

The phone roused me at what turned out to be 9:07 A.M.

"I'm here. Where are you?" Seth Frankel's earnest voice asked.

"My God! Sleeping. Would you believe it? Seth, I'm really sorry. Rough night." I couldn't stifle the yawn. Cats suddenly made an appearance, rubbing up and down various parts of me, lobbying for breakfast. "Look, I'll be there in half an hour. I spoke to Alfie last night. He knows that you'll be doing the spokesing. Haven't seen the papers or even the eleven o'clock news. Oh, shit! We need to draft a statement and—"

"Not to worry. I did, I did, and I did. Speculation about Stover's 'troubled building' and all that. One tenant mouthed off to the *Post* about what a bastard Zeibach was, but the rest of 'em seem to've had the brains to keep their mouths shut."

"Which tenant? Was it . . . was it an old woman?"

"Ada Fauer, from the tenants' committee, you mean? Nah. This was some would-be-actress type. Probably just wanted her name in the paper. I called the reporters and assignment editors and told them I'd be representing Stover. You'll see the draft statement when you get here."

"I'll love you forever, Seth Frankel."

"Hah!"

I threw on a burgundy body suit and matching skirt and panty hose. I grabbed a new, sinfully expensive Chanel scarf—black with jewels printed all over it—to tie around the neck. Even in my rush I remembered that I'd be seeing Percy later—and that while business was on my mind, it wasn't the only thing on my mind.

Half an hour later I was at the office, as promised.

"Aren't we chic this morning," Morley greeted me. "Want to return calls first, or should I let Seth know you're in." He handed me a stack of pink message slips, which I flipped through, looking for Ike's name even before I realized that's what I was doing. No message from him—or from Art Blyfield. But Vi Royal had called, and Margaret Rooney, and Ray Mentone.

"Buzz Seth, but ask him to give me ten minutes, okay. Also, would you be wonderful and—"

"Get you a cup of coffee, I know."

I closed my door and dialed Vi first. Whatever she wanted was going to be easier to deal with than Ray or Margaret. After the way I'd screwed up with Bobbie and then Ike last night, I figured I'd better do some serious thinking before I spoke to either of them.

"Vi? Hi, it's Liz."

"I'm glad you caught me. I had one foot out of here."

"What can I do for you?"

"I think I need to talk to you . . . to someone anyway."

"I guess I qualify as someone, though recently I'm not too sure."

"Could we maybe get together tonight?"

"Gee, I'm sorry. I'm representing Stover International, and if you saw this morning's paper you—"

"Oh, that guy who got killed. Sounds like he was a real bastard. Your life is kind of eventful these days, girl."

"You might say."

"How about coffee, then? Tomorrow morning, early. I could come to your place."

"Fine. Eight-thirty too early?"

"That's okay. I'll see—"

"Vi, would you transfer me to Bobbie?" Maybe it was all okay. Art had found him, sobered him up and . . ."

"Not in. 'Fact I tried him at home 'bout ten minutes ago. We got a deal going together on his exclusive at the Beresford. His roommate said he's down with the flu—too sick even to come to the phone." Oh, God! Bar-hopping with no jacket in February. I was sorry he'd gotten sick, but far more relieved that he'd gotten home.

"Well, switch me to Arlyne, then." Something Bobbie'd said

in the heat of the scene last night had just bounced back into my head.

"Our 'broker to the stars'? She getting to be a buddy of yours?"

"Hardly know her. She doesn't seem so bad though. All that name-dropping's kind of fun, really." Morley set a steaming mug of black coffee in front of me and exited as silently as he'd entered.

"Makes me puke. You wouldn't love her so much if you talked to some of the folk she worked with at Elliman. One tough bitch! And you can't let her near your customers—steal 'em right under your nose. She's real thick with Bobbie though. Made a big point of wanting to sit next to him, and of course poor Dee Johanson got bounced out of her seat to make way. I'm just looking over at Arlyne's desk. Doesn't look like she's here either. I'll switch you to reception—you can leave her highness a message." I did, and got her home number at the same time. But she wasn't there either.

Before calling Ray Mentone, I decided to call Art Blyfield to find out how Bobbie was doing.

"Hello." Art's voice—taut and anxious.

"Art, it's Liz Wareham. I'm so glad Bobbie's home safe. I mean, I know he's sick, but—"

"He isn't."

"Isn't sick?"

"Isn't home." The coffee I was in the process of swallowing went down wrong, and I coughed myself teary-eyed while absorbing what he'd said. "I . . . I just said that when what's-her-name called so that . . . Well, what else could I say? That he's off on a bender and maybe . . . maybe *dead?*" His voice broke. "I'm sorry, I've been up all night. I've checked out all the places we used to . . . I've called everyone. Goddammit, why'd you have to—"

"Art, I botched it. I should've called *you* first. I didn't realize. I thought Bobbie and I were good enough friends . . . I thought I could handle it—and I couldn't."

"Forget it. It's done."

"Have you . . . have you called the hospitals, or the police?" I asked gingerly, hating to upset him even further.

"Hospitals, yes—at least the ones in neighborhoods where I figured he might be. Police, no."

"Maybe you should."

"Are you kidding? I couldn't do that—even if Bobbie weren't a convicted felon. We faggots don't tend to run to the police a lot," he said bitterly. "Especially to enlist them in an all-out search for our drunken lovers. They'd laugh me out of the precinct—tell me to do a bed check of our friends." A knock at the door.

"Come in, Seth," I called. "Look, Art," I said into the phone, "maybe I can think of something. I have to go now, but I'll call you back within the hour. Meantime, if—uh—anything changes, please let me know." I gave him my office number and hung up.

I turned my attention to Seth, seated in one of the two chairs opposite my desk, hands clasped behind his head and short legs stretched out straight in front of him. He looked at his most relaxed, but then, he always did when he was on top of an assignment in this business he claims to hate so much.

"Sorry to keep you waiting," I said, my mind still on the disturbing conversation with Art.

"No problem. Here." He handed me his draft of the Stover media statement.

"Great," I said after I'd scanned it, "only one thing—cut out where you have Stover calling Zeibach 'a veteran professional.' "

"But—"

"I *know* it's pretty faint praise, but the guy was a scumbag, and the more that comes out—and it will—the more we're going to have to dissociate Alfie."

"I disagree. Stover *hired* the guy. He can't just call him a scumbag now that he's passed away."

"Died, Seth. He died. He didn't pass away. I *hate* that."

"So sue me. My mother always said 'died' was bad manners. Okay, you want it out, you got it out." He peered solemnly at me through his thick hornrims. "I told you you wouldn't love me forever."

I laughed. It felt unaccustomed. I scribbled a note to Alfie on my personal pad and tore it off. "Give this to Morley on your way out, would you? Tell him to fax it to Alfie, along with your draft statement. I'll get back to you soon as I know more." He grunted and turned to leave. "Don't sulk, Seth," I said, "I *do* love you. It's just that my love isn't worth very much these days."

I flipped a mental coin about whether to call Margaret Rooney or Ray Mentone next. Mentone won. I still had no idea about the best way to deal with him, but I knew that over the phone wasn't it.

"Good morning," he said by way of greeting, his tone making it clear that he was liking the morning about as much as I was. "I think we need to get a coupla things straight."

Only a couple? I thought, but didn't say. Smart-ass didn't seem the ticket somehow. "Umm-hmm?" Noncommittally.

"If we're gonna work together, we've gotta do some air clearing, you and me." Was he going to take over Zeibach's duties on Westover? God, I hoped not! "Specially since I now understand you work for the Iron Maiden."

"Excuse me?" I responded, though I understood him perfectly well.

"My dear former partner, Miss Rooney. There're some things you're gonna have to understand."

"Nothing I'd like better, Ray—because right now there are some things I don't understand at all." At least, I *hoped* I didn't.

"Tell you what I'll do, I'll buy you lunch." The big-man-to-little-girl note in his voice came dangerously close to activating my knee-jerk squelch reflex. On the other hand, I *did* need to talk with him, and lunch was probably as good a time as any.

"Fine."

"Arturo Grande. One o'clock." It was not a question.

"Fine," I repeated, but I think he'd already hung up.

I knew I had to return Margaret Rooney's call, but I hardly relished the prospect. It was a no-win situation. Either I told her about Bobbie, or I didn't. And I couldn't, just couldn't—not until I was a lot surer of my ground. I'd made that decision last night when I'd kept my mouth shut with Ike, and I guessed that

even the astonishing information Art had dropped hadn't
changed my mind. I gritted my teeth, reached for the phone,
and dialed the Rooney office. I lucked out. Margaret was in a
meeting.

"Well, just tell her I returned her call, Selma, but," I added,
"she won't be able to reach me—I'll be in meetings out of the
office. Tell her I'll call her later." If I could duck Margaret till
after my lunch with Mentone, maybe I'd have a better idea of
what the hell might be going on. I buzzed Morley. "If Margaret
Rooney calls, say I've gone off to a meeting and I'll call her
later."

I spent the next hour and a half catching up on work for the
other clients who helped subsidize my kids at Brown and Stanford and me at Bergdorf's and Saks. Almost everything was
going smoothly, and none of my staff needed me to step in and
take over, for which I was profoundly grateful. Judging by my
recent track record, had there been a problem, my intervention
would only have made it worse.

John Gentle was out of town for the day, so I didn't have to
provide him with hourly action bulletins, and the phone was
relatively quiet. Elvira Treemor called to report that Alfie'd had
his interview with the police. "Two of them. Lovely, they were—
specially that Irish one. Such blue eyes. I always was partial to
. . . There I am, goin' on like a silly old cow. Anyway, Alfred
said to tell you 'e'll call you later." Just before she hung up, she
added, "You know, Liz, 'e was a bad lot, Zeibach. Not to speak
ill of the dead, but I can't be all that sorry." Elvira didn't have a
millimeter of hypocrisy in her makeup—one of the reasons I'd
always been so fond of her.

"I feel exactly the same way," I said, "and I met the man only
once."

"You're fortunate. Some around 'ere might feel quite different, o' course," she said with a heavy insinuation in her tone,
which puzzled me for a moment, until I remembered the person
that tone, and the words "some around 'ere," used to be reserved for: Alfie's wife.

"Doreen? I mean Dolores?" Mentone had said his brother-in-

law screwed around, but . . . "Are you saying that Zeibach and—"

"Pay me no attention, dear. I talk too much."

"I pay you lots of attention, Elvira," I said. "Did Alfie know about—uh—what was going on?" It never occurred to me to ask if she was sure anything *was* going on. I knew her observations to be pretty damned accurate.

"Don't know, do I? Some around 'ere do all kinds of things, and you'd think Alfred was none the wiser. And then . . . well, I 'ave to go now, the other phone's ringin'. 'E'll call you later." And she was gone, leaving me with at least three more questions unanswered.

My mind raced around some funny corners. Elvira had never had much use for Doreen—a shared dislike that had strengthened our relationship. If she thought Doreen and Zeibach were having an affair, and she told Alfie, would he . . . ? The idea of Alfie as the cuckolded husband driven to murder his rival seemed an absurdly poor fit. Alfie's prime passion was, as far as I knew, his business. If Alfie'd killed Zeibach, it would have been more likely out of revenge for a screwed-up Westover than a screwed wife.

It beat hell out of me what Doreen—or any woman—might see in Jerry Zeibach anyway. But whatever it was, Doreen Stover clearly wasn't the only one susceptible. Maybe his attractions were something like that special whistle only dogs can hear.

My only other call was from my mother in Florida. She'd heard about the Zeibach murder on television and remembered that Stover was a former client of mine. Her opinion had much in common with Elvira's, and she hadn't even known Zeibach.

"Trying to throw people out of their homes. No wonder somebody killed him. You start monkeying around with people that way, it only leads to trouble. But then, that Stover, I knew he had no sense. He fired *you.*" Which in her book was incontrovertible evidence. My mother's judgments are far from evenhanded. It didn't seem the best idea to bring up that I was working for Stover again.

"How are things down there, Mother? Playing much golf?"

"Every day, baby. What's happening with the apartment? Sell it yet? I feel a little strange about you moving in with Ike. Call me old-fashioned, and I suppose I am, but—"

"You don't have to worry, Ma."

"What?" Her voice was suddenly wary. She's known me a long time.

"I'm not moving in with Ike," I said, determined to keep my tone quietly neutral.

"Oh, Lizzie"—her concern for her chick surged through a thousand miles of phone wire, wiping out the previously expressed doubts about propriety—"what happened?"

"Nothing," I replied, feeling instantly disgusted with myself. Why the hell had I brought it up if I wasn't prepared to discuss it? "I'm just not ready. I don't know. I think Ike's not . . . I think we're not right for each other."

"Nonsense. You're *just* right for each other. Look, I have known that boy since he was ten years old. He was at the house all the time. Dad taught him the piano."

"Mother, would you stop?"

"Now, you listen! That boy is strong-minded and smart and nice. And you always liked him. No matter what you said, he was always the one. You let him go now, you're a . . . a fool."

"Mother!"

"I'm sorry to say it, Lizzie, but—" An opportune knock at my door.

"Just a second," I called. "Ma, I can't talk about this now." I noticed with annoyance that my eyes were watery and my throat lumpish. "I'm late for a meeting. I'll call you." We said mutual strained "love yous" and hung up.

"Come in," I called, my gut grinding a bit with the abrupt gear switch.

Seth strode in purposefully and sat down. "Know how Zeibach died?"

"Uh-uh. How?"

"Air bubble injected in his jugular vein—you call that really going for the jugular, right?" He grinned at his joke, exposing a set of broad pink gums. "A coupla minutes and pfft!" He snapped his fingers. Kessie at the *Post* told me. He got an exclusive source in the medical examiner's office—anonymous, of course. He scooped the TVs on it." Seth sat back triumphantly, vicariously sharing the scoop. "That means the killer knew about that kinda stuff."

"What kind of stuff?"

"Needles. Injections. You know, medical stuff. That you could kill a person by injecting air. Anyway, that's what Kessie says the cops are thinking."

"He have an anonymous police source too?" I asked, imagining the steam coming out Ike's ears, if that were the case.

Seth shrugged. "Thought you'd wanna know. Any ideas who dunnit?"

Needles. Air bubbles. Percy Tuthill wrote mysteries. . . . well, I *read* them. Certainly the old air bubble shot was a genre mainstay, but actually knowing how to *do* it was something else. Ada. Hadn't she said her late husband was diabetic? She probably knew . . . that's ridiculous!

"Not a one," I said.

Chapter 20

Arturo Grande is one of the maybe hundred interchangeable, expense-account Italian restaurants that punctuates the long side streets east of Fifth Avenue—the kind where men in suits cut for paunch camouflage energetically cut deals while consuming overpriced, not-bad pasta, veal, and fish. The maître d' showed me to Mr. Mentone's table—a cozy corner one—with a courtly smile. It was still a few minutes before one and he had not yet arrived. "Mr. Mentone be here soon, Signora," the maître d' assured me with a smile. "He *always* on time." I ordered a San Pellegrino, sat back on the cushiony red leather banquette, and tried to pull my thoughts together.

Needles. Rats. Somehow it had to fit together, but, like a particularly stubborn crossword puzzle, whatever I slotted in across didn't seem to work down.

"Well, hello," Ray Mentone said with a smile that didn't make it as far up as his raccoon eyes. He reached for my hand as he slid into the banquette catty-corner to mine, and squeezed it with something that might be mistaken for affection. I wondered whether this show of intimacy was meant for the waiter, who was just bringing my San Pellegrino, or me, who knew as well as he did that we didn't even like each other.

"Hello," I said, retrieving my hand and wrapping it around the damp, frosty glass.

"What for you, Mr. Mentone," the waiter asked, "Rob Roy?"

"You got it, Carlo. Make it a perfect—Chivas. Can't we interest you in something a little stronger, Liz?" he asked with a conspiratorial grin at the waiter.

"'Fraid not," I replied, forcing an answering smile, "I think I'm going to need my wits about me today—those I have left anyway." I sipped the mineral water. It felt good in my mouth, which I realized was dry with nervousness.

Mentone leaned toward me and gave me a long look with his
sexy eyes. "Hey, Liz, can I give you a little advice?" The question was rhetorical, as such questions always are. "Lighten up.
We're gonna be working together—could be a situation very
good for both of us. Know what I mean?" Another smile, but
just a little one.

"No, Ray, I don't know what you mean, but you said some air
had to be cleared, and I couldn't agree more." His drink arrived, and he took a long, savoring swig.

"You got something on your mind, and I bet I know what it
is."

"I bet you do too." Even drunk, Bobbie had almost certainly
called Mentone the minute he'd left my apartment. "Can we
just get it out on the table?"

He held his hands out expansively, palms up. "Shoot."

"Okay. Are you employing Bobbie Crawbuck to play dirty
tricks on Margaret Rooney's clients?" I asked it with the throw-
away casualness that TV lawyers use to such good effect.

He sighed and shook his head. "Do I look dumb to you?
What are you talking about, dirty tricks? Tricks are chickenshit.
Hey, I may not be your cuppa tea, but I'm not into chickenshit."
I didn't answer. "Look, Liz, when Crawbuck left your place last
night, he called me, okay? Poor fag was hysterical. It was hard
to follow what he was saying. Something about how I set him
up, and he was being framed for killing somebody. What is it
with this stuff? Hey, I'll be straight with you. I'm starting a
residential brokerage with Alf—Stover Residential, we're calling it. I say *with*, 'cause I got a piece of the action on this one,
follow? I hear Crawbuck's a good performer, so I offer him a
job. You got some problem with that?"

I tried to read his face, but it didn't tell me anything. "I don't
know. Maybe I do."

"Why? 'Cause he works for Miz Margaret Rooney?"

"Yeah. Lots of brokers around, why go fishing in her waters?"

He smiled slightly. "You're a smart lady. Why do you think?"

What the hell? "Because it's soul-satisfying to screw someone
you think has screwed you."

The smile reached his eyes this time and grew broader. It was kind of appealing in a funny way—as though a coat of tough-guy stage makeup had been instantly removed. "You're okay," he said, shaking his head slowly. He polished off his Rob Roy and summoned the waiter, who hopped to with a pair of over-size menus.

"You ready to order, Mr. Mentone?"

"Yeah, but I don't need that thing." He gestured at the menus. "Trust me to order for you, Liz?"

"Sure," I answered. His enthusiasm had an almost boyish quality, which was surprisingly infectious. No one but a real drag would've insisted on picking out her own spaghetti.

"Bring us the caesar salad for two and the steak pizzaiola. But first bring me another one of these." He pointed to the empty Rob Roy glass. "Come on, Liz, you gotta drink some-thing besides water."

"A glass of red wine, then," I said.

"Bottle of the classico," he said to the waiter.

"No, really, Ray. I have to work this afternoon. A glass'll be—"

"I'm gonna drink some with the steak too. Not to worry. It's left over, it'll be left over." After the waiter had gone, he reached his hand out to me. "Friends?" he asked.

"A little premature," I answered, leaving both my hands in my lap. "I think we have to talk some more before I can give you an honest answer."

He shrugged. "What can I tell you? That I hate that dried-up bitch? She should've stayed in the nunnery and saved everybody a lot of grief. But I got a question for you. What's all this stuff Crawbuck was blabbing about—this murder he thinks is gonna be pinned on him? He can't mean Jerry. He didn't even *know* Jerry."

His fresh Rob Roy arrived and the waiter wheeled over a cart with all the makings of a real caesar salad—the anchovies, raw eggs, fresh parmesan, rich garlic croutons, and bristling, sturdy greens—a rare treat, since what most restaurants dare to call caesar salad is a pallid bunch of chickory drowned in viscous bottled dressing.

"No," I said, turning in toward Ray, my back to the waiter,

who was beginning to prepare the salad with the absorbed expertise of a surgeon making a first cut. "The murder he meant was an accidental one—at least I think it was." There was no way I could extract information from Ray without providing some. And he'd learn what I was about to tell him from Bobbie anyway, whenever Bobbie turned up. "Ray, I mentioned before that someone's playing dirty tricks on Margaret's best clients. She thinks—with some justification—that one of three brokers in her office is responsible."

"And Crawbuck's one of them?"

"Right. Margaret also thinks that some competitor's behind the whole thing."

"Ah-ha. The light dawns. What kind of dirty tricks?"

I told him. "All those things—the lye in the face cream, the doctored scotch, the paint in the shampoo—they all can hurt people, but not kill them. And the exploding log was probably meant to be more of the same, only—"

"Yeah, I got it." He sighed, the eyes narrowing as he took it in. If he was acting, he was pretty proficient at it.

The waiter placed heaping portions of caesar salad in front of each of us, and departed with a *"buon appetito."* I took an appreciative whiff and realized I was starved. As I chewed an initial forkful of the exuberant blend of textures and flavors, it occurred to me fleetingly that this garlicky lunch might not enhance my appeal to Percy Tuthill this evening. I took another bite and told myself I'd brush my teeth, or gargle or something, but the stuff on my plate was just too good to pass up.

"This is terrific," I said, taking a morsel of bread and a sip of gut-warming, deep red Chianti. The bread was so-so, but who cared?

"Thought you might like it," he replied, pleased. "You said three of Margaret's agents were under suspicion. Who are the other two?"

"Norrie Wachsman and Arlyne Berg. Maybe you offered them jobs too. You know, really stick it to Margaret."

He looked at me strangely and put down, uneaten, the forkful of salad he'd been ready to pop into his mouth. "Let me tell you a story," he said. "Once upon a time there was this guy—Italian bozo from Brooklyn, parents straight off the boat from Napoli. Well, this guy, he wanted two things in life. He wanted to be somebody and he wanted to get married to a beautiful girl—live happily ever after, you know?" I nodded. I knew, all right. My own dream was simply the female version.

"Something the matter, Mr. Mentone? You no like the caesar today?" The waiter hovered at Ray's shoulder, ready to make whatever reparations might be required.

"No, Carlo. It's fine. Just not as hungry as I thought. You can take it." Which Carlo did, but not before refilling the wine-glasses. "Well, school was never his thing, this guy in the story, but he found out pretty early he was good at selling. So after he got out of the navy—this is 'seventy we're talking about—he goes into real estate. And he does well, real well. Rolls up those commissions. Top producer of the year. Now, in that same office there's another top producer, okay? Pretty blonde, and boy can she hustle."

Carlo returned with two huge plates of steak smothered in red sauce that looked delectably bumpy and smelled great. But my appetite seemed to have gone the way of my companion's. I looked down at the steak and took another sip of wine.

"So," he continued, "these two hustlers figure, why work for somebody else when you can work for you? She comes up with a chunk of start-up money, and they're off and running with their own business. Things go good. More than good. So he has a lock on the first part of his dream. He is *somebody.*"

"And the second? Does he fall in love with this pretty blonde?" It suddenly occurred to me that maybe, at root, *that* was what his hatred of Margaret was about—suitor spurned.

"In love with *Margaret?* Are you kidding?" The incredulity in his tone sounded too spontaneous to be anything but sincere. "God, that'd be like . . . well, never mind. Back to the story. He *does* fall in love though. She was called Camilla, Cammy." His voice caressed the name. "She was blond too—like her sister," he added with a wry half smile.

"Sister? Then that's Margaret's younger sister, you mean?"

"I'm surprised she told you. She never . . . she stopped talking about Cammy after . . ." He clamped his mouth shut hard.

"Look"—he pointed down at my cooling steak—"why don't you eat some of that? It's good stuff. Just 'cause I—"

"I'm not really that hungry either. I kind of pigged out on the salad."

"C'mon, just a bite." Which summoned up memories of the way I'd coax Sarah when she was two and didn't like anything edible except chocolate. I complied.

"It *is* good," I said, cutting a second piece. His eyes, as he watched me, looked mournful and tired. "Please go on with what you were saying—about Cammy."

"Cammy. You said Margaret told you about her?"

"No. I was in Margaret's apartment and I saw a picture of two little girls with bikes. I recognized the older one as Margaret and assumed the other was her younger sister."

"I know that photo. The father's in it, right?"

"Yes—at least I guess it was her father. Margaret never mentions her family. I don't even know if her parents are dead or alive."

"Mother's dead. Cancer while Cammy was still a baby. And the father's as good as. May be by now, for all I know. He cut out to join some monastery, no less—a lay brother, running around in a long skirt. Big deal Cath-o-lic. Can you imagine? Leaves those two little girls flat and calls himself *religious.* Left it to his mother to bring them up. And they all three used to tiptoe around like he was some fuckin' saint! Irresponsible bastard is more like it." I tended to agree with him, but didn't think his fire needed any more fuel.

"I think I saw a picture of the grandmother too. Looks just like Margaret. I remarked on that and she . . . she seemed to want to get off the subject."

"I'll bet she did," he snorted. "Don't know how she can stand to keep a picture of old Hortense around."

"Why?"

"Never mind." He reached over for the wine and poured the rest of it evenly into our glasses. The waiter, horrified at being less than Johnny-on-the-spot, bustled over, but Ray waved him away.

"What about Cammy, though? Didn't Margaret approve, you

know, of the two of you?" Whatever tact I possessed seemed to have dissolved in the wine, leaving me free to ask whatever I felt like.

"She did at first. Why not? I was a successful Catholic boy, never married. And what screwing around I did, Sister Margaret didn't know about. Sure, I was fine with her, even though I was an Eyetie."

"So what went wrong?"

"Cammy and I fell in love—like I said. And we made love. We didn't screw around, or have an affair. We made love. She was beautiful. God, she was beautiful!" He looked down into his wineglass. "Cammy got pregnant."

"Well, why didn't you just get married?"

"That's the sixty-four-thousand-dollar question! Why didn't we? I wanted to. She wanted to. I'll give you the sixty-four-thousand-dollar answer. Sister Margaret. Before she got finished with her sermons about how dirty, how disgusting, how sinful Cammy had been—how disappointed Daddy-the-saint would be . . . Well, she finished Cammy off. You gotta understand, Cammy was fragile—not a toughie like Margaret . . . or me," he added bitterly.

"What happened?" I asked softly, dreading the answer.

"She killed herself," he answered just as softly, looking straight into my eyes. "My girl jumped off the balcony of my apartment. Landed on the balcony one floor down, crashed right into the geraniums." His laugh was as poignant as a sob. "Would you believe, I was showing that apartment when it happened? My downstairs neighbor gave me the exclusive on it. Cammy and I'd been hassling. She was crying about the last shellacking from Margaret, and saying that a marriage founded on sin—I guess that was the way her dear sister put it—could never work. I just blew up—told her if I heard one more word about her fucking sister, *I'd* back out of the marriage. Then the doorman buzzed from downstairs. My customer was there to see the apartment. I told Cammy to wash her face, get real— that I'd be right back. I was just showing the guy the kitchen when I heard the crash."

"My God." I said it inadvertently as I lowered my eyes. I just couldn't look at him.

"Yeah, can you beat that? My girl . . . and my baby. My life is over, and what am I doing? Showing a goddamn apartment. Guy bought it too. Full commission—thirty-one thousand four hundred fifty-seven bucks. I'll always remember that number. Hey, Carlo," he called suddenly to the waiter, "bring us some espresso." Then he turned to me again with a smile that was painful to see. "I don't make love anymore, little Liz. I get laid a lot, but I don't make love."

Chapter 21

It was almost four when I got back to the office, slightly woozy from the wine, and more than slightly depressed.

"Well," Morley said, "I guessed you'd be back before five. Seth didn't think so, but you know how he is. Chris at Baker Bank called. She said to tell you she hates the way the new brochure looks."

"Chris hates the way everything looks since she broke up with her latest boyfriend," I replied gloomily.

"Also, Margaret Rooney called back."

"Uh-huh. Anyone else?"

"Nope." So Bobbie still hadn't turned up. Nor had Ike called. Hell with him.

I walked into my office, shut the door, and sat at the desk. I propped up my face with clenched fists and mused on the unspeakable things people did to each other in the name of . . . well, all kinds of noble sentiments.

My lunch with Ray Mentone had been chillingly illuminating about why he and Margaret hated each other. But I still didn't know whether he was behind the dirty tricks. I also didn't know whether Bobbie was the only Rooney broker Ray had recruited for his new firm. When I'd asked about Norrie and Arlyne, he'd ducked answering me. Jesus, if he was involved with *all* of them, I was back to square one!

Just as I was about to pick up the phone to ring Baker Bank and try to convince Chris that she really *loved* the brochure, it rang.

"Trying to reach me?" Arlyne Berg's brash voice was warm and a bit breathless, as though she'd been running. "I've been at a closing all goddamn day. Three and a half mill, and they're fighting about the light fixture in the bathroom! What can I do for you?"

"I need to talk to you, Arlyne."

"Sure. I'm glad to work with you. Some interviews set up? You know, I had my own press agent for a while—just fired her. Maybe—"

"It's not about press, Arlyne. Bobbie's missing." Silence. Did I hear her catch her breath? Maybe not.

"Well," she said after a moment, "missing's a strong word. Did you call his lover?"

"Yes, I did. Art doesn't know where he is. Do you?"

"Me? How would I know? I mean, we were friends, but not all that close." She was definitely nervous.

"Look, I think we should meet. If you came to my office, we could have some privacy."

"Privacy?"

"Arlyne, let's not fence. I saw Bobbie in Ray Mentone's office, and when I faced him with it, he panicked. He also mentioned you. Said he wondered if his 'good friend Arlyne' was trying to pin something on him." I wasn't at all sure of my ground, but I wasn't risking much. If she weren't involved, she wouldn't know what the hell I was talking about. But she did.

"I'll be right over," she said in a voice much smaller than the one I'd become used to hearing.

I fetched myself a mug of coffee from the kitchen, called Chris, and succeeded in convincing her to at least meet with me and discuss her problems with the brochure. It felt good to succeed at something for a change.

Morley knocked at the door, opened it, and stuck his head in. "Arlyne Berg to see you. She's got some Italian designer's whole collection on—Versace, I think."

"I know what you mean. Bring her in, and ask her if she wants a cup of coffee."

"I did, and she doesn't." He disappeared, and a few seconds later Arlyne walked through the door, preceded by the Giorgio scent she favored. She was dressed in a bicolored suit—chartreuse on one side, burnt orange on the other—with a thigh-hugging short skirt. A silk scarf printed with peacocks was slung around her neck. She sat down in one of the chairs opposite my desk, put her large orange purse on the floor next to her, and crossed her legs, causing the skirt to ride up even higher on her plump thighs. Her face, pale and worried, was from a different movie altogether.

"I don't want to fence with you either, Liz," she said. "How much do you know?" The appraising intelligence those black eyes trained on me overrode the silly outfit.

"Not very much, Arlyne, unless you count some educated guesses."

"Let's hear them. You got an ashtray?" I found one under a large yellow pad and pushed it across the desk to her. I've got no objection to people smoking, except that it makes me want to, even after eight years, especially when I'm nervous. She fished a pack of Pall Mall Gold and a gold Zippo from her bag, lit up, and dragged deeply. I hadn't seen her smoke before.

"You have some kind of deal going with Ray Mentone," I began. Her expression didn't change, nor did her eyes waver from mine. I continued. "You quit Elliman and came to Rooney to woo Margaret's top performers over to Ray's new brokerage." I paused. No change. No response. "And maybe to sabotage her best exclusives with dirty—"

"*No!*" she shot out. "You're right about the first two—but not the tricks. Not me."

"Somebody."

"Use your head, Liz. I don't know you that well, but you're not dumb. Would I do that to my own clients? Hell, the Leonaideses were *my* clients. Besides, I don't have to damage Margaret Rooney to keep my people loyal. They'd follow me anywhere—to Elliman, or Rooney, or Berg and Mentone."

"Berg and Mentone?"

"That's what we're calling the new business." A prideful smile lit her eyes. "Ray wanted to put my name first, you know, because of my reputation."

In the midst of all this confusion I'd finally come upon one thing I was certain about. "Arlyne, I know Alfie Stover pretty well, and let me assure you that no matter what Ray Mentone told you, there is no way on God's earth that Alfie will finance a business without putting his own name on it. Think about it. Stover International, Eastover, Westover. The only thing that brokerage is *ever* going to be called, if it lives to see the light of day, is Stover Residential—which is, in fact, the name Ray mentioned to me."

Her dark red mouth opened to a soundless "O," and a flush crept up her neck to color her sallow cheeks. She crushed her cigarette out in the ashtray and lit a new one. "That bastard," she said in yet another voice—quiet and cold. "That bastard."

I don't know what I'd expected, but the extreme reaction had taken me by surprise. I'd hit her where she lived. "Is the name that important?" I asked.

"You bet it is. And he knew it . . . he *knew* it!" She smoked silently for a while, with desperate concentration—as though she expected someone at any moment to take the cigarette forcibly away from her. "The name was everything to me," she said finally. "It's the reason I went along."

"I know it's nice to have your name on the door, but . . ." I finished the sentence with a hands-out gesture that indicated how puzzled I was.

"Illegitimate." She fired the word. "I called *him* a bastard. *I* was the bastard—and a *poor* bastard at that. You don't know what that's like. I can tell by looking at you! Where'd you grow up—Great Neck or someplace? Nice big house? Daddy a lawyer, or a doctor, maybe?"

She wasn't far wrong. "Forest Hills. But you were right about the house—and my father. He was a doctor. How'd you know?"

"It's my *business* to know! Why d'you think I'm so good at real estate? It's not just the connections. I can psych people out, is why. I know what they want in an apartment before they do— because I know who they *are.*" She'd certainly figured out who Bobbie was in a hell of a hurry—his hunger for money. Her own was probably as strong. Stronger, maybe. Just what Mentone needed to start his new business and destroy his old partner.

She filled her lungs with smoke and blew it out slowly. "My mother and me, we lived with my grandma in a three-room apartment in the Bronx, on East Tremont. The roach motel. Gram sold makeup in Lord & Taylor. She got Essie a job doing the same thing—that was my mom, Essie. Esther really. Pushing makeup—what a waste! She was smart, Essie was. Went to

Bronx Science, till she had to drop out after she got caught. That's what Gram always used to call it, 'caught.' 'My Essie got caught,' she'd say to me. 'You see it doesn't happen to you, baby. Hear me?'

"This was still the fifties, remember. You got 'caught,' you dropped out of school—got married, if the guy would marry you. If you even knew who the guy *was*. Not like today, with special classes and all for pregnant teenagers. Those two broads, mother and daughter, got on the D train every day, all dolled up—they loved clothes, just like I do—to stand on their feet all day, selling makeup to the rich ladies who shopped at Lord & Taylor." She laughed, not unpleasantly. "Liquid Gold. That was the name of one of the products—moisturizer, I think." She paused to light a third cigarette.

"I was a smart kid too. Just like Essie. I got into Bronx Science—and I *didn't* get caught. The two of them put my diploma in this gold carved frame—like it was a Rembrandt or something—and hung it up on the wall. Arlyne Berg. Essie spelled it with the Y so it would be special. She always used to say, 'You be proud of your name. People are gonna hear from Arlyne Berg.'" Her smile thrust her chin upward. I noticed her eyes were moist.

"Well, they have, Arlyne. 'Broker to the stars' and all that. You're pretty famous. Your mother must be proud of you."

"Would've been if she'd lived long enough. Heart attack. Essie liked these things as much as I do. Haven't had one in eight months, but the hell with it!" She gave the cigarette a defiant little wave.

I figured this wasn't exactly the time for an antismoking lecture. "How'd you happen to become a broker?"

She smiled that wonderful transforming smile I'd seen the first time we'd met. "My second career. Started out as a hooker."

"Probably the only one in your graduating class," I said. She guffawed appreciatively at that, and I joined her, "or maybe not," I added.

"At least the only one I know who was up front about it. I was a sexy kid and a smart kid. I read a tell-it-all book by a call girl,

and figured out pretty fast that I could make more money selling me than selling Liquid Gold." She shrugged. I got to meet
some high-powered guys. They talk in the sack, you know—
afterward. I was a quick study—learned a lot about business.
After a while it occurred to me I could make out even better
selling apartments than I could selling my bod—to the same
customers and their buddies. It worked out. Boy, I love it—the
hunt, the negotiating. And that commission check. Better than
any orgasm I ever had!"

"But you still miss having your name on it."

"Yes, I miss it." She leveled those smart eyes at me again.
"Ray knew that and he conned me. I'll never forgive him for
that. *Never.*" She stubbed out the cigarette and glanced down at
her watch. "I've got to go. I have a showing." She leaned forward in her chair. "So, what're you going to do? Tell Miss Margaret?"

"It would be better if *you* did," I said.

It took her a long silent minute to process the options. "Well,
I'll tell you," she said finally, "the way I see it, we never had this
conversation."

"How do you know I didn't tape it?" I asked.

She looked at me, head to one side, weighing the possibilities.
"You didn't," she said. "That's not who you are."

Unfortunately, she was right. I wasn't smart enough. "So
what *are* you going to do?" I asked, wishing like anything to be
on a plane headed somewhere away from the whole goddamned
mess.

"I'll think of something," she said, rising, a smile of a different kind playing on her lips. "I always do."

I stopped her at the door with one more question. "Who else
did you recruit for Ray? Norrie, by any chance?"

"You've got to be kidding. Who'd want *her?* She couldn't sell
her own bod to a shipwrecked sailor. No, Bobbie was as far as I
got."

Chapter 22

Arlyne? Bobbie? Ray? Close your eyes and pick the trickster. Suddenly an idea presented itself. What if Ray'd had the other two smuggle him into those apartments as a phony customer without saying what he was up to? That would explain the disturbing coincidence of the rats in my fridge. Ray was probably quite familiar with his brother-in-law's ways and means. As I batted it around from right brain to left, a dull ache began to beat just behind my eyebrows.

I shook two aspirin out of the bottle I keep in the top drawer and gulped them down with the remains of my cold coffee. I mulled the idea over some more, and it didn't fall apart. Ike would have to be the one to question them. That was no task for amateurs. The main thing was *it worked!*

The excitement made my heart pound hard—my head, too, but I didn't care. The phone bleeped and Morley told me that Margaret Rooney was on the line. After a second of panic I took a deep breath, straightened my shoulders, and decided how much I was going to tell her. Nothing. Not yet.

"Hi, Margaret. Just taking off my coat," I lied. Clients aren't thrilled when they have to call you twice to get hold of you.

"Where have you been?" Her voice was edged with irritation.

"I had an emergency with a client—Stover International, actually. You may've read one of their people was killed last night." Did she know Mentone worked there?

"Oh, yes, Jerry Zeibach. Disgusting man! He was married to my former partner's sister. I believe Ray Mentone is at Stover also," she added almost too casually.

"Yes. Yes, that's right." I sounded as uncomfortable as I felt.

"I didn't know Stover was your client." Storm brewing.

"Wasn't—until yesterday afternoon. I mean, Alfie *was* a client a few years ago, and he called us in yesterday to handle a project. Next thing I hear, Zeibach's been murdered." Well, the main facts were true.

"You might've come to me," she said sharply. "You knew Ray Mentone and I . . . well, there could be a conflict of interest here."

"I hardly think so, Margaret. Stover's retained us to handle the Westover project. Period. That's no conflict. Besides, I never met Ray Mentone till yesterday afternoon. I had no idea he worked there."

"We'll see," she said, her voice far from happy. That man has the morals of a . . . a tomcat. I want no connection with him, do you understand? *None.*" Her last word grated in a voice hoarse with emotion.

"I understand." I certainly did. What I was going to do about it was another story.

"Let me tell you why I've been trying to reach you. Liz," she said, sounding more like herself, "I've had a very disturbing call." She paused. For effect? "From Arnold Wachsman." It took a beat to register. I'd thought of him as Attila for so long that I'd almost forgotten Norrie's ex-husband's first name.

"What about?" I was instantly wary. Whatever it was, Attila would not be not a bearer of any good news for Norrie.

"About Dr. Shepperton. You know, the dentist who got sick on the bad scotch—the second dirty trick. I think I mentioned that they were classmates in dental school."

"Yes?"

"Well, Wachsman seems to think Norrie is responsible for putting the ipecac in Shepperton's scotch bottle."

"What!"

"It seems that he heard about the incident from Shepperton —who's, by the way, perfectly fine now—and thought it was his duty to call me and report that this is just the kind of thing his ex-wife would do. She's done it before. I'm quoting almost word for word."

"That fucking bastard! That—"

"Hold it, Liz. I know she's your friend. I'm upset about it too, and—"

"Don't you see what he's doing, Margaret? He hates Norrie

for leaving him. He's never forgiven her. He's the kind of sadis-
tic—"

"That may be true." Her voice was tight and calm. "And then
again, there may be something to it. The main thing is, Shepperton's canceled his exclusive with us."

"Well, of *course* he has. His good buddy feeds him this shit"
—I was upset enough not to censor my vocabulary as I normally
did with Margaret—"what can you expect? But that doesn't
mean—"

"What it *does* mean is that we've lost a great exclusive after
only a month, and the gossip will hurt us—even if the whole
story doesn't come out, it'll hurt us. This is what the tricks were
meant to accomplish, and it's working! I have to let her go,
Liz."

"Margaret, *you can't!*"

"Please don't tell me what I can't do," she said frostily. "Norrie Wachsman is a lackluster performer. She made exactly nine-
teen thousand dollars last year—didn't even cover the cost of
her desk. I can't jeopardize—"

"But it's so unfair. Everyone will think she—"

"Played the tricks? Maybe she did. At this point, that's for
the police to find out. If there are no more tricks, we'll know
that—"

"You *won't* know! It'll just mean that whoever it was got
scared off when a man actually died and the police got involved." Or when I stumbled onto the Ray-Bobbie-Arlyne connection, I added silently. Suddenly I ached to tell Margaret all
about that. But as far as I could see, it would only make things
worse. And it wouldn't do Norrie a bit of good. Atilla had accomplished his mission with resounding success. Norrie was history at the Rooney Property Company.

"Look," Margaret said, "my first responsibility is to my pro-
ductive agents. I can't put the company at risk out of pity for
Norrie. It simply wouldn't be fair." Mother Teresa of the classi-
fieds had spoken. I'd've liked myself a lot for responding that
I'd seldom heard such a load of self-serving bullshit, but I gritted my teeth instead.

"Have you told Norrie yet?" I asked after a moment.

"I told her that Dr. Shepperton had dropped the exclusive and that I'd have to let her go, essentially because of her numbers. I think she understood my position." I just bet she did! Ray Mentone, with his tomcat morals, suddenly seemed an ideal partner for Margaret, who, as far as I was concerned, had all the human empathy of an umbrella stand.

"What about O'Hanlon?" I asked. She'd certainly tell Ike about Attila's call. I couldn't even fault her for it. I just hoped she hadn't done it yet.

"I left a message for him, and when he called back I was out. I'm sure we'll connect before the day's over." She added, her tone resharpened, "Liz, this is confidential—as you know. I would not take it kindly if you spoke with Norrie about her husband before the police do. I'm sure *they* wouldn't take it kindly either."

Fuck you—and them, I thought. "I hear you," I said very quietly.

After we'd hung up, I sat there, feeling paralyzed and impotent. I *would* talk to Norrie—*would* tell her about her scummy ex-husband's accusations. She was my friend, and, client confidentiality or no, she deserved better from me than to sit back and let Ike blindside her. She'd been through enough losing her job—and in a way that would make everyone at Rooney suppose that she was guilty.

I dialed her home number, sure somehow that she wouldn't be there. But she was.

"Norrie," I began in the tiptoe voice you catch yourself using with a cancer patient, "I . . . I just heard from Margaret—uh—"

"Lighten up, Liz. She fired me, she didn't *kill* me. I'll bet she'd fire my two fellow suspects also, if they weren't such hotshot moneymakers. *I'd* fire Arlyne anyway, just to get rid of that damned stink of Giorgio."

"Norrie, I need to talk to you. Can I come over?"

"Really, I'm okay. Besides, tonight isn't good, I—"

"I didn't mean tonight. I meant now." I checked my watch. "It's four-thirty. I can be there in twenty minutes." Norrie lived in Chelsea—West Twenty-first Street.

"Is it that important, Liz?" she asked, sounding far more concerned than she had about her lost job.

"It's that important," I answered, and put the phone down before she could say another word.

I was out of breath when I arrived at Norrie's door. I'd run from the F train stop at Twenty-third and Sixth—four-thirty being a tough time to get a cab in New York—and then up the three flights to her apartment.

"I guess I'm pretty out of shape," I panted as she opened the door.

"Come on in and get off your feet," she said, taking my hand. "God, your hand's ice cold."

"So's yours." I shrugged off my coat and hung it up on the tall bentwood rack. Norrie had taken the top floor of a turn-of-the-century brownstone and transformed it from a small three-room apartment into a single-room aerie. Somehow she'd gotten her landlord's permission to take down the bedroom and kitchen walls, and had created the dwelling that every twenty-year-old girl with Mary McCarthy fantasies dreams of leaving her parents' home for. The large room, with its charmingly irregular nooks, was painted stark white. The clean-lined sofa was white too, and so was the damask spread on the chaste single bed against the wall. A square white rug sat on the mellow pine floor. A small, armless Victorian oak rocker and an upholstered armchair, covered by a white chenille spread, faced the sofa. The only touches of color were the large Braque and Miró prints on the walls. The last winter-afternoon light was fading and a white-shaded brass lamp lit the room with a gentle glow.

I sat on the rocker, liberated my feet from their pumps, and tried to let the surroundings work on me. "This is a great place," I said. "Such a sense of—I don't know—awayness. Peace."

"You got it." She smiled ruefully. "The still center, et cetera. I'm having a cup of tea. Want one?"

"Sure. Black, please, no sugar."

She poured two steaming white mugs, placed them on the small antique trunk that served as a coffee table, and slid her-

self gracefully onto the sofa, crossing her long, jean-clad legs.
Her hair hung down almost waist-length in a single loose braid,
and her face was more relaxed than I'd seen it in quite a while.
She picked up her mug and took a small sip of tea. "So what's
the emergency?" she asked.

"Norrie, this is going to upset you, but I think you have to
know it." I took a deep breath, hating in advance the effect on
her. "Your ex-husband has been spreading nasty stuff about
you."

"What else is new? In case you haven't heard, he doesn't like
me much."

"He called Margaret and told her that what happened to
Shepperton is just the kind of thing that you'd do—*have* done."
I blurted it out fast and felt my face flush.

Her mouth·tightened as she took it, the only clue that she was
at all upset. Her doe eyes were wide as they perused my face.
"Do you believe that?" she asked mildly.

"No." My gut gave a nervous jump. "I'm here, aren't I?
Breaking all kinds of rules," I added. I picked up the hot tea
mug with both icy hands and took a grateful sip.

"Thank you," she said simply.

"Margaret hasn't reached Ike yet, but she will. He'll be coming to—uh—talk to you."

"Question me, you mean. I won't say you warned me, don't
worry. Well," she continued with forced brightness, "Margaret
got a twofer, didn't she? A reason to cut loose a piece of dead
wood and a scapegoat for her crime spree." She laughed bitterly. "Lucky I didn't get to sell your apartment, isn't it?
Would've muddied the waters for her." I must have looked as
stricken as I felt. "Sorry," she said immediately, her face and
tone snapping back into friendly focus, "I appreciate your coming to me like this. You're a good friend."

"Norrie, is there anything . . . I mean money or—"

"No. I can manage," she said, making it clear that the subject
was closed. She leaned her head back and fixed her eyes on the
ceiling. "You're wondering whether Arnold can back up what
he said about me, aren't you?"

She was right, but there was no room in our friendship for me to ask the question. "It's your call. Do you want to tell me?"

"You deserve to know. He's going to tell them about the bees. Arnold's allergic to bee stings. Shortly before I left, a few of them got loose in our bedroom. He thinks I did it." Since the only two words that leapt to mind were "did you?" I kept quiet.

Norrie shrugged. "Bees get into old houses in spring," she said. "The exterminator got sick and had to cancel an appointment to do the annual spraying. He was coming the following week. My dear husband didn't believe that. He thought"—she held her hands out, palms up—"shortly after that, he found out I was having an affair. I told him I wanted a divorce, and he went bananas." She looked down at her hands, now in her lap. "He tried to have me put away."

"Put away?!" I exploded. "Getting rid of him was the sanest thing you ever did." We looked at each other and the tension broke in a mutual laugh. The phone rang and Norrie reached over and grabbed it from the oak end table next to the sofa.

"Hello . . . oh, hi . . ." She looked over at me meaningfully. "Yes, Ike. Of course," she said, her voice controlled and careful. "Half an hour would be just fine. It's the fourth floor—walkup, I'm afraid." After she hung up, she folded her arms and crossed her legs around the other way. "I guess Margaret reached him. You'd better disappear before he gets here."

Chapter 23

I had an hour before my date with Percy Tuthill and decided to spend it covering the two miles up to his place on foot. The biting weather had softened a bit. Also, when I'd left for work, I'd managed, for a change, to grab two lined gloves that were not for the same hand. I pulled on the gloves and a black wool knitted hat and set off up Eighth Avenue.

As I waited for the light on Twenty-fifth Street, I replayed my theory about Ray Mentone as the trickster. Ray had a clear motive to damage Margaret Rooney—the only one of the suspects who did, as far as I knew. He might've given Bobbie and Arlyne any one of several credible reasons to smuggle him into the strategic Central Park West apartments where he could do his damage. He could've said that he wanted to refamiliarize himself with properties and prices, or that he wanted to see the quality of exclusives they'd be able to bring to the new broker-age, or—

"Why'ntcha look where you're goin', lady?" an irate Jersey driver hollered out the window of his Buick as he squealed to a life-saving halt.

"Sorry," I called back sheepishly, and high-tailed it to safety. It still made sense to me—good sense. I'd sleep on it and call Ike first thing in the morning.

I stopped at a street phone to give Art Blyfield a call and see if Bobbie'd come home yet, but all I got was their machine. With any luck, they were out at an A.A. meeting, helping Bobbie back on the wagon.

As an afterthought I checked in with my own machine. Two messages. The first began with much shuffling and sniffing. When the speaker finally started, she said, "It was you. I *know* it was you," and hung up. I recognized Ann Marie Zeibach's voice and hoped fervently that she wasn't leaving the same message with media all over town. The second was simply breathing, close to the mouthpiece and full of menace—at least it would certainly sound that way alone, wakened from sleep at three in the morning. At six-thirty in the evening from the security of a bustling street, it was, well, just disturbing.

I arrived at Central Park West and Sixty-second a few minutes before seven-thirty, feeling invigorated by the exercise and kind of excited about seeing Percy. I'd felt that way this morning —but this morning seemed years ago. I pushed Percy's buzzer and waited for a moment. No answer. Probably it didn't work. I swung open the rusty door—lock still broken—and walked into the vestibule, not knowing what to do next. Find a phone and try to call him, maybe, but I didn't have his number. If he were unlisted . . . The inner door opened to reveal a wispy blonde of about thirty in a balding gray persian-lamb coat, a chubby toddler in a yellow, hooded snowsuit holding her hand.

"Hi," she said cheerfully, showing a set of white, slightly buck boarding-school teeth, "you're here to see . . . ?"

"Percy Tuthill." The child—girl, I guessed—was working up a full head of suction on the red and white pacifier in her mouth.

The woman reached into her coat pocket, extracted a piece of lined yellow paper, and glanced down at it. "Your name?" she asked briskly.

"Liz Wareham. Is the intercom broken?"

"Uh-huh. We have to cope with it one way or another, so we take turns on door duty. Percy's expecting you. I'm Weezie St. John, and this"—she looked down and smiled fondly—"is Courtney. She is being such a good girl," she added, emphasizing each word in that tone peculiar to mommies of young children.

"Well, I can see that," I responded in kind. I was, after all, a long-standing alumna of that sorority. I made a mental note to speak to Alfie about this first thing in the morning.

"I remember your name. You're the PR woman. Ada told me about you just before she left. She said you're going to make some changes around here. True?"

"True," I said firmly, "starting with the intercom and the

front door. Meantime, why don't you get hold of a security guard right now. I guarantee Mr. Stover will pay for it."

"Well," she said, her smile a bit tentative, "I don't know. Look, I don't want to sound ungrateful, but we're looking for a lot more than stopgap measures here and we wouldn't want to send the wrong message, you know? I think we'll have to vote on it."

Great, I thought with a flash of irritation, a self-righteous bunch who can't take yes for an answer. But I pulled myself up short. These people had been jerked around pretty thoroughly and had good reason to be suspicious of anyone working for the Stover organization. "Weezie," I said carefully, "the security guard is only a small first step. There will be others, especially now that . . . well, Mr. Stover's going to keep a much closer eye on how this building's managed. I'll tell you what, *I'll* call the guard service. With any luck, they can have someone here in a couple of hours."

She still looked dubious. Courtney advanced on me, smiling around her pacifier, and reached up with a battered red plastic truck that was minus a front wheel. "Nice truck," I said, kneeling down and pushing it around in a small circle. Courtney dropped to her knees, reclaimed her vehicle, and crawled it back toward the elevator. I stood up. "She's cute. How old?"

"Two and three months." She turned and called, "Courtney honey, drive the truck back now. Come on, show Mommy how fast you can drive it back to me. Look," she said, switching her back to her grown-up voice, "why don't you discuss it with Percy. If he says it's okay, then it is."

I declined to remind her that Stover hardly needed her permission or Percy's to engage a security guard for his own building. The fence-mending required here was monumental, presuming it could be accomplished at all. If the tenants had gotten to the point where they'd rather score off Alfie than see the broken doors and intercoms fixed, then Zeibach's damage was irreparable. Damn him! Dead or alive, damn him. The thought didn't even make me feel guilty.

"Where's Ada gone?" I asked. "You said she left."

"Yes, she did," Weezie said vaguely. She knelt beside Court-

ney, unzipping the child's snowsuit. "You're getting a little too
warm, sweetie. That better?" She stood. "I don't know where
Ada went. She left right after Courtney and I came down to do
our door shift. She was carrying a wonderful big, round hatbox,
you know, like the old-time models used to use? And she had
this cab waiting for her. She gave Courtney a kiss and said she'd
be gone for a little while and she'd bring her girlfriend—that's
what she always calls Courtney, her girlfriend—a nice present
when she came home. I was kind of surprised, actually, because
Ada's never gone away before. I mean, we've lived here, oh, six
years now, Chet and I, and she hardly ever leaves her apartment."

"Probably she was feeling spooked about the murder and
went to stay with a friend. It *did* happen right next door to her."
Or maybe, I added silently, she was afraid the police would find
out about her experience in giving diabetes shots and think . . .

"Well, maybe," Weezie conceded, sounding dubious, "but I
had the idea that all her friends were here in this building,
and—"

"Mommy, I want juice." Courtney's order came out with remarkable clarity, considering that the pacifier was still lodged in
her mouth—early oratorical training, like Demosthenes and his
pebbles.

"What's the magic word, sweetie?" Weezie rummaged
through her red canvas shoulder bag, produced a small carton
of apple juice with a little straw stuck in it, which she held up as
though it were a dog biscuit.

"I wannit!" Courtney wailed, her lower lip protruding and
her chubby hand outstretched.

"Okay, sweetie. Okay. You're tired, I know." Weezie pulled
the plastic plug from Courtney's mouth, stowed it in her coat
pocket, and handed over the juice. "Mommy'll hang on to your
nunu for you while you drink. That's what she calls the pacifier
—her nunu," she confided with we-know-about-these-things
smile.

"Please," said Courtney gravely after a long pull at the juice.
Magic doesn't always occur on demand.

"It was good to meet you, Weezie. And you too, Courtney," I

said, bending down. I straightened up and shook her extended hand. "You people have a lot of good reasons to be wary of the Stover Organization, I know that. But let's say the past died with Zeibach, and see how we can work things out starting now." Other than the obvious repairs and such, I had no brilliant ideas on that subject. This was hardly a case of miscommunication. The tenants wanted to remain in their apartments, and Alfie Stover wanted them to disappear. They understood each other perfectly.

Percy's apartment occupied the eastern corner of the eleventh floor. His front door looked as though it had been transplanted from the Beresford or San Remo, its smart forest-green paint and antique brass knocker a shining example—or a reproach—to its battered brown neighbors. I rapped the knocker twice.

"Well, hi." Percy's forest-green turtleneck, the color an exact match to the door, complemented his russet hair and beard. It hadn't been a mirage. He was as attractive as I'd remembered. He gave me a confident, welcoming smile as he ushered me inside a Japanese cocoon.

Straw matting covered the floors, and shoji the windows—except for a pair of large single panes on the east wall, which offered full views of Central Park. The living room contained no furniture except for two folded white futons and two rectangular tables low enough to accommodate them. The walls, a pale beige, were entirely undecorated.

"Percy, this is . . . well, it's very special." I sounded artificial to my own ears.

"That's okay," he said with a laugh, "it takes most people a while to get used to. Here, let me take your coat. And, if you like, you can take your shoes off." I looked down at his feet, bare in their scuffs. "But only if you like," he added.

"When in Rome," I said, "or I guess Tokyo's more appropriate." I kicked off my high heels and wriggled my feet into a pair of the guest scuffs by the door. Felt good. "What's that wonderful smell? Shaving lotion?"

"Sandalwood candle." He pointed to a pair of fat white candles burning sedately on one of the low tables. "I get them in

Chinatown. Come, sit." He motioned toward one of the futons. I lowered myself into it and curled my legs under me. "What would you like to drink?"

"Sake?" It was a question rather than an answer. I don't really love the stuff except with sushi, but what the hell?

"Hey, you don't have to go that far. This isn't a theme park— just the way ah like to live. Guess ah grew up with too many things around—Old South ancestry and all that. Speaking of Old South, I'm going to have some bourbon."

"Scotch for me. But I want credit for being a sake volunteer."

"You got it." He slid back a shoji to reveal a comprehensive bar. After he'd poured a pair of generous drinks, he joined me on the futon, placing himself pleasingly, but not pushily, close. "To you, Liz, the first good thing ah can say about Alfred Stover," he said, raising his glass.

"Cheers," I said safely, giving it a clink with my own. "I met your neighbor, Weezie St. John, downstairs on door duty."

"Yeah. She's great, Weezie is. Husband's an actor. You've probably seen him in commercials."

"I told her I'd put on a security guard till the door was fixed. She told me to check with you." I sipped my scotch. His response would tell me a lot about where we stood.

He laughed. "Obviously, ah don't have to give Mr. Stover permission to send a security guard to his building. Want a phone?"

"Sure." He reached over to the floor beside him and produced a cordless phone. "Defender Industries is a good one. The number's 555-8739," he said as he handed me the phone.

I dialed while I still had the number in my head and arranged for twenty-four-hour service until further notice. They'd try to get someone there by nine.

"Looks like you're gonna kill us with kindness," he said, "twenty-four-hour service, wow!"

"Now, don't make fun of me," I kidded back, "I'm just trying to do my job, sir." I took in a bit more scotch and put my glass down on the table. "But seriously, sounds like you're not unacquainted with guard services."

"At the beginning, when Stover bought the building and let

the doorman go, we used them all the time. Those who could afford to, paid. Ah did. Weezie did. You'd never know it from those thrift-shop clothes she wears, but her trust fund's pretty substantial. Before long, some of the others—Ada, for example —started to feel like we weren't equal neighbors anymore; like they were charity cases. The feeling in the building changed. Then Weezie and Ada came up with this plan. When the intercom gets broken, we take turns on door duty till nine P.M. After that, anybody who's expecting visitors can just go down and let them in."

"Makes sense," I said. "I take it Zeibach was aware of all this?"

"Oh, he was delighted when we got the security guard and all the dissension started. Ah guess he'd been in his dirty business long enough to know that when the tenants start fightin' among themselves, the landlord wins."

"Uh-huh," I said cautiously, "but look, to you Alfie Stover's some kind of ogre—the landlord. I understand why that is, and I'll admit that it was damned dumb of him to sign on with a sleaze like Zeibach. All I can say in his defense on that score is that this is his first experience with residential real estate in America, and he believed a lot of stuff that . . . well, he should've known better. Do you think you might be able to go back and start from square one with him, and see if maybe we can work out something fair?"

He looked at me without answering and took a contemplative sip of bourbon. Maybe I'd gone too far too fast. "Fair to whom?" he asked. "If ah were Stover, ah'd want us all out too. After all, he bought the building, why shouldn't he do what he wants with it?" He paused, russet eyebrows raised. I stayed quiet and raised my own brows in response. "On the other hand, Ada and some of the others have made their homes here for a long time. They don't have any money to speak of, and they don't want to leave. Why should they have to?"

"And what about you—and Weezie. You have the money to live probably anywhere you want. Why should you be Alfie Stover's responsibility?" I smiled as I said it, making clear—or trying to—that we were talking philosophy.

"Where we want to live is here. Ah rented this apartment twelve years ago, in good faith. Ah've always paid my rent. The law says Stover can't throw me out or jack my rent up—no matter what ah can afford."

"How much rent do you pay?"

"Seven eighty-two—and seventy-three cents."

"I don't know much about rents, but it sounds to me like about what? Half the market rent for an apartment like this?"

"More like a third—even with the broken door and intercom," he said calmly.

"But is that fair? I mean—"

"That's how the rent control laws in this city read. Stover should've checked them out before he bought the building. Caveat emptor."

"I'm not talking law or slogans for a second, I'm talking *fair.*" I tipped up the glass and drained the last drop of scotch from it.

He put a warm hand on my shoulder. I looked down at the tapered fingers, so different from Ike's square-topped ones, and felt a thrill of unfamiliarity. "And *ah'm* talking refill," he said with an appealing grin, taking both our glasses back to the bar.

"You sound kind of like Trask," I said, referring to the hard-boiled hero of his mystery series.

"Not too surprising, is it?" He settled himself back onto the futon, a tad closer than before, and handed me my drink. "Trask *is* me in a lot of ways."

"Funny pair, the two of you—tough black detective and white southern writer. Doesn't sound like too much in common."

"Ah'm pretty tough," he said softly. "Maybe it doesn't show —effete southern accent and all. And every white southerner has a black piece of him, where he feels isolated, wary—me against them. Every white southerner with any imagination, that is. Comes of the way we live together. It's different up north. Whites and blacks, too close—and not close enough."

"I . . . I'm not sure I know what you mean, but maybe I do." I thought about blacks in my own life. Freddie Mae Riggins, the dancer who cleans my house once a week. We were fond of each other. She'd once saved my life, in fact, but our relationship was circumscribed by services bought and paid for.

Vi Royal. We talked clothes, had had dinner a couple of times—
and I didn't know her at all, I was forced to admit.

Percy's arm found its way around my shoulder and pulled me,
ever so gently, closer. I didn't pull away. Stupid? Unprofes-
sional? Maybe, but it felt good after the buffeting I'd taken the
last few days. "As to tough," I said, "your southern accent
doesn't fool me a bit. Let's get back to fair though," I went on
as though we were still sitting a foot and a half apart, his hand
in his lap. My agenda with this man was too mixed to try to sort
out, and at the moment I didn't feel like trying.

"Okay, back to fair," he said, reaching under my scarf to
stroke my neck, "would it be fair to ditch my friend Ada? To say
ah can afford to move, and you can't, so good-bye and good
luck. Stover wants this *whole* building empty, not just part of it.
What good would it do if Weezie and ah and some of the others
left. A few *did* leave with bribes—didn't change anything. My
rent *is* low, ah'll give you that. Think ah should give myself a
voluntary rent increase? Would *you?*"

"No," I admitted. And I didn't know anybody who would.
New York renters lucky enough to have snagged controlled or
stabilized apartments bragged about the fact—even if they were
millionaires. It was a victory against the System. Everyone likes
to win. The stroking on my neck was feeling awfully good—too
good, maybe. "Look," I said in a burst of prudence, "maybe we
should go out and eat now."

"Don't have to," he said. "Ah had them send the sushi in. Ah
thought we might find it more . . . comfortable." He stopped
the neck activity, dropped his hand to my shoulder, and gave it
a friendly squeeze. "Not to worry. Ah like you, Liz. Ada said ah
would and ah do. Ah'll go get the food. You can have sake now
if you want, but ah'm going to have some Pouilly-Fuissé. It's a
pretty good one," he added, hoisting his six one out of the futon
and starting toward the kitchen.

"I'll skip the sake. The wine sounds great," I called after him.
I stood up, walked to the window, and gazed out at the park.
Those two windows framing the park like a pair of mammoth
paintings were startling and wonderful against the starkness of
the room. If Westover went up according to plan, Percy would

certainly lose that view. Even if he could somehow keep his apartment, it would hardly be the same. Suddenly I heard my friend Barbara Garment's voice. "I'd *kill* for that view," she'd said as we first gazed out the living room window of the Conquistador apartment she now owned. She hadn't, in fact, killed for it—just paid a great deal of money. Would anybody literally kill for a view? The question scampered across my mind before I realized it existed. A hand touched mine and I jumped.

"Sorry, ah didn't mean to startle you. Wonderful, isn't it?" He gestured at the window. "With that to look out on, it seemed silly to hang pictures on the wall."

"I agree." I turned to look at him. This tall, ginger-bearded man, so appealing, so bright. I tried to picture him, needle in hand . . .

"What are you thinking?" he asked softly.

You wouldn't want to know. "Oh, nothing special. Just enjoying the view—and you."

"Ditto. Let's go tuck into some sushi and wine." We did. The large polished-wood platter of sushi on the low table was a minor work of art, the whorls and spikes of each piece designed to showcase its elements to best advantage. Two simple stemmed goblets of wine had been poured, and the bottle sat waiting in a tall earthenware cooler.

I sat and spread a large white napkin on my lap. "God, this is gorgeous. Is there no end to your talents?" I asked, picking up a pair of polished chopsticks.

"Ah just ordered the stuff, ah didn't make it. But, to answer your question, we'll see." He smiled with just the right touch of suggestiveness.

Of *course* he didn't kill Zeibach, I told myself. Only a nut would do something like that. Elizabeth Gail Herzog Bernchiller Wareham, you are becoming a female Inspector Clouzot: "I suspect everyone . . . and no one." Now, get off it, and stop being ridiculous. "Weezie told me that Ada's gone away for a few days," I said after swallowing a melty piece of yellowtail accented with scallion and preserved ginger. "She seemed surprised. Said Ada's only friends are here in the building."

"Did she?" I waited for him to continue, but he picked up a plump salmon roll and popped it into his mouth.

"She did. Do you know where Ada went?"

"Not exactly. And if ah did, ah might not say."

"Really? Why?"

"Because she has her reasons, and ah'm going to respect them."

"Am I dumb, or what? Because something's going on that I don't get."

"Look, Liz," he said slowly as he refilled our glasses for a second time, "Ada is not in danger, nor has she done anything wrong. We . . . she decided it would be a good idea if she made herself scarce for a while."

"But—"

"And that's all ah'm going to say about it," he cut in, his smile not compromising the firmness of his tone a bit.

I backed off. At least by the sound of it she was okay—and it really *wasn't* any of my business anyway. "Percy," I asked, "is there any ground at all that you see for negotiation with Stover? Because if the only thing that'll satisfy you is for him to turn his back on Westover and take his loss, there's very little I can do to help. Oh, maybe I can see that basic repairs are made—for a while, but Alfie's not going to just climb into a red suit and play Santa. You wouldn't in his place."

"Ah probably wouldn't," he said after a moment. "What's he prepared to offer? And ah don't mean just money."

"Hmmm." I took it in. "I don't know," I said honestly, "but I'll talk with him. Maybe we can come up with something." Something that makes everybody concerned just unhappy enough to know they've made a compromise, I added silently.

"Let's give this real estate a rest. Ah want to know about *you* now," he said, topping up our glasses from a second open bottle, which had somehow appeared.

"Okay," I laughed. "The short version. I grew up in Queens. My dad was a doctor. He's dead. I have a mother who spends a lot of time in Florida and a sister who teaches English at Columbia. Everything else, I have two of: two kids, two cats, two ex-husbands."

"And no current husband?"

"No current husband."

He put down his chopsticks, leaned over, and kissed my cheek. His beard brushed against my neck. It felt strange and wonderful. I sat there, hardly breathing, feeling excited and numb at the same time. He moved closer, wrapped one long arm around me, and untied my silk scarf with his other hand. His tongue flicked at my ear, and I think I cried out. Then without warning he reached under and scooped me up, the way grooms used to when they toted their brides over the threshold. "Oh, Liz," he murmured into my ear, "my new, beautiful Liz."

As he carried me into the bedroom, a tremor of alarm made its way through the haze of alcohol and attraction. Suddenly I saw Ike standing there, naked, looking at me. Just looking. My breath caught in a gasp. Then, just as suddenly, he was gone. But it had been enough to make me break out in a cold sweat. Percy placed me gently on the bed and started to take off his shirt.

I sat bolt upright, my head spinning with scotch and wine, "Percy, I . . . I . . ."

"What's the matter, darlin'?"

"I *can't.* I just can't, that's all." Oh, my God! I was acting like that most infamous of high school villains—at least when *I* went to high school—a *cocktease.* Only I was over forty, and that made it much, much worse. I'd flirted. I'd . . . well, why couldn't I just go ahead with it? He was goddamned attractive, and nice, and . . . I ought to be locked up. At very least, I ought to go back into therapy. "Percy. I . . . I have to go home!"

I bolted out of the futon and ran into the living room as though pursued by wolves. I slipped out of the scuffs into my heels, grabbed my bag and coat, and flew out of there—all in the space of about fifteen seconds. Percy didn't come after me. Who would have?

Chapter 24

The squat security guard monitored my frantic exit from the building with the uninquiring glance of someone who knows enough to know that he doesn't want to know more. I dashed to the corner of Central Park West, my hand raised in the posture of an attacking marine. No one was pursuing me. I knew that, but my desire to be home was intense, and every second of delay only made it more so. That's why, when a cab lurched to a halt to pick me up, I was astonished that I blurted out 66 Charles Street instead of my own address.

Ike's house. Why the hell was I going to Ike's house, I wondered as I sat taking long, calm-down breaths and willing my hot face to cool. Maybe Jeannie, the soignée stockbroker, would be there. Well, *I'd* been playing footsie with Percy Tuthill, why shouldn't Ike . . . I nursed the thought, almost relishing it. At least it would provide the misery I deserved. You're turning into some atavistic Old Testament Jew, I told myself disgustedly. Stop dramatizing—he probably won't even be home. Then you can turn right around and go back to Central Park West and the only thing this ridiculous self-immolation will have cost you is an extra ten bucks on the meter.

"Here you go," I said as I paid the cabbie, "but would you wait a second to be sure I get in okay. I—I'm not—uh—sure my friend's home."

"No problem." The flicker in his eye said, another nutty broad. I couldn't have agreed more.

I pushed the bell and waited, heart pounding. Lamp on in the living room, but that didn't mean anything one way or the other. I counted forty seconds and rang again. Now I thought I heard footsteps. "Who do you suppose it is, darling?" she asked in my imagination, her voice spiky with the irritation of arousal interrupted. "Hang on." Ike's voice for real as his feet cantered down the stairs.

The door swung open, leaving us face-to-face, no more than a foot apart. I felt as surprised and unprepared as he must've, even though it was I who came here.

"To what do I owe—" he started to say, slipping into irony to cover the moment.

"Stop it, Ike!" I blurted out, not knowing what I meant or wanted or why I was there. "No smart-ass talk. I can't! Take me to bed. Just take me to bed. I—I need to make love to you." Was that what I needed? I laughed. What about Jeannie, lying there waiting for him? Things were getting curiouser and curiouser. All at once I was aware that I was trembling—legs, hands, lips.

One warm plaid wool arm clamped around my shoulder hard and snug, followed by the other one. We stood there like that, close up against each other till my shaking stilled. Then Ike took my hand and, without a word, led me upstairs to the huge bedroom, which is the entire top floor of his house. The room was dark except for the small, focused glow of the bedside lamp on his side. The bed was empty, its dark red coverlet rumpled and pulled carelessly back in a morning-rush-off-to-work mode.

My coat still on, I began to unbutton his shirt. Its wool felt rough and substantial under my fingers. I pulled it off him. Then I unhooked his jeans, lifted his white T-shirt up high and bent to kiss his hot, hard stomach. My mouth traveled up his chest, licking his nipples. Suddenly the tantalizing preliminaries were more than I could bear. I threw my coat off and got out of my clothes in about three seconds, with no regard for fractured zippers or shredded panty hose. I looked at him, naked now but for his socks—which made him seem vulnerable somehow, and boyish. I knelt and took him in my mouth. My heart fluttered as though taking an adventurous little break from its metronomic chores. I might die of excitement—and was ready to welcome it. I pushed him backward, and we bounced onto the bed without changing position. Then we got lost in a way that doesn't happen often—even in bed.

I woke with a start, disoriented, and turned over to find Ike, propped up against two pillows reading Anthony Burgess's autobiography.

"What time is it?" I croaked.

"Four thirty-seven," he said, turning slightly bloodshot blues on me in a wait-and-see gaze.

"Ike, I . . . I'm sorry. I—"

"Sorry? You burst in on a poor unsuspecting bachelor, have your way with him, and then you're *sorry?*"

"I . . . I have to go home." Just what I'd said to Percy, I realized with a twinge.

He gave a hard-edged laugh. "What am I supposed to do now, ask you demurely if you'll still respect me in the morning?" I started to get out of bed, but he reached out and pulled me back. "You are not going to tear-ass off in the middle of the night again. Not if I have to deck you."

I blinked my eyes shut and opened them. They felt rusty sore, the way they do the morning after an all-night flight. "I am a crazy person, Isaac, and you are well rid of me," I said quietly, my voice as rusty as the eyes.

"That may be, but you're dynamite in bed. Hey, if you call me Isaac, should I call you Elizabeth?" He reached both arms out, and the Ike-smelling warmth of his body was irresistible, so I didn't try. I let him make love to me this time and lay back and enjoyed the hell out of it.

"You can call me anything you want," I gasped when it was over. We lay there silently for a while, thinking our separate thoughts. I wasn't a bit sleepy.

"Want some coffee?" he asked after a while.

"Yeah. My robe still around?"

"And your toothbrush and makeup and underwear. Lucky you showed up, I was just about to give them to my new—"

"For God's sake! Would you—"

"Well, don't ask dumb, coy questions." He zipped up his jeans, pulled on his T-shirt, and headed for the stairs.

I showered, shampooed, belted my white terry robe around me, and followed the scent of brewing coffee.

The main floor of Ike's firehouse is one huge loftlike area with open kitchen at the front end and sliding glass doors onto a deck at the back. He was seated, chin on fist, at the seven-teenth-century English tavern table that he'd won years ago in a poker game—it being what they were playing on, and the last thing his host had had left to lose. The coffee was just finishing dripping through. I went behind the counter and poured us each a mug.

"Ike," I said as I slipped into a chair across from his, "I need to talk to you about something."

"Uh-huh," he said neutrally but with a slight expectant note.

"I have an idea that these two cases you're working on may be connected in a funny way."

"Yes?" His eyes narrowed.

"Oh, I don't mean that Zeibach's killer is responsible for the tricks. I have no idea who killed Zeibach. But I think Ray Mentone may be the trickster—and since he was also Zeibach's brother-in-law, not to mention coworker—"

"That would explain the coincidence of your rats," he finished. "Also, I understand, Mr. Mentone has ample reason to dislike Ms. Rooney." My surprise must have registered. "Liz," he said wearily, as though being patient with someone, as they say now, mentally challenged, "you pay taxes, in part to fund a police department. What the hell do you think we do?" The patience was wearing thin. "Play with ourselves while you un-cover information we're too incompetent to find?"

"No," I said, staring into my coffee while I absorbed the sting. "I assume you've found out that Mentone was starting a residential brokerage for Stover?"

"We have, madam, no thanks to you." He leaned across the table and grabbed my arm. "You knew this yesterday, dammit. Maybe if you'd used half a brain and told me, your buddy Crawbuck wouldn't be loxed out in a hospital bed."

"What!"

"After you threw your bombshell at him the other night, Mr. Crawbuck went for a jaunt in Central Park—but not before taking a detour over to Columbus Avenue to pick up a quart of vodka. Silly bastard passed out. Fortunately, a uniform found him along about three in the morning, feeling no pain, but half frozen to death, minus his watch and his pants."

"His pants? Was he—"

"Raped? No. Some coked-out mugger must've gotten the idea that it would be fun to lift the pants as well as the wallet and watch. Bit of poetic justice, wouldn't you say, for a former dope dealer?"

"That's rotten! He's already—"

"Paid his debt to society," Ike finished. "I know, I know. I don't mind the liberal, but does your knee have to jerk quite so fast?"

"Where is he?"

"St. Luke's. He's delirious—high fever. We haven't been able to question him yet. Got the ID only a few hours ago."

"Then how—?"

"Fortunately, his friend Mr. Blyfield was a bit more sensible than his friend Ms. Wareham. He filled us in."

"Oh, God, Ike!" I shut my eyes and felt tears of self-recrimination burn the lids.

"I'm not going to tell you not to cry. You *deserve* to feel rotten about it. Look, I can't swear he wouldn't've gone on a bender if I'd nailed him on it, but Christ, Liz, I'm a *professional* in this—and it's not a game!"

"*You* look! Deck me if you want to. Maybe I have it coming. *But don't you patronize me!* I know it's not a 'game.' " I mimicked his tone on the word. "I did what I thought was right and . . . it wasn't." I ran out of steam. "I guess you know about Arlyne too?"

"What about her?"

"That she was Mentone's initial recruit—the person he sent into Margaret's office to woo her best brokers."

"Umm-hmm." He *hadn't* known. "When were you planning to reveal this?" he asked in a voice that could've stripped three layers of old paint.

"Now," I responded defensively. "I've known it only since this afternoon. I haven't said anything to Margaret because I don't have any proof. Arlyne'll deny it. She said she would, and my hunch is that Margaret would rather believe Arlyne than me —especially the way she's feeling at the moment. I'd've called you, but you were at Norrie's—" Oops.

"How did you know that?" he asked quietly.

"I . . . I . . ."

"I'll help you out." His eyes made the February dawn outside look friendly. "Margaret Rooney told you about her call from Arnold Wachsman, and you rushed over to warn your friend before I could catch her unawares, squeeze a confession out of her, and clap her in irons."

What could I say? Essentially, he was right. I sipped my coffee silently.

"Where's your pal Ada Fauer?" he asked coldly.

"I have no idea. Her neighbor, Weezie St. John, saw her climb into a waiting cab with a suitcase around seven tonight. But I imagine you know that." He investigated my face. "It's the truth," I added sullenly. What I *didn't* add was that Percy Tuthill might know exactly where she was. You have to take some things on gut faith, and on that basis, I knew that Ada Fauer, even if she were the fastest insulin shooter in the East, hadn't murdered Jerry Zeibach. Not that way. If she'd had the strength, she might have bashed his skull in with her Louisville Slugger, but not a calculated game plan with a hypodermic. Besides, if Zeibach had been sacked out in the next-door apartment, how would Ada have even gotten in? Those doors lock when you close them. "You think Ada killed Zeibach?" I asked, trying for nonchalance.

"No, I don't," he answered coldly, "but I need to get hold of her. Lizzie, if I find out that you know—"

"I don't," I said. I looked up at his large grandfather clock. Past six-thirty. "I've got to go get dressed. I have an early meeting." I started up the stairs. "Thanks," I said, my own voice as chilly as his, "thanks for . . . everything."

Chapter 25

I shut the cab door behind me and strode into my lobby, feeling purposeful despite the light throbbing almost-pain of an incipient headache. During the ride uptown I'd made a resolution that would simplify my life immeasurably: to pretend I was a nun until this whole miserable business was finished. I nodded good-morning to Gus and punched the elevator button.

I'd been a blithering moron to begin a flirtation with Percy Tuthill, nice as he was, under these circumstances. Even if there'd been no murder to complicate things further—even if my single concern had been to represent Alfie Stover in negotiating with his angry tenants, I'd compromised my own position and Alfie's, flouncing around like something out of an old Doris Day movie.

I opened my apartment door, gave the waiting cats perfunctory pats, which didn't interest them much, and fresh food and water, which did. I marched down the hall, chin high with anger and resolve. I'd make it right. I would! I'd been in PR a long time. If I couldn't deal with people, I ought to find some other way to make a living.

I threw my coat on the bed and glanced at the message machine. It registered three. Two I'd already heard when I'd called in the previous night—the obsessed widow and the breather: a pair of real winners! The new message was from Elvira Treemor, saying that Alfie wanted to meet with me Thursday, today, at eleven-thirty. Good. He and I needed to get things on track, but, I acknowledged with a disturbing twinge, the tracks we had in mind were likely to be different. I'd half expected that Percy might've called—bewildered or, more likely, pissed off at my strange about-face. But he hadn't, or if he had, he'd hung up without leaving a message. I'd have to call him. My bedside alarm read 8:07. Vi Royal had said she'd be here at eight-thirty, and brokers tended to be prompt.

I slipped into some fresh clothes. The zipper on my skirt was a casualty of last night's revels, if I could call them that. I put it aside to take to the cleaners for replacement. Then I reached for the phone. May as well get it over with. I checked Percy's number, dialed it, and waited, chewing my thumbnail, for him to answer. One ring. What'll I say? Two. Matter-of-fact, that's the ticket. Apologetic, but matter-of-fact. Three. Jesus, maybe he's gone out and I'll have to rev myself up for this all over again. Four. He picked up in mid-ring.

"'Lo." The voice had a sleepy, stretching languidness.

"Percy. I'm sorry to wake you, but—"

"Who is it?" Funny time we live in. You carry someone to your bed but you can't place her voice on the phone.

"It's Liz," I said, embarrassed, "I wanted to apologize for—" A blur of sound at the other end.

"Hang on a second, would you?" I heard the muffling of a hand covering the mouthpiece. ". . . some business, darlin'. Ah'll be right off. You go back to sleep now." Was that sound a *kiss?* "Yes, Liz. How're you?"

"Fine, Percy. Just fine," I assured him dopily, not certain whether my relief was entirely free of a flash of outrage—as though I'd been jilted. Shape up, I told myself sternly. A nun, remember? "Look, I wanted to apologize for our—uh—misunderstanding last night and"—I speeded up to get through the rest of this ridiculous, hypocritical sentence—"I hope it won't in any way damage our working together."

"No reason it should," he replied benignly. At least it sounded benign. "Ah'll keep your scarf for you. Take good care of it." Was there a touch of insinuation in the way he drew out the word "good"?

"Thanks," I said crisply. That should make me feel at least a tad better, I reasoned. Brand-new two-hundred-fifty-dollar Chanel scarfs don't grow on trees. "I'm meeting with Mr. Stover today, and I'll be in touch later. How's the guard service working out?"

"Just fine. Ah have to go now, Liz. Good to hear from you."

As I replaced the phone, the comedy of the situation reached out and tickled me. The seduction-over-sushi. The *Gone With the Wind* carting off to bed. The reluctant-virgin runaway. The immediate substitution of some interchangeable "darlin'." I giggled. The giggle grew to a full-fledged laugh, which somehow brought Norrie to mind. This was just the kind of slapstick vignette that used to reduce the two of us to mirthful tears. Without mulling it, I punched in her number.

"Good morning." Her voice sounded downright cheerful.

"Hi, Nor, it's Liz. Sounds like you're feeling better."

"I am. I'm finished selling real estate. And if *that's* not something to be thankful for—" A strident, long buzz.

"Oops," I said, "the downstairs buzzer. It's Vi coming for coffee. Look, I have to go, but I called to see if you want to come over tonight for a pizza or something. I've got a belly-laugh story for you. Be good for both of us."

"Great," she said after a pause long enough to make me think she was going to say no. "Eight or so?"

"See you then," I said, and ran to the house phone just as it produced another insistent buzz.

I put on a quick pot of coffee and ran to the door just as Vi turned the corner on her way from the elevator. Her glossy sweep of black mink rippled elegantly as she walked.

"What becomes a legend most?" I asked with a hand flourish.

"Not much this morning," she answered with a smile that looked, at most, half-hearted.

"That is *some* coat," I said. "Let me hang it up at your own risk. I may never give it back. New?"

"Yeah. My last commission check was a biggie." She shrugged the coat off and handed it to me. Underneath she was wearing jeans and a sweatshirt—uncharacteristic work clothes for Vi. "Here. Take it away. Right this minute I couldn't care less."

"What's the matter, some friend of animals try to spray-paint you?" I asked. "A major mink isn't exactly the most politically correct—"

"I don't give a damn about that issue," she snapped. "That's for candy-ass white ladies from Larchmont with nothing else on

their minds. Far as I'm concerned, these little buggers were
born and raised to be coats, and until you stop wearing leather
shoes or—"

"Hey, I was just kidding. Mink coats aren't *my* issue either."

"I'm sorry, Liz." Her voice sounded weary and troubled. She
ran long, red-tipped fingers through her aureole of hair.

I noticed, on closer look, that her face, devoid of its usual
makeup, matched the voice. "What's the matter, Vi?" I asked
as she followed me into the kitchen.

"Big trouble. It finally got to me so bad today that I canceled
my showings. You got an aspirin? I woke up with this real
pounder."

"Bottle of Excedrin right over next to the Cuisinart," I said,
pouring out two mugs of coffee. "Shit! I don't have any milk. I
could put some ice cream in it and I've got some English muffins in the freezer. Oh, would you shake me out a couple of
Excedrin too?" The drums of my own headache had just started
to march down Main Street.

"The ice cream'll be fine—but just a little. I'm gonna pass on
the muffins though."

I lucked out and found some vanilla next to the Heath Bar
Crunch and spooned a dollop into her mug. We downed our
pills and took our coffees into the living room.

"So what's the big trouble, Vi?" I asked.

"I'm out of the running as a suspect in this dirty-tricks thing,
right?"

"Right."

"Wrong."

"Wrong?" I asked, feeling a bit like Abbott and Costello.

"Yeah, wrong," she sighed. "I was there at the Leonaides
place. I could've done it. I didn't—but I could have."

"Well, how come your name wasn't on Arlyne's show sheets.
Did you show the apartment without telling her?"

"No, she knew about all my showings. Just like her records
said, I hadn't showed it for a while. I meant I was there—at the
party."

"But . . . but that's impossible! *I* was at the party. I'd've
seen you."

"Maybe you would've," she said with an odd, ironic smile, "but I was betting nobody else would. *I* saw *you* there though, and that's when I left—in a hell of a hurry." She stopped and sipped her coffee.

"I'm not very swift this morning. Would you please spell it out for me? Who were you there with? And didn't they find it strange that you just up and left?"

"I was there with the Party Perfect Maid Service, and yes, they did. They were pretty annoyed, actually, that I left them short-handed."

"*Maid service?* You're one of the most successful brokers in New York. What are you doing moonlighting with a maid service?"

"Researching an article for *New York* magazine."

"I didn't know you were a writer. What on?"

"A lot of things about me you don't know. The article's about not having a face—about being anonymous. Anonymous and black. They go together, you know. Or maybe you don't," she added, her voice taking a bitter turn.

"Maybe I don't," I agreed.

"I'm in and out of these buildings every day. I buddy up to the doormen—tip them, talk about the weather, their families, whatever. And you know what? All they see is the package, the black broad with the mink, the Armani, the jewelry. I wore the damn coat today only to get past your doorman. Those women at Rooney. 'Oh, Vi,' they say, 'you always look so smashing.' And I smile and we talk clothes."

I winced slightly at her mocking tone. She and I had had precisely that exchange more than a few times. "Well, you *do,*" I said, feeling estranged and, somehow, sheepish.

"You know *why* I do? Because I have to. Because if I don't, I'm gonna have a repeat of what happened my first week in real estate. I came to preview an apartment. Doorman thought I was a maid. Before I could say a word, he gave me a key to some other apartment—said that Mrs. Whoever had left it for me, along with a fresh jar of Easy-Off and the message that I should scrub the stove out good."

"Oh, Jesus!"

"You like that? It was raining that day. I was wearing a rain-coat—just a regular London Fog thing and a silk scarf on my head. Let me tell you, I'd just come here from Boston after my divorce. All I had was my settlement money from my ex—and until you've met Wilfred Weems, boy accountant, you don't know the *meaning* of stingy! So, bottom line, I didn't have a whole lot of money. But you know what I did? I went right over to Saks and spent three thousand four hundred and seventy-two dollars and eight-six cents on clothes. I'll always remember the number, 'cause when I signed that American Express slip I almost passed out. But it worked. No doorman has ever tried to hand me the Easy-Off again."

"Shit," I said inadequately.

"I've got to live in your world to make a buck—at least the kind of bucks *I* want to make. You know a funny thing? I love to wear pants, flat heels, informal stuff. Lots of brokers do, 'cause it's comfortable. But I *can't.* I'm as professional as any broker in New York, and I don't have the same freedom to wear what I want. There's always someone looking over my shoulder, watching out for me to step wrong—to be *too black*—so they can say, 'We're just not *comfortable* with her, somehow.' " Her imitation of a pinky-extended society type wasn't half bad. "That's what they did to my brother."

"Who did?"

"His law firm. Cliff was an associate with Wallace and Myerson, back in Boston. He was a show nigger, my big brother." I flinched at the word, as she'd intended when she chose it. "Went through their schools on scholarship—Boston Latin, Harvard, the whole nine yards. He was up for partner. Thought he was on real solid ground, so he took the chance of speaking up about a candidate the firm was getting behind for Congress. Guy was a racist and Cliff said so. Refused to go to some fund-raiser for him. Well, the partners were pretty embarrassed on account of they were gonna deliver this tame black face, sticking out of a good tux. After that, Cliff's partnership kinda went away. They weren't *comfortable* with him anymore." She arranged her mouth into a smile as sarcastic as her tone.

"I hope he told them to shove it and went to a different firm."

"That's what *you'd* do, right? Well, Cliff's not you, baby. He's a black man who played by their rules all his life. He showed his balls *once,* and they cut them off. Since he doesn't have any left, he's still there—oldest living associate. Know how that makes me feel?"

"Furious, I imagine," I said quietly.

"You got it. I deal with white people all the time, even have myself a white guy sometimes. It's always there though, the anger—anywhere from a rock in my throat to a pebble in my shoe. You're a good woman, Liz. I like you, but even with you the pebble doesn't go away."

"I suppose I could say I know what you mean—being Jewish, but it wouldn't be true." I chewed my thumbnail. The Excedrin had done its job, sort of. The drumming was still there, but it was wrapped in wads of cotton batting.

"No, it wouldn't, but maybe you can get why this project was so appealing—kind of a way to stick it to them."

"The *New York* magazine thing?"

"Yeah. It started at an EWOC meeting. Executive Women of Color—it's a group I belong to, maybe the only place I really do relax. Well, anyway, we got to discussing how anonymous and interchangeable black women are in your world."

My world. I felt for an instant like telling her about my phone episode with Percy, and how interchangeable *white* women— black ones too, for all I knew—were in *his* world, but I didn't want to sidetrack her.

"And I said," she continued, "that I bet if I walked into a building dressed like a maid—a building I go to all the time— that the doorman wouldn't recognize me. Well, Toni Odom— she's an editor at *New York,* just joined EWOC last summer— loved the idea. 'Go to it, girl,' she told me. 'Try it and see. Write an article about what happens and I'll get the magazine to print it.' "

"Don't tell me—"

"I *am* telling you. I figured what the hell, I *have* to do this— not just for me, but for all of us. I picked the Conquistador because there's so much security—not just the doormen, but concièrge and the whole thing—and I show in that building all the time. Well, I knew about the big party, and I figured I'd just slip in along with the catering crowd. So much help coming in, nobody'd question. I know I kind of snubbed you out on the street Monday, but I was rushing home to get into my maid clothes, also I was starting to get spooked as hell about the whole idea. Wish I'd listened to my gut and just . . . But I didn't." She looked at me intently with large, tip-tilted eyes. "You know, Liz, nobody even looked at me twice. Not when I came in, or signed in, or walked into the apartment." We sat there, face-to-face, our eyes searching each other's for a stretched-out moment. "So you see the spot I'm in," she said finally.

"I do, yeah." She'd taken a huge risk with a career she'd worked damned hard for, and it looked as though she was going to lose. "When did you actually leave the party, Vi? I got there on the late side—shortly before the murder." Did she flinch just slightly at the word? Her anger—the pebble that never went away. Could she have—?

"I spotted you over near the fireplace, talking with the Leonaideses and some other people, and I bolted."

"Uh-huh," I said, still taking it all in—or trying to. Vi, *there!* Suppose she—

"Can you imagine Miss Priss-ass Rooney hearing this? Hell, she'll think the whole *idea* of the article was a dirty trick on her —and I'm history."

"What would've happened if there'd been no murder? The article would've been published and, if I know Margaret, she'd have gotten rid of you anyway."

"Oh, I'd've quit. I had something lined up through this dude I was seeing, but it fell apart. I told him about the article and he backed out. Fucking racist!"

I figured Vi would be poison at most brokerages after that article, and wasn't at all sure I'd call it racism. That was a philosophical question to explore—but not now.

Vi took a last sip of her coffee. "So what do you think I

should do, Liz?" She laughed thinly. "You wanna be my public relations adviser?"

I gave my thumb another chew and thought for a minute or two. "I'm going out on a long limb with this, Vi, but I think you should do exactly what you just said—minus writing the article, of course. You should get hooked up with a new brokerage right away, and I mean *today*. Don't tell Margaret a thing, except that you're leaving. You won't have any trouble. Corcoran, Brown Harris—I bet they'd jump at you."

"Uh-huh." She was liking it, but I wasn't too sure how she'd take the rest of it.

"But before you do even that, get hold of Ike O'Hanlon. I wish I could run interference for you, but believe me, you couldn't have a worse ally at the moment. Tell him all of it, including that you're leaving, and ask him—don't try to sell him, just ask—if he can keep it confidential."

She shook her head decisively. "No. I'm not gonna do it. That'd give them all they need, Goddamned mick cops—an easy black scapegoat!"

"Ike's not like—"

"I'll just bet! Anyway, nobody recognized me that night. Why should I go tell on myself?"

"Because he'll find out," I said, shaking my head slowly at the truth of what I was saying. "Somehow, he *always* finds out."

Chapter 26

After Vi left, I poured myself a fresh mug of coffee and phoned Morley.

"Hi, it's me. Look, I won't be in till—oh—one or two. Anything up?"

"Your boss. John's been up and down the hall at least four times, looking for you."

Shit! He was back in town—the last thing I needed. "Tell him I'm out at a meeting."

"That's what I told him. Where are you?"

"Home," I admitted, "but I have an eleven-thirty at Stover. Any calls?"

"Art Blyfield to tell you Bobbie's at St. Luke's Hospital and he's going to be okay. Chris Maclos's office confirmed her three o'clock with you over here—I've reserved the conference room. And that crazy person—the one who came here the other morning? She called. Just kept saying that she knew and wouldn't give up till you admitted it. Didn't leave her name."

"I know her name," I said wearily. It looked like I'd have this woman and her obsession on my back for a long time. "Seth there?"

"With two phones glued to his ears, at least since I got in. Hang on."

After a couple of minutes I heard a crisper than usual "Seth Frankel."

"Hi. I've got an eleven-thirty with Stover. What's going on?"

"Yesterday was zoo time—pretty quiet today. What I did is I punched up some of Zeibach's press coverage from the last couple of years on Nexis. Did you know Jerry-boy was involved in the Kraskow project—row of brownstones over on York Avenue? Well, that one went bust. He couldn't get the tenants to move. He tried some pretty rough stuff, but it didn't work. In the end, Kraskow had to pay off in some law suits. Embarrassed a lot of people, including some lady in the Kraskow organization that the *Post* said at the time was sleeping with him."

"Uh-huh, sounds familiar, now that you mention it. Not good news for Alfie. Foreigner or no, he should've checked out his help."

"Well, I kind of suggested to the reporters I talked to that some of the enemies Zeibach made then might have long memories. I figured it would keep them off Stover's back—at least for a while."

"Remind me to Indian-wrestle John and get you a raise," I said.

I took my coffee into the living room, settled myself in the Eames chair, and tried to sort out the increasingly untidy basket of scraps in my mind. Zeibach's murder; the dirty tricks, ending with Steed Leonaides's death; the rat in my own fridge; Ann Marie's insistence that I'd been getting it on with her husband.

One of the tenants could have murdered Zeibach. God knows they had reason, and Percy Tuthill, at least, was cool and knowledgeable enough to pull it off. But none of those tenants would have motive or opportunity to come into my apartment with rats. I was back to that connection. Zeibach was the rat man, and the Rooney brokers had access to my apartment.

There was only one link between the two: Ray Mentone. I'd already decided that he'd put Bobbie or Arlyne up to the dirty-tricks campaign, or had them take him into apartments to pull the tricks himself.

He just as easily could have gotten into *my* apartment after a call from his brother-in-law about my meddling. "Throw a scare into her." I could see Zeibach's hard, handsome face saying that. And Ray had done it, or ordered one of his tame brokers to. They were both in my apartment that day. I shuddered as I pictured first Arlyne, then Bobbie actually dumping the rats out of a sack next to the San Pellegrino.

I preferred to think Ray had done it himself. But if he had, he'd done it knowing that just a few hours later he was going to kill his brother-in-law. Why? I mulled over Ray as devoted brother, killing his sister's philandering husband. It didn't fit, somehow. Another possibility occurred to me. What if Alfie Stover, furious about Zeibach's brutish tactics and the damage they were doing, had said to Ray, "Tike care of him or 'e's out —and so are you," and Ray . . .

Ray. One way or another, it came back to Ray Mentone.

I arrived at Alfie's office about ten minutes early for our eleven-thirty meeting, just in time to bump, almost literally, into Doreen Stover marching out. She looked so mad that even the hairs on her sable seemed to bristle.

"Good morning, Dolores," I chirped. A sniff was her only response as she swept past, chin jutting sixty-five degrees north. They do have chins, these Englishwomen.

The receptionist told me that Mr. Stover was ready for me and I made my way through the double doors, down the hall, and around the corner to his office. I didn't run into Ray, as I half expected to. That meant either that he was out—good news, or that he was waiting for me in Alfie's office—not good news at all.

"Good morning, Ms. Liz," Elvira's chirp resembled my own greeting to the disgruntled Doreen—only her sunniness seemed a good bit more genuine.

"Good morning, Ms. Elvira. Alfie ready for me?" His door was closed.

"Ready and eager, I'd say."

"Terrific." I stopped with my hand on the knob, trivial curiosity having gotten the best of me. "By the way, I noticed Doreen leaving in kind of a hurry. She didn't look happy."

"Shouldn't think so," she said with a quick wink. "Some around 'ere may not *be* around 'ere very long—if you get my drift." So Alfie was going to dump Doreen/Dolores, if I understood Elvira correctly, for her peccadillos with the late Jerry Zeibach. Hmmm.

"Sit down, Liz, sit down," Alfie greeted me, a semi-scowl underscoring the froglike aspect of his face. Ray, I noted with relief, was not there.

"Hi, Alfie," I said blandly as I put myself into one of the wine velvet chairs opposite his desk. This was going to be tricky. I

needed to persuade Alfie that he could no longer delegate negotiating with the tenants—especially not to a man who might
any minute be accused of all sorts of unpleasant things, including murder. Trouble was, I couldn't say it in those words. In
fact, I couldn't seem to bad-mouth Ray at all, not after I'd
clashed with him so openly at our first meeting. John Gentle
was right—it had been a vain, stupid thing to do, and I was
paying for it now.

Questions started to leapfrog around my head. Had Ray told
Alfie about the Rooney dirty tricks? How much did Alfie know
about Ray's broker-recruitment program for Stover Residential? I forced myself to pull the reins in. One thing at a time. "I
was over at the building last night," I began.

"Good, good. You met with the old lady?"

"No. She seems to be off, staying with friends."

"Preparing to move out?" The hopeful note in his voice made
me feel slightly ill.

"No way," I answered more sharply than I'd meant to.

His scowl renewed itself. "But she's the key! She—"

"I met with Percy Tuthill, who's the *real* leader. Oh, Ada's
important, but she's the head of the committee mainly for media purposes. Tuthill's the main decision-maker."

"And 'oo *is* this Tuthill?"

"A very well-known mystery writer. He writes under a different name—Mark Christmas."

"And this . . . this millionaire probably 'as a rent-controlled
apartment in *my* building! I'm supportin' the bloody—"

"Rent-stabilized, but yes, he certainly can afford to pay market rent. The law, unfortunately—"

"I don't care about the bloody rent, I want 'im *out*. I want 'em
all out."

I took a deep breath and prepared to bite that bullet. "Alfie, I
don't think that's going to happen."

"Well, what am I *paying* you for, then?" he exploded.

"To help you get the best outcome possible for Westover—
and to tell you the truth. Look," I continued, eager—maybe too
eager—to say at least part of my piece before his temper
erupted in full force and made that impossible, "you've tried

quick cash offers and you had a couple of takers, but that's all. You've tried . . . or, I should say, Jerry Zeibach tried bullying and intimidation, and that backfired. It hurt you badly, Alfie, because it's made the tenants automatically resistant to *anything* you propose and—"

"Zeibach's over. You 'ave to make 'em understand that. It's Ray now. Ray knows 'ow to smooth people. 'E's—"

"Alfie," I said levelly, "I don't think that's the best way to handle things."

"What do you mean?"

"I mean that I think your best shot is to deal with those tenants yourself."

"What on earth are you talkin' about?! That's entirely out of the question."

"Think about it for a second. The tenants don't know you. All they know is what Zeibach did in your name—and he did bad things, Alfie. He did bad things on other projects too, in the past. I don't know if Ray told you about Zeibach's history, but he worked on a development with Peter Kraskow a few years ago, and it was abandoned because they couldn't get the tenants out. They tried cash and turning off the heat—even hired thugs and moving homeless people into the empty apartments they'd warehoused. None of it worked, and Kraskow had to pay out in a few law suits, to boot." God bless, Seth.

Alfie's face flushed pink. "But this was *different.* My people *never* 'ired thugs. Westover's not like Kraskow's project—not at all. Ray said there'd be no problem."

"Ray was wrong," I said, "there's a big problem. But you've also got something going for you that only *you* can make work."

"What's that?" he asked, his voice suspicious.

"That you're a foreigner. That you're a fair-minded business-man from another country who depended on others to tell him how things were done here."

"A fool, you mean?" he asked caustically.

"Not necessarily. If the bottom line on your deal winds up favorable, you were very smart—even if you have to be more generous to the tenants than—"

"What the 'ell do you expect me to do," he roared, "start a

charitable foundation for 'em?" His face was well on its way from pink to puce. He stood up and pointed a stubby finger at me. "You are a bleedin' 'eart, that's your problem!"

No, you're a cement-head, *that's* my problem. "When I went to the building last night, the intercom was broken and the tenants were taking turns on lobby duty. That would be rotten publicity for you just now, so I've put on a guard service till it's fixed, which you should see to as soon as possible. Also, you should have some kind of part-time superintendent come and clean the lobby and halls a couple of times a week."

He glared at me, frog eyes popping. "Because," I continued, willing my voice quiet, "if you *don't* do these things, you are throwing out the money you're paying us. Public relations won't help you a bit."

He didn't answer, but he did sit back down—a good sign— and his complexion returned to normal. After a few silent minutes he hollered, "Elvira!" She opened the door so quickly, I suspected she'd been standing right outside it. "Get the intercom repaired at that bloody building and 'ave Tom come by once a week to clean the 'alls and keep an eye on things." She nodded and left. "Twice a week is too often," he said sullenly, "I'm not Father Christmas."

I departed Alfie's office with my stomach twitching. Score two points: He'd given the order to repair and clean the building, and he hadn't fired me. Could've been a lot worse.

Just as I reached the double doors to the reception area, I felt a hand on my shoulder. "Hi, there, little Liz. Weren't you even gonna drop by and see me?" Ray Mentone.

"I didn't—" I cleared my throat nervously, feeling as though he were somehow privy to all my alarming speculations about him, "didn't know you were in."

He smiled. "Where'd you think I'd be, playing nasty tricks on Miz Rooney's clients?" He laughed at my obvious discomfort. "Never mind, I'm just teasing. By tomorrow thing's'll be all cleared up. You'll see." He patted my shoulder again. His mood was on a definite upswing, at odds with anything like reality as I knew it. "Get squared away with Alf?" he asked buoyantly.

"Depends what you mean by squared away." No point in

pussyfooting, Alfie would tell him what I'd said anyway. "I advised him to go out front and negotiate directly with the tenants."

"Good idea," he said, throwing me an unexpected curve. "This damn thing's gotten to be one colossal mess, thanks to my late, great brother-in-law. Swear to God, if somebody else hadn't put his lights out, I could've done it myself!"

Since this rendered me just about speechless, all I managed was a quick good-bye.

Chapter 27

I arrived at my office just before two, carrying a brown-bagged turkey and ham with Russian, which I gobbled at my desk while I speculated on the why of Ray Mentone's unexpected upbeat mood and the how of managing the next step in Alfie's tenant negotiations. No brilliant ideas presented themselves on either front—but the sandwich, washed down with warmish Perrier, was delectable, its flavor enhanced by my suddenly ravenous appetite and the fact that John Gentle was out at lunch—a long one, I hoped.

At a quarter of three I forced both the Stover and Rooney situations into a back-of-the-mind holding pen and tried to focus on Baker Bank and the right words to get Chris Maclos reenthused about the Fiscal Fit brochure. I'd decided to meet with Chris one on one. Cormac McCafferty, who'd written the thing, was apt to get smart-ass and defensive. Seth didn't work on the Baker account at all, and Angela Chappel, the aide who did, was still off under some palm tree—a pity, because convincing people that black was white was her special art form.

When Chris arrived, looking stiff and grim, the floppy bow on her Brooks Brothers blouse tied more vehemently than usual, I concluded on the spot that persuasion was a fool's errand. Once we'd closeted ourselves in the sleek gray conference room, I ignored the stacks of memos, copy, and layouts assembled to support my case, and just sipped the fresh coffee Morley'd laid on.

"I don't know, Chris," I said mildly, "maybe you're right."

"How do you mean?" she asked, sounding suspicious.

"Well, the Fiscal Fit could be wrong for Baker's market identity." Ray Mentone wasn't the only one who could throw a curve. "It may be a bit too current, too . . . young."

"But we're going after the young customer with this."

"I know, but maybe the vigor of it is too startling. I mean, Cormac's a very creative young man and he approached it with the Ivy League light touch. You know, kind of Gary Larson. And the graphics have the same flavor. It may all just be too zippy for where we are right now."

"Zippy is what we're trying for," she replied indignantly.

"I know, I know. All I'm saying is perhaps it was too much too soon."

We continued in this reverse-sell mode until Chris, over my objections, insisted on taking another look at the material and getting back to me by the end of the week. I'd have loved to run from the room right then—before she could change her mind, or I could screw things up. The closest I could come was to change the subject. So for the next forty-five minutes we talked about how inadequate men were, especially those who, like her recently decamped boyfriend, "couldn't love," for whatever reason. I'm ready to bet that for better or worse, business meetings between males never include these conversations.

I saw Chris to the elevator, knocked on John Gentle's door, brought him selectively up-to-date on the Stover account, and felt, as I slipped on my coat to go home, pretty pleased with myself—a refreshing change. Even God had cooperated by seeing to it that Margaret Rooney didn't call.

When I got home, I changed into jeans and a stretched-out black sweater, and was just pouring some Dewar's over ice when the phone rang. I hoped it wouldn't be Norrie canceling. "Hi." Norrie's voice. Well, maybe there'd be something good on television. "I'm at Bloomingdale's. I think I'm in love with a red sweater, and I'm winning the argument with myself about how fifty-nine ninety-five plus tax won't deal the death blow to my fragile finances. I may be just a little late, okay?"

"Sure. Whenever." I was relieved. I was looking forward to the evening, relishing in advance the laughter that would soothe the residual sting of the Percy debacle.

The phone again. "Hello."

"Liz"—the voice sounded strained and odd—"it's Margaret. I need you here right away."

Shit! God had fallen asleep at the switch. "Margaret, what's the matter? You—"

"I need you here—*now.*"

So much for my girl-talk evening with Norrie. "Okay, but—uh—where's here?"

"My office." She hung up with a harsh click.

I slipped into boots, debated for a second about whether to change to a sweater in better condition, and decided the hell with it. No way I could reach Norrie. I scribbled a note to leave, along with my keys, with Juan at the door, saying I'd been called away, would be back ASAP, and why didn't she go up and have a drink and wait for me.

In the cab I played Russian roulette, wondering which of the volatile elements had exploded to make Margaret summon me at almost eight P.M. in such a clipped, peremptory tone. Arlyne's treachery? Or Bobbie's? Had Vi confessed after all about the planned *New York* magazine article? Had she found out that her old enemy Ray Mentone had nailed her with exactly the dirty-tricks plot she'd suspected and feared? Worst of all, had she somehow discovered that I'd been holding out on her?

She'd fire us. No question about that. And John would fire me. No question about that either. I'd withheld crucial information from a client, shielded people I should have reported, and hadn't even had the sense to cover my ass by telling him what was going on. I *should* be fired, I thought in a satisfying burst of masochism.

I paid the driver and walked into the lobby through the side swinging door, the revolving ones being locked for the night. A gray-uniformed guard, seated at a lectern, stopped me.

"Where you going, Miss?"

"Sixteenth floor, Rooney."

"You wanna sign in?" He handed me a pen, and I did, checking my watch for the time—eight-fifteen.

The sixteenth floor, with only a couple of ceiling spots listlessly lighting its beige carpet, had that stage-set look that bustling daytime offices get at night when everyone's gone home. I turned left toward Margaret's office. The reception area was dark. My hand, as I groped along the wall for a switch, felt sweaty. Margaret *had* said her office, hadn't she? Why was the light off? I snapped it on and let out a deep breath. Being alone in the dark scares me, always has—enough so that I leave an all-night lamp on in the Hilton Whatever and find it more comforting than embarrassing.

Margaret's office door was closed. I knocked. I knocked again. I called her name. No answer. Nothing about this felt right. I turned the knob and opened the door—or started to. Eight inches or so was all it would go. It was as though something had been shoved against it. I peered inside, but couldn't see anything in the darkened room. Now was clearly the time to leave, but curiosity, at least for me, tends to be uncontrollable, blotting out even fear, or good sense.

I shrugged my coat off and slipped through the narrow opening. Then I fell flat on my face. I lay there, panting with terror and surprise. It took me a second to realize that nobody had pushed or pulled me. I'd simply tripped on whatever the bundle was that was blocking the doorway. I stood up and looked down. The bundle was Ray Mentone.

His raccoon eyes stared at me vacantly, and his mouth was an *O* of mild surprise. The dark, wet-looking hole in his glen plaid lapel was small and neat. I knelt down and touched his hand. It was warm. As I bent close to him, hoping for a breath or heartbeat, I noticed the smell of urine and wondered, irrelevantly, if that would've bothered him. Probably not. He'd have shrugged and said, "What can you expect? Lady shoots a man, he pees his pants. Only human, little Liz."

I swallowed hard. Margaret had killed him. She'd found out what he was doing and gotten him here and . . . But would she really do it *here* in her own office, and then set me up to find the body? Where the hell was she anyway?

I edged back out the door, picked up the phone on Selma's desk, but before I could dial, I spun around to a familiar voice.

"What the hell are you doing here?"

"Vi!"

"What's wrong, Liz? You look—"

"There's a dead man in there," I said—measuring out each word as though that would somehow keep things calm.

"A dead man? Who?"

Without answering, I dialed Ike's office, praying I wouldn't have to go through a rigmarole to get hold of him.

"O'Hanlon."

"Ike, it's me. I'm at Margaret Rooney's office and . . . and Ray Mentone's been murdered."

A beat went by. I heard Vi gasp. "Liz," I guess I didn't answer promptly enough. "Liz," Ike repeated, sharper this time.

"Yes."

"Anyone there but you?"

"Vi Royal. I don't know, there may be others—down the hall in the salesroom. I'm in Margaret's office. That's where he is."

"Uh-huh. Look, you stay there—right outside her office. I'll have the precinct troops over in just a couple of minutes, and I'm getting in my car right now. You okay?"

"Yeah, I'm okay."

"Ray? Murdered?" Vi asked softly, as though begging for the negative answer she knew she wasn't going to get.

"You know him?" I asked.

"Yes," she said, her eyes not quite meeting mine.

"How?" I asked, but a split second later the answer hit me. "Of course! He was the one who offered you the job, and then pulled back when you told him about your article. You said you were 'seeing him.' You mean *sleeping* with him?"

"Why're you surprised?" Her chin trust upward in challenge. "I told you I got it on with whiteys sometimes. No big deal. Nothing serious for either one of us."

"I get laid a lot, little Liz, but I don't make love." Ray's voice echoed in my head. Fucking racist, Vi had called him. Could all that anger have finally exploded and—

"Hey, quit staring at me. *I* didn't do it." She gave a small laugh which petered out halfway through.

"Anybody else in the salesroom?"

She shrugged. "Dee Johanson, Mac Stitt, a few East Side brokers. Also, Ms. 'broker to the stars.' Lots of people in and out. I wasn't paying much attention—too busy cleaning out my desk and getting files bundled to take home."

Arlyne Berg. Margaret wasn't the only one with reason to hate

Ray Mentone. Hadn't Arlyne said she'd never forgive him for
lying to her about the name of the new firm?

"Did you do—uh—what we talked about yesterday?" I asked.

"I sure did." She smiled radiantly, as though forgetting for an
instant what lay behind the door. "I start at Stribling Monday.
That's why I was getting my stuff together. I'm gonna give Margaret the word tomorrow."

"Did you reach Ike?"

"No," she admitted, lowering her eyes. "I was going to do
that tomorrow too."

"Terrific," I muttered.

If she'd been going to say anything more, I never got the
chance to hear it, because all at once the place was crawling
with cops.

"Wareham! Who's Wareham?" called a short, squarish kid,
his Fu Manchu mustache as feathery as a gosling. The name tag
on his parka read Slonski. I raised my hand. "Homicide said
you found the body."

I nodded. "He's in there," I said, gesturing toward Margaret's
office. Three men and a woman in plainclothes crowded in just
then, impatient to get past us.

"Let's step outside and let these Crime Scene types get
started. You got here pretty fast, Doc," he said to a dessicated
man with a stethoscope around his neck. "Lieutenant didn't
even come yet."

"Gotta keep the taxpayers happy with the service," the medical examiner responded with a ghoulish grin as he sidled
through the narrow opening into Margaret's office and closed
the door.

"Okay," Slonski said after we'd staked out a quieter corner of
the reception area, "your full name, address, phone." I gave
him that information, as well as the name and address of "the
decedent."

"Now, who's this lady?" he asked, jerking his head at Vi.

"My name is Violet Royal. I work here," Vi responded with
regal composure.

"Were you with Miss Wareham here when she discovered the
decedent?"

"No, I was not. I was in the salesroom, cleaning up some paperwork."

Just then I heard the elevator doors open and Ike appeared along with Joe Libuti, who was lighting up one of his ubiquitous Camels.

"Hi, Lieutenant, Sergeant." Slonski greeted his elders with the deference we used to display to our teachers.

Ike nodded at me and drew Slonski aside for a private huddle, after which they went into Margaret's office. Joe Libuti cocked a bushy black eyebrow. "You turn up all over the place these days, don't you, Liz?"

"Joe, I—I'm sorry about the other night. You know, getting you to sign me out of the Leonaides party early with that story. I hope that you didn't . . . I mean I hope that Ike didn't land on you for it."

"Hey, no sweat." He dragged deeply on the cigarette. "The lieutenant and me, we got a long history. He gets his Irish up sometimes. But he's one of the good guys—best I ever worked with, and I knew his pop too. But you shouldn'a run off like that. I guess you had your reasons, but it wasn't the right thing." He shook his head slowly. I glanced at Vi and saw her suppress a smile.

Ike came back out, dispatched Slonski someplace with a pat on the shoulder, and walked back toward us. "Ms. Royal, anybody in the salesroom besides you?"

"A few others. At least there were when I walked over here and found Liz."

"We didn't see anyone leave," I added, "and Slonski and the others got here awfully fast, so I guess they must still be around. One of them is Arlyne Berg," I added.

"Uh-huh," Ike mumbled, but his eyes flickered interest. "How come you happened to walk over here, Ms. Royal?" he asked casually.

"I was on my way to the ladies' room and saw the light on."

"That it? You didn't hear anything unusual?"

"No." I closed my eyes for a second, willing Vi to tell Ike about the maid masquerade at the Leonaides party. I can't say it worked, but something did—maybe just good sense. "Lieutenant, I have some things to discuss with you," Vi said, her head high, her voice resolute. I gave silent thanks to God—or someone.

"About this murder?" Ike asked.

"Uh, not really," Vi said after a pause.

"Then I'm going to ask you to go back to the salesroom with Sergeant Libuti and answer some questions first." He motioned Joe aside and spoke to him quietly for a moment.

"It's *you* I need to talk to, Lieutenant," Vi said with an urgent edge.

"I hear you, Ms. Royal," he said. "I'll be with you in about twenty minutes, as soon as I finish with Liz." He gave me a flash of bright blue headlights—high beam—for the first time since he'd arrived. I realized, uncomfortably, that I was about to be grilled, if not filleted. Okay, O'Hanlon, I said silently, go for it. You don't scare me. You don't even attract me. I'm a nun till all this is over.

He settled us in a pair of sofas in the far corner of the reception area and said curtly, "Let's have it."

"Margaret called at—uh—about a quarter to eight, I guess, and said she needed me here immediately. So I jumped into a cab and came—and I . . . found him," I finished, shaken by a sudden mental replay of Ray lying there, his face frozen in unexpected death.

"But no Margaret?"

"No."

"What did she say, exactly, when she called?"

I shut my eyes and summoned up the sound of her. I'm pretty good at that—auditory memory. Back when I was acting, by the time a play was halfway through rehearsal, I was letter-perfect in everyone's part. "She said, 'Liz, it's Margaret. I need you here right away.' I asked her what the matter was and she said, 'I need you here—*now*.' I wasn't sure where 'here' was, so I asked. She said, 'my office' and then she hung up."

"You're sure that was it?"

"Uh-huh."

His eyes narrowed in concentration. "How'd she sound?"

"Nervous. Tense. Kind of . . . strange."

"Strange in what way?"

I chewed my thumbnail, thinking how to describe it. I remembered my English teacher in the senior year of high school telling us, punctuated by spirited poundings on his desk, that if we couldn't put it into words, it wasn't a clear thought. "Well, her voice was clipped in a funny way. And then she hung up so fast."

"Stay right here," he ordered, disappearing into the hall on the run. I tried to organize my thoughts, but they were far too scrambled for that. My favorite suspect was dead and my client was God knows where. Before my brain left the starting gate, Ike was back.

"What happened when you got here?" he asked. I told him. "Did you touch or move the body?"

"I may've by an inch or two when I pushed the door open. And I touched his hand and checked that he wasn't breathing. Then I called you." I figured that at least here my conduct had been unexceptionable.

"You shouldn't have pushed that door open," he said flatly.

"Oh, for God's sake, Ike, do you have to find fault with *every—*"

"Even you must have noticed that something was wrong when you get summoned to a strange meeting at night and the place is dark and your client doesn't answer when you call her name and the office door is blocked and—"

"Okay, okay," I snarled, "enough!"

"You should have gotten the hell out of there and called 911. How did you know a perp with a gun wasn't behind that door, waiting for you?" he snarled back, that angry white line beginning to edge his lips the way it does.

"And how did I know Margaret wasn't lying there, minutes away from dying?"

"And who are you, Florence Nightingale? It was a stupid risk, with all that's been going on, and you damned well know it. You should've called for help. You've been playing cute games in this whole thing, Liz, *and it's got to stop!* I'd shake you till you rattle if I thought it would do any good. I know you've been holding out on me, probably for some fucking misguided idea of client loyalty or friendship—"

"Why are you wasting time hollering at me?" I hollered. "Why aren't you out rounding up—" I broke off when I realized that the only way to finish that sentence would be Margaret Rooney.

Ike finished it for me. "Joe's on his way to Ms. Rooney's apartment as we speak. Did you have any idea Mentone was coming here?"

"No. But come to think of it, I saw him at the Stover office this morning, and he seemed, well, almost euphoric. I remember he said that after today, things would be all cleared up."

"That's what he said—exactly?" I nodded. "What did you think he meant?"

"I—I didn't know. I'd just had a rough meeting with Alfie Stover and I guess my mind was fixed on that."

"What about this thing your friend Royal wants to discuss with me? Know something about that, do you?"

"What makes you think so?" I asked, but he had me skewered.

"Don't ever think of becoming a secret agent. You haven't got the face for it."

"She's going to tell you that she's not out of the running as the possible perp of the dirty tricks." He smirked at my use of the jargon, but contained any sarcastic response. "Also, that she knew Ray Mentone."

"Uh-huh. I'm all ears," he announced with exaggerated affability.

"Let *her* tell you. I'm out of it. She came to me this morning and I told her to go to you."

"I have not been incommunicado. Did I miss a message from her, perhaps—or from you?"

"No," I snapped. "Can I go home now? All hell is going to break loose over this, and I have to—"

"I know, talk to your client and deal with the media. As for your client, not a chance in hell of your getting to her until I'm finished with her. And if you even try—"

"Stop it!" I screamed as the sting of tears surprised my eyes.

"Go home," Ike said, sounding suddenly depleted. "You'll have to come down and make an official statement tomorrow." I nodded and went to retrieve my coat. "Be careful, Lizzie," he said to my back as I stood waiting for the elevator. "Be very careful."

I didn't answer.

Chapter 28

I walked out of the building into a media maelstrom. Channels 7 and 4 had arrived, along with WINS, the *News* and the *Post*. Slonski and a compact nut-brown female cop were doing what they could to hold the hungry reporters at bay.

"Liz Wareham," I heard one of them say. "That's Liz Wareham. She's the Rooney flack." Two mikes stopped their thrust four inches from my mouth. Shouted questions tripped over each other.

"Who's dead up there?"

"What happened?"

"Did you find the body?" This from Kessie of the *Post*. "You gotta stop doing that, Liz," he added with a half smile, referring to my discovery last year of the body of another client, King Carter. I couldn't have agreed more.

The rain of questions continued to pelt. Slonski stepped in front of me. "Leave the lady alone. Want me to put you in a cab, Miss Wareham?"

I'd've loved it, but I couldn't just give the finger to the reporters like a normal citizen. I happen to be in a business that depends on them. "Tell you what," I said quietly, "if you could flag me a cab, I'll talk to these folks for a couple of minutes and then make a quick getaway." I held up my hands in a futile attempt to quiet things down. "I'll tell you everything that I know, okay?" I shouted. That accomplished what my arm-waving hadn't. "But I'd like to do it only once," I continued in a more normal tone, "so gather in with your mikes." I paused. Channel 2 had just arrived, scrambling out of their car, minicam ready for action. "At a little after eight I arrived here for a meeting and found Ray Mentone dead."

"How?" "How'd he die?" "Do they know who did it?"

"Wasn't he Rooney's ex-partner?" The questions erupted like kernels of popping corn.

"He'd been shot. I have no idea by whom. Mr. Mentone was a former partner of Ms. Rooney's, but that ended more than six years ago. Mr. Mentone had no association with the Rooney Property Company."

"Anybody else up there?" "Where's Margaret?" "Was it a break-in?"

"I understand there were several brokers working late at the other end of the floor. I don't know which ones. I have no idea about a break-in. Ms. Rooney is not in the building." I spoke mechanically, trying to avoid anything blatantly untrue, yet not wanting to provide more information than I had to.

"I don't know any more than I've told you. Lieutenant O'Hanlon is in charge. I'm sure he'll speak to you when he comes down." I let Slonski clear a path for me and jumped into the waiting cab.

It wasn't until we were halfway through the park that I remembered my date with Norrie Wachsman. I glanced at my watch. It was almost nine-thirty. She'd probably gotten tired of waiting and gone home.

Juan was on the door. "You friend, the real estate. She upstairs," he said as he helped me out of the cab.

I opened the door to *Le Nozze di Figaro* rolling gloriously out of the speakers. Norrie, in jeans and a bright red turtleneck, was sitting on the sofa, her legs crossed Indian-style, a cat on each thigh, and what looked like scotch over ice in her hand. When she saw me she raised her glass. "L'chayim. Conquering heroine. I was beginning to give up hope, but I was having such a good time playing with these guys that I decided to stick around." She scratched Elephi and Three affectionately around the ears. They ducked their heads in responsive pleasure.

I poured a short neat scotch for myself, walked over to the stereo, and turned off the Mozart. Its abounding joy would have been an obscenely unsuitable accompaniment for announcing a murder. I sat next to her on the sofa and saw her face change from surprised to worried.

"Something's terribly wrong," she said. "What is it?"

"Somebody's been murdered. Shot—in Margaret's office."

She stared at me, the brown doe eyes wide. "You're not kidding," she said at last.

"Wish I were. His name's Ray Mentone. He used to be Margaret's partner. They hated each other—with very good reason. Turns out he may've been the one behind the dirty tricks."

"And she killed him? In her own office? Were you there when it happened?

"No. Margaret called, telling me to get over there right away. When I arrived, I found Mentone's body but no Margaret. I don't know that she killed him. It would be a pretty dumb way to do it, pointing to herself like that."

"Unless she just lost her marbles with hatred. You *did* say she hated him. But if she had a gun, that means it was planned, right?"

"Yeah." I nodded. "I suppose it could've been a double switch. I mean, killing him there in her own office was so obvious that someone like Margaret would never do it. So maybe she did just that." The possibility had started to germinate in the cab home, and I felt disloyal as hell to my client as I heard myself voice it.

"Ironic, isn't it?" Norrie said, a smile twitching at one corner of her mouth, "Margaret, a suspect." Elephi batted at Three's ear, and they both abandoned Norrie's lap and streaked toward the kitchen.

"God!" she said, a new thought hitting her. *"I* might've been the one to find the body. I was there to clean out my desk, and I wanted to drop in and tell Margaret good-bye or fuck you or something. I walked over to her office right before I left. Her door was closed. I saw the light under it, so I thought she must be inside. I kind of stood there in the hall for a minute, but I couldn't make myself knock—just *couldn't.* I knew she'd be the oh-sooo-gracious lady—put that arm around my shoulder and wish me well, and I'd be supposed to say thanks and no hard feelings. And I just couldn't play that little scene, so I wimped out." Her shoulders slumped.

"What time was this?" I asked sharply.

"Right before I left—about a quarter of seven. Let's see"—

she turned her eyes up and calculated—"I guess I got there just before six. Got my things together and spent a little extra time catching up with Bobbie. He's been sick, you know. Looks awful."

"Bobbie was there?"

"Uh-huh. Why're you so surprised? He dropped in to pick up a check from his closing last week. Didn't stick around. He was still feeling kind of rocky, but the lure of money waiting around with your name on it is, how you say, irresistible."

So Bobbie'd been there too. "Look," I said, pushing this new element to the back of my mind, "you ought to contact Ike and tell him about seeing the light under Margaret's door. Her office was dark when I got there, and that means—"

"Gotcha. I'll do it."

The phone shrilled, and I got up to catch it. Kessie, the *Post* reporter, trying to wheedle some extra tidbit. While I was up, I realized that I should've called Alfie Stover the minute I walked in the door. I did it then.

His reaction to the news of Ray's death was uncharacteristically subdued, but characteristically self-interested. "Trouble," he said, quietly enough to be talking to himself. "That man's been nothing but trouble since I clapped eyes on 'im." A pause. "See that I don't get 'urt too bad in the papers, won't you?" It was only after we'd hung up that I realized Alfie had asked not one question about who might have killed Ray Mentone, or why.

I returned to my place on the sofa, the kitchen cordless phone in my hand, kicked off my shoes, and tucked my legs up under me. I was going to have lots to do, but I didn't quite know where to start. Another few minutes with Norrie wouldn't affect things one way or the other. Having her there felt comforting, and the scotch didn't hurt either.

The phone again. This time a second of heavy breathing, followed by a hissed "Bitch!"

Shit! Pity bumped up against a flash of anger. Her brother was dead now too, in addition to her philandering husband, and here she was, playing phone games. "Look, Ann Marie," I said wearily, "don't do this. Whoever it was screwing your husband, it wasn't me." No answer, but she was still there. "I know you're upset, but this has got to stop."

"Bitch," she repeated, this time punctuated by what sounded like a sob. Did she even *know* yet that Ray was dead? Then she hung up.

"What was that about?" Norrie asked.

"Ray Mentone's sister."

"His *sister?* What's she got to do with you?"

"Long arm of coincidence. That fellow who was killed, Jerry Zeibach?" She nodded. "Mentone was his brother-in-law. I met Zeibach once, the night before he died—saw him intimidating an old woman, so I butted in. His wife keeps calling me. She somehow got the idea that he and I . . . Dreadful guy, by the way. Ironically, from what I've heard since, I was one of the few women in New York he *wasn't* screwing."

"Why does she think you were?"

"I don't know. Claims my name was all over his appointment book—which, of course, nobody can find. If that asshole were *my* husband, which he'd never be, they wouldn't have to look very far to find out who offed him. And I'd want a public service award for it."

She chuckled. "You are a funny lady, Liz."

"Praise from the champ! I could never get up in a club and do stand-up the way you did. Boy, you were good."

"A long time ago," she said with an upside-down smile, "a very long time ago—and you can never go back."

The sudden sadness that crossed her face touched something in me that wanted to go back as much as Norrie did—and knew, as she knew, how impossible that was. I felt my eyes fill up. Maybe the scotch was working too well. I had to break this new mood. "You think my reflections on Slimeball Zeibach are funny, let me tell you about last night with Darlin' Percy." Which I proceeded to do—the whole damned thing, including his swooping me romantically off to bed, and my last-minute change of heart.

We laughed together like the girlfriends we'd been twenty years ago. "So you ran out of there in mid-seduction and came home?" she asked, wiping a laugh tear.

"Yes," I said, coming back to earth with a thud. Running off to Ike's the way I had was something I felt too rotten about to mention, even to Norrie, who'd have understood. "But," I finished, delivering the punch line even though the serendipitous mirth of the moment had abruptly left me, "I call up this morning to apologize—after all, I *do* have to work with the guy. Well, he says, 'Oh, fine, no problem, darlin'' and then I hear him talking to *another* darlin' lying right next to him. She was under the bed for all I know, ready to move up when I ran out."

Norrie laughed a new burst. "You'll have to fix me up with that one. Sounds like just my speed."

"Only if you play your cards right." I finished the last bit of scotch and shook my head slowly. "There seems something so wrong about my sitting here laughing when— Look, I have a million and a half calls to make about this and—"

"I know. I'm leaving. Glad I was here when you got home though. Don't beat yourself up for the giggles, Liz. You had a shock and you had to come down off it. This was as good a way as any." Her brow furrowed with a thought. "I wonder if he was in there with Margaret when I left."

"Quarter of seven? Maybe. So then you went over to Bloomingdale's? The sweater's good, by the way."

"Yeah. Thanks." She held her arms out and swiveled in graceful parody of a showroom model. "Brave new red—what the unemployed will be wearing this year."

Chapter 29

I spent the next hour or so on the phone, propped up in bed. I hadn't heard from Margaret, which probably meant that she was still being questioned—or that the police hadn't yet found her, or that she'd run off to Mexico or somewhere. No, strike that one. Margaret would never run away. I left a message on her machine and rang Selma Weidenfeld, her secretary. If anyone knew where Margaret was, it would be Selma.

It turned out, the police had figured the same thing. Joe Libuti had just left her apartment, in fact—and taken Margaret downtown for questioning.

"Margaret was at your place?"

"Yes. Oh, Liz, something . . . something *terrible's* happening."

"You're right, Sel. I'd certainly describe a murder as terrible."

"Of course," she said impatiently, "but that's not what I mean. What's terrible is that someone tried to *frame* my Margaret for it!" The melodramatic TV-show verb sounded odd passing her motherly lips.

"Uh-huh," I said neutrally, hoping she'd go on.

"Judge for yourself. I was just putting my Weight Watchers in the microwave, and the doorman rings up. It's Margaret."

"You weren't expecting her?"

"No. I'd just left her at the office. She practically pushed me out the door—said I'd been working too hard lately. I begged her to leave too. It was almost six and she looked so tired. But she said she couldn't. And then there she is, looking frantic with worry. Liz, can you imagine? Some . . . some monster called her up and said he was my super. Said I'd had a heart attack!"

One sure way to get her out of the office, I thought. But, hot on the heels of that thought, came another. *Who knew whether Margaret ever actually got that call? It was only her word.*

"He was an evil man, that Ray Mentone," Selma said, her voice vibrating with intensity. "He was responsible for the death of Margaret's little sister, did you know that? Might as well have killed that girl with his own hands. I'm not sorry he's dead. But for someone to kill him in my Margaret's office—to try to . . . to ruin her life . . ." She was speechless with the indignity of it.

"Sel," I asked, trying to make it sound not too important, what time did Margaret get to your place?"

"Six-thirty," she said, sounding absolutely certain. "Oh, Liz, what are we going to *do?* Margaret's worked so hard to get where she is, and now *this!*" Her voice shook with incipient tears.

I tried to calm her down, say some right things. They seemed to help a little. Whether or not I believed them myself was another story. I told her, if she heard from Margaret, to ask her to call me.

I called the *Times* and, as it happened, got an old real estate reporter who'd recently been exiled to hatch, match, and scratch duty.

"Wondered if you were planning to do an obit on Ray Mentone, Murray. I mean his murder'll be all over page one, but—"

"Sure, Liz, why not? But who's your client here? I can't see that Margaret would care about Ray's final notices." A cynical chuckle. "Considering she punched his ticket."

"I'm not at all sure she did—and the police aren't either," I added. "But, to answer your question, I'm representing Stover International."

"Back on track with Alfie, are you? Congratulations! I knew Ray was over there, for what now, year or so?"

"About that," I replied, realizing that I had no idea at all how long he'd been with Alfie.

"Lost touch with Ray after Margaret dumped him. What was he up to those five years, till Stover took him on?"

Beats hell out of me. "Some independent brokering. A little investing." It was probably true. "You got his vitals in your computer? Alfie was—uh—too upset to fill me in."

"Sure thing. Let's see. Last update Mom still around in Brooklyn. Pop dead. Brother an accountant in Teaneck. Sister in Cedarhurst. Boy, is she some unlucky broad, or what? First her husband then her brother."

"She sure is that."

"Ray was a good guy. I liked him. No way him and Margaret were ever gonna make it together though—too different. She came up with all the cash to start that business, you know. Ray never had a dime to kick in. Good salesman, but he spent everything he made before it ever hit the bank. So you don't think she shot him, huh? Maybe not, but she's tough enough. There was a lotta talk back when that grandma of hers died so conveniently, and abracadabra, our girl has the bucks to open a fancy office. And then when that sister of hers took a swan dive. Didn't hardly blink an eye, Margaret. Hey, my other line's goin'. Good to talk to you, Liz. Don't you worry. I'll give Ray a good sendoff."

A lot of talk? I remembered the photo in Margaret's apartment, the resemblance so strong I'd first thought it was of Margaret herself. What had Ray said about the grandmother spinning in her grave? Plain and simple, these people were implying that Margaret had killed her grandmother for money to start her business. Two days ago I'd've passed it off as malicious nonsense, but now . . .

I got John Gentle at home.

"You're a regular Typhoid Mary," he began jovially. John's sense of humor often suffers major lapses. "Is this going to rebound on us with Stover? The fact that your client Rooney probably killed his guy." On the other hand, nobody's ever accused him of taking his eye off the ball. Stover was potentially a much more lucrative account than Rooney.

"I don't think so, John." In fact, I didn't know whether Alfie had any idea we represented Rooney. "Look, all we know is that the man was killed in her office, not that she killed him. Are you suggesting we resign the account? And how come, all of a sudden, she's *my* client, not *our* client?"

"Whoa! Don't get snippy, kid. We're in business here, and we need to know what's what."

I managed to get off the phone without further snip and rang Seth, who was about to ring me, having just seen my impromptu press conference on the eleven o'clock news.

"Not bad, Liz. I think you handled it well," pronounced the recently crowned media-spokesperson maven.

"Thank you," I responded gravely. "Try and catch the morning network coverage, and have Morley order the transcripts of everything as soon as you get in. Look, I may buck some of the media calls to you, if you don't mind, so brief yourself, say as little as possible, and do not, repeat, do not comment on Mentone's relationship with Margaret Rooney. Okay?"

The call-waiting tone beeped. I said a hasty good night to Seth and flicked the button. It was Ike.

"You all right?" he asked laconically.

"Umm-hmm," I answered in kind.

"Are you alone?"

What did he have in mind? Did he want to come over? As cop or . . . ? You are a *nun,* idiot! "Uh, yes," I said.

"Well, *are* you?" he asked impatiently.

"Yes, sir. I am," I answered with military crispness. "But I really have to get to bed, I—"

"The question was not amatory." My face flushed with embarrassment and anger. "Liz"—his tone took a quick turn to serious—"some of the things going on aren't making sense to me yet. But others are beginning to. We're dealing with some pretty cute cupcakes here. Cute and dangerous. I am asking you, not bullying," he added quickly, *"please* do not, repeat, *do not* get yourself involved."

"What do you mean 'involved'? One client's right-hand guy has just been murdered in another client's office. I can hardly get on a plane to Paris—appealing as that might be. Look, did Norrie Wachsman get hold of you?"

"She did."

"So you know that when she left at a quarter to seven, Margaret's office light was on—she saw it under the door. When I found Margaret at eight-fifteen, the room was dark. The murderer must've turned the light off before leaving. Now, during that hour and a half—"

"Nancy Drew, get your ass into that blue roadster and drive the hell out of my case!"

"Good night, Isaac," I said sweetly, and hung up before he could answer.

I yawned extravagantly, suddenly exhausted. Lucky I was already in bed, I thought; it would've been too much trouble to get there if I had to. . . . The thought didn't progress any further before I fell into dreamless oblivion.

I woke at six-forty with an industrial-strength headache. I lay there for a minute or so and let it bash. Finally, I pushed the cat barricade aside and got up. This was not fun. My tongue was glued to the roof of my mouth, my eyes were puffed and bleary, and the jeans and sweatshirt I'd slept in felt, well, slept in.

Before turning on the shower, I made my painful way down the hall to the kitchen to feed the cats and make some remedial coffee. As it started to drip through, I reached for the Excedrin bottle on the counter and popped two, washing them down with the last half bottle of San Pellegrino left in the fridge. I'd have to restock over the weekend. Head still throbbing, I opened the front door, took in the *Times,* and flipped through it. Ray's murder hadn't made that edition. They'd have a later one at the office.

Back in the bedroom I turned on *The Today Show* in time to catch the tail end of a wrap-up of the story. ". . . had made a comeback in New York real estate, working for British developer Alfred Stover. Mentone is the second Stover associate to be murdered this week." Cookie Battistessa's earnest face filled the screen in a tight close-up. "Last night his life ended in the office of his former partner." For *Channel 4 News,* this is Cookie Battistessa reporting." Quick cut to a commercial. *His former partner.* Cookie's words reminded me that I still hadn't heard from Margaret. Where the hell was she? We had to talk, not just about the media, but, even more important, about reassuring her agents, and clients, and customers. There needed to be meetings, memos, letters. Shit! Why hadn't I started to draft some stuff last night.

I stripped off my gamey clothes and turned on the shower

taps full blast. Midway through my shower, just as I was rinsing
the shampoo out of my hair, I began to feel markedly better. By
the time I stepped out to towel off, there was a definite spring
in my step. All of what had happened wasn't so terrible, I realized. Life was, after all, a continuum. Maybe Ray was better off
in some other world, with his Cammy again and . . . Maybe
Steed Leonaides was too. And my father. Had they all met one
another by now?

I walked back into the bedroom and let the towel slowly un-
furl from around me and drop to the floor. Well, maybe intro-
ductions didn't happen so fast there. After all, Ray had died
only yesterday. Where was "there"? The Big Rock Candy
Mountain. *That's* where it was. I smiled to myself and started to
sing. I remembered all the words. What a smart girl! I ran my
fingers through wet curls and went to the window. Still kind of
dark, but it would be a beautiful day. You could tell that by the
colors—the rosiness hiding just behind the slate blue.

Suddenly I looked at my big black bag lying on the floor next
to the bed and felt sad as I realized that it had been alive once.
Just like Ray. Strange, I'd never thought of it as a calf gambol-
ing happily with its mother, only as a bag—a convenience.
Crass. How could I have been so crass?

I picked Elephi up and hugged his furry gray body close. "I'm
glad you're not a bag," I whispered in his ear. "You'll *never* be a
bag. I promise!" He meowed and jumped down.

It seemed like a good day to wear red. I flung open my closet,
pulled out a long red silk shirt, and put it on. It slicked back and
forth on my still-damp skin. A walk in the park. Wouldn't that
be a great idea?

I ran out the door and heard it slam shut behind me. The hall
carpet felt prickly on my bare feet. Why wait for the elevator?
Time was ticking away while people wasted it waiting for elevators and not walking in parks and not playing with their kids.
Where were Scott and Sarah, I wondered. Must've gone off to
school early with my sister, Roo. Well, *I* wasn't going to school.
It was too pretty out for that. I was going to play hooky with Ike
O'Hanlon. He'd let me. I'd make him let me—even if I was only
a girl. I'd go live with Ike too . . . No! A cloud crossed my sun-

filled mind and brought me up short. We're not going to think about that, are we? I laughed as I bounded down the fire stairs.

"Good morning, Gus," I called gaily.

"Mrs. Wareham!" How serious his voice was. A bad night, maybe. "Let me help—"

He reached for me, but I darted away. "No, you don't," I called out, "you can't catch *me.*" This game was fun! I ran out into the clear cold morning. Exhilarating. I should do this every — Suddenly a large yellow creature, a huge beetle, rushed at me out of nowhere and lifted me up—high up. For a split second I was suspended thrillingly in space, before I fell on its hard yellow back. Then swirling purple. Then just black.

Chapter 30

Sirens, flashing lights, faces thrust up against mine, breath smelling of coffee and garlic, hands reaching out to get me. "Get away!" I hear myself shout. I flail my arms around and try to stand up. I can't. They're holding me down. I scream "let me go," but they don't. They tie my hands up and wrap me up in a cocoon, so I can't move. I scream again. They will take me to a concentration camp. I know it. The showers. The ovens. Hopeless. I cannot do anything about it. I shut my eyes and try to escape to a sunny place behind them.

I was dimly aware of time passing. A needle jabbed my arm. A cuff tightened on my upper arm. I slept and woke, and slept some more. Once I woke lying on a gurney in a small, curtained cubicle—then, again, in a large, cold room with mammoth equipment hanging over me. Finally I opened my eyes and found them looking directly into Ike O'Hanlon's tense blues. I was tucked tightly into crisp hospital sheets. I moved my arms. They were not tied down. My mouth was so dry I could barely move it to talk.

"Hi," I said in a voice that was almost inaudible, even to me.

"Hi," he answered, sounding blessedly familiar, yet strange, somehow. I was profoundly glad to see him.

"Could I have some water?"

"Sure." He filled a glass from a carafe on the night table, pressed a button to raise my head up, and brought the glass to my lips. "Slow, now, Lizzie. Don't gulp."

I concentrated on doing as he said, letting the small sips irrigate my parched throat and mouth. It seemed to take a very long time. I shifted in the bed and almost yelped with the pain. "What . . . what happened? I hurt!"

"I bet you do. No broken ribs, fortunately, but you've got some pretty bad bruises."

"Tell me what happened to me, Ike!" I clenched my fists against another burst of pain and tried to sit up.

"Easy!" He pressed the button again and raised the top half of the bed a little more. Then he smiled, a vintage Ike smile that made his eyes disappear. "You're sounding more like yourself." The smile retreated. "You got hit by a cab," he said. "Wasn't his fault. You ran right in front of him. Luckily, he slammed on his brake and just nicked you. You got thrown up on his hood. That's how you hurt your ribs. Your legs aren't going to feel too terrific either for a couple of days, but, all things considered, it could be a lot worse."

"What the hell are you talking about? Why don't I remember any of this? Something . . . something's very wrong with me." Had I suddenly lost my marbles? I felt myself break out in a sweat of terror.

Ike put his hand on my cheek and stroked it. "Shh, don't be scared. You're fine now. Nothing's wrong with you. You were high as a kite on acid, is all."

"What?!" I sat bolt upright, and damn the pain.

"You dropped some LSD this morning. I had tests run on the stuff in your medicine cabinet and in the kitchen. About half the pills in your kitchen bottle of Excedrin had been treated."

I was too stunned to say anything for a moment. "Half?" I asked finally. "Why half, do you suppose? If somebody wanted to do this to me, why not all?"

"Because maybe your friend the trickster thought it would be more fun that way."

It sank in. My friend the trickster. I took a deep, extremely uncomfortable breath. "Do you have any idea which of my friends we're talking about?" I asked, wanting urgently, and not wanting at all, to know the answer.

He sat on the side of my bed and looked at me intensely. "All four suspects have been in your apartment this week."

"Five, Ike. *Five* suspects. Ray Mentone's dead, but he could've come into all those apartments—including mine—with Bobbie or with Arlyne, posing as a customer."

"They both say not, when the most convenient thing would be to finger him, precisely *because* he's dead. But, okay, five. I'm including Crawbuck, even though he may be out of the running as Mentone's killer. He claims he left the Rooney office at six thirty-five and the lover was waiting for him downstairs to go to a seven o'clock A.A. meeting way the hell down in TriBeCa."

"Mmmm," I mused, "so if Norrie saw the light under Margaret's door at quarter to seven . . . Hey, that clears Margaret, too. She showed up at Selma's apartment before that."

"Maybe," Ike said tonelessly. "But let's table that. Sorry I brought it up. I'm pretty sure the trickster drugged you, but that's a separate issue from who killed Mentone. So let's go over again who was at your place, and when."

"Bobbie, Arlyne, Vi, and Norrie were each there on Monday. All of them except Arlyne have been there since." As I played it back in my clearing head, something occurred to me. "Vi was over for coffee yesterday morning, and we both took Excedrins from the kitchen bottle. If she'd been the one, she wouldn't've—"

"Could you swear to that? Were you the one who took the pills out of the bottle?"

"N-No, I wasn't. I was preparing the coffee and—" I stopped and thought about it. "No," I said, firmly this time, "I *couldn't* swear that the pills either of us swallowed came from that bottle." A wave of nausea swept over me. I swallowed hard.

"You look a little green," he said, his voice abandoning its interrogator mode of a moment ago. "I've pushed you too hard."

"No . . . no, it's okay. Could you—this is going to sound crazy—could you get me a toasted bagel with vegetable cream cheese and a cup of coffee? I think I'm starved."

He smiled and leaned over to kiss my damp forehead. Could I ever give this man up? "Be right back."

I stopped him with his hand on the doorknob. "What do you mean 'maybe'?"

I didn't think he was going to answer. "I want it on the record," he said after a second or two, "that you're taking advantage of your situation and my basic good nature. We know that Margaret arrived at Selma's at six-thirty. The doorman substantiates it. Maybe Margaret slipped out the service entrance, went back to her office, did Mentone, and hippity-hopped back to Selma's."

"But Selma said— Besides, how'd she get back in without the doorman seeing her?" I asked with a gotcha overtone.

"I can see you're starting to feel better." Ike grinned. "Ms. Selma could've been waiting for her at the service door, just listening for a knock. Are you going to deny that there's anything that woman wouldn't do for her precious Margaret?"

"I guess not. So that's your maybe, huh?"

"I have another one. Maybe Norrie's lying about that light under the door at six forty-five. If she is," he added over his shoulder as he walked out the door, "not one of them has an alibi worth shit."

Chapter 31

Ike returned with the food fast enough to make me suspect he'd marched into some coffee shop and declared a police emergency. Some coffee shop? What one? I realized that I had zero idea of which hospital this was, or even the day and time. But for once, hunger outranked curiosity.

I took a huge bite of crisp, chewy bagel, with its tangy topping, and followed it up with a couple of sips of fresh hot coffee that tasted hardly at all of cardboard.

"Where am I?" I asked, sounding to myself like a Victorian damsel recovering from a case of the vapors.

"New York Hospital. The EMS guys were going to take you to Bellevue. Can't blame them—drugged-out broad, half naked." A wave of embarrassment engulfed me as I remembered from some faraway dream dancing out the front door, a long red silk shirt flapping around my bare thighs. "You owe your doorman a bottle of good scotch. Apparently, he fought like a son of a bitch till they agreed to take you here instead." A bottle? A case was more like it, I thought.

"What time is it? And what day, for that matter?"

"A little after midnight. Twelve-thirteen, to be exact," he said with a glance at his watch. "So, I guess it's Saturday—at least technically."

"When can I go home? What about the cats? Does my office know where I am? Does—"

"Whoa! Eat some more of your bagel. It's getting cold."

"But—"

"Now. Or you don't get any dessert."

I smiled in spite of myself. "Yes, Mother."

As I munched away, Ike provided answers—to at least some of my questions. "You can leave here in the morning, but you're not going home."

"But I—"

"You are not going home." He said the words slowly, giving each equal emphasis, the way some people speak English to non-English-speakers. "I don't yet know whether any other cute tricks are waiting for you there, and neither do you, so—"

"But—"

"But me no buts. Look. I know you don't want to stay with me right now." A cloud flickered over the blue eyes, but only for a second. "So be it. I called your friend Barbara. You'll stay with her for a few days. The Conquistador is near you, so you can stop by your place to keep an eye on the cats and pick up anything you need. To answer your second question, the cats are fine. I stopped by and fed them a couple of hours ago."

"How did you get in?" I asked, as it came to me that nobody but Freddie and I had keys to the new locks, and mine were inside the locked apartment.

"Ve haf our vays," he replied, his Irish mug trying unsuccessfully for Otto Kruger. "You now have a brand-new bottom lock. I had some extra keys made. I also brought your bag and some clothes. They're in there." He motioned toward a narrow closet door.

"Thank you," I said, my voice husky with a sudden throat lump that threatened to dissolve into tears.

"Don't say thank you as though I'm some kind stranger. I happen to have a curious fondness for you, Christ knows why."

"I'd be surprised if he did," I said, trying determinedly for the lighter note. "Did you happen to call Morley and let him know?"

"I did so happen. I told him it was food poisoning and that you were going to be fine, but were too sick to take any calls. I said you'd be in touch as soon as you got out of here."

"Thank—I mean . . . I don't know what I mean." I threw my hands up and finished off the bagel. I'd just come through a preview of dying. I'd dropped off the edge of the world in the middle of fourteen different crucial responsibilities. And guess what? Everything moved on without me—but I had no idea where to. "By the way, did Arlyne admit that she'd been shilling for Mentone's new brokerage?"

"Don't push. You always want confidentiality for your various buddies. Arlyne deserves the same from me, whether or not you happen to like her."

"Where's Margaret? I gather you haven't arrested her or anything." I turned my head toward the night table, searching in vain for a phone. "She's probably been trying to get hold of me and—"

"Shhh." He pressed the button to lower the bed flat, and leaned over to tuck the sheets in. "You'll be in better shape in the morning if you try for some sleep now."

I reached my arms up around his neck, pulled his head down, and kissed him seriously. "I have a curious fondness for you too," I said.

After he left, I lay there and gave the multiplying questions free rein to play tag in my head.

Why would any of them have pulled this LSD stunt on me? *Any of them.* In English, that meant Vi, Arlyne, Bobbie, or Norrie, whose name I felt a twinge of guilt even including. Or Ray Mentone—clearly the candidate of my choice, especially since he was conveniently dead. But that raised the question of who'd killed him? As far as Ike was concerned, nobody had a firm alibi. Margaret had the strongest motive. If she'd found out he was stealing her best agents, engineering lethal tricks to kill her business, and she already considered he'd as good as murdered her sister—well, she could shoot him point-blank, without a second thought, and consider it simple self-defense.

Norrie, I noted with some relief, hadn't been an agent worth stealing, so she hadn't known Ray. But the others had. To Vi he was a racist, who'd let her down. To Arlyne he was a bastard, who'd played on her fondest hopes to trick her into serving his interests. For Bobbie, he'd caused the raking up of a dope-dealing past and a narrow escape from death. Was any of it enough to make one of them pull the trigger? I didn't have a clue.

Drowsiness crept over me, giving no quarter to recently drunk coffee or disturbing thoughts. Next thing I knew, I was sitting in a huge yellow cab—a Macy's Thanksgiving Day parade float, sailing high above a festive, cheering crowd. Ada Fauer sat next to me, her round model's hatbox on the seat between us, whistling, "Come Away with Me, Lucille." The driver turned around and called out, "Way to go, Bubby!" I was surprised to recognize Elie Halevi.

Chapter 32

"Come now, let's put some clothes on. Your friend is here to collect you." The skinny nurse's West Indian lilt roused me. I'd dozed off again after the dawn patrol had woken me to check various systems and inquire how I was feeling. Sleepy is how I was feeling.

"Hi, Barbara," I said on the tail of a yawn, and tried getting out of bed. Shit! It'd seemed easier when I managed to do it sometime in the middle of the night to get to the bathroom.

"Let me help you." The nurse reached out her experienced hands and half lifted me while I swiveled my hips and got my feet on the floor. When I stood, Barbara wrapped both her long arms around me in a hug, which produced an inadvertent gasp of pain.

"Oh, God, I'm sorry. Your ribs!" Barbara sprang away from me, her strong, cheekbony face worried.

"Hey, it's okay," I reassured her, "just a preview of our glamorous eighties."

"From what I hear, you almost blew the chance to find out how they're going to be." She attempted a smile, but it was undermined by the alarm in the amber eyes behind their tortoiseshell glasses. Barbara Garment and I have been close friends for twenty years—since playground-mommy days, when we were married to our first husbands and thought we always would be. Now neither of us is married to anyone, and Barbara, through her books and numerous appearances on *Oprah* and *Donahue,* has become the guru of why men and women will probably never make it together.

Recently, we'd talked a lot about aging. Not whether we would or wouldn't lift faces or color hair, but whether there was really any *good* way to be an old woman. If my aching creakiness of this morning truly were a preview, I had my answer—and I didn't like it.

The nurse helped me off with the hospital gown and I saw for the first time the blue and purple bruising around my lower breasts and middle. It looked even worse than it felt. "I think I'll skip the bra," I said as I took the big black sweatshirt from her and slipped it on.

Barbara gave the cabbie my address and asked him to wait while we made a quick pit stop there to feed the cats and pick up some supplies that Ike had omitted from the hastily packed bag he'd brought to the hospital.

I took Gus's hand as we walked into the lobby. "Thank you," I said, "I hear you kept me out of a Bellevue straitjacket."

"Well, Mrs. Wareham"—he smiled, half pleased, half shy—"I know my people. I knew you weren't . . . you wouldn't . . ."

"Be doped out of my mind? I appreciate your faith in me."

"Ya know, later on some reporters were nosing around, but I didn't tell 'em nothing. Just that you got sick to your stomach and had to go to the hospital."

"Thanks for that, too." It jibed with Ike's food-poisoning story. With any luck, I hadn't made the papers. It occurred to me that I must really be out of it. Not until this moment had the possibility of publicity even entered my head.

My apartment looked exactly the same. That in itself felt weird—wrong. The place had been violated. Somebody's sneaky, malevolent hands had tampered with its contents. That should *show*. All at once I was furious. *I* had been violated, toyed with, dangerously manipulated—and not by a stranger. I went mechanically through the motions of petting and provisioning the cats. Then I clicked shut the bracelet of my watch, which instantly made me feel more like myself, and gathered my stuff as quickly as I could. I gave a fleeting thought to asking Barbara whether we could take Elephi and Three to her apartment, but decided that would be overkill. Ike had just changed the locks and I wouldn't be bringing in any potentially threatening guests.

"Let's get out of here," I said tensely.

*   *   *

Barbara's apartment is on the fourth floor of the Conquistador, which makes the view of Central Park quite different from the panoramic one that you get at penthouse level. Here, you really feel *in* the park, not above it, and sometimes I like that better.

She'd bought the place after the huge success of *In the Enemy Camp: Loving Men Who Can't Love Back,* and furnished it with the advance from *Combat Zone: Men Against Us.* Most people who knew her expected that she would live in a brisk environment of tweed, leather, and brushed steel, and were surprised when they saw quite the opposite. They just didn't know her well enough. The graceful French Provincial fruitwood, the flowery printed fabrics, the Limoges, were part of the Barbara who approached a blind date with hope, and arrived, bearing homemade chicken soup, at the door of a flu-plagued friend.

"Want a cup of tea? A snack?" Neither of those items was a particularly appetizing prospect chez Barbara. The tea would be Lemon Zinger or Peppermint Something, and the snack some kind of gerbil food from the health food store. At least you could add salt to her chicken soup.

"Tea would be great," I said.

"I'm going to give you some A and E. And some C too. I know you don't believe it, but they'll help you heal faster."

"I'm in your hands. And I can't think of a more comforting place to be," I added. "You're a lifesaver, Barb." I reached my head up and kissed her cheek. "Look, I need to hole up with the phone for a while, okay?"

"Sure. Come on." She picked up my bag and led me to the second bedroom, which looked like a country bed-and-breakfast you'd want to stay at. She patted the pile of variously shaped plump pillows stacked at the head of the pineapple-posted double bed. "Lie back and jabber all you want. I'll get the tea."

I reached over and put the cream-colored phone on the flowered spread next to me. My first call was to my home phone. I'd been so eager to get out of there that I hadn't taken the time to debrief my message machine. I was unprecedentedly popular. Morley, Seth, Vi, Bobbie, John, Norrie, Elvira Treemor, and last but not least, my favorite heavy breather, Ann Marie Mentone

Zeibach—only this time, before handing up, she spat out, "Think you're hot shit, don't you, L.W.!" No, I answered silently, not really. Not at the moment. Why hadn't Margaret called?

I dialed Elvira first, while the home number she'd left was fresh in my mind.

"'Allo!" warbled her bird voice.

"Hi, Elvira."

"Liz. I know you must be awfully busy with this dreadful thing that's 'appened to Ray, but I did need to talk to you."

So she didn't know anything about my hospital stay—the alleged food poisoning. "What can I do for you?"

"I 'ope you'll excuse me for gettin' you at 'ome. I didn't like to speak from the office, with Alfred about."

"Yes?"

"I 'ad an idea, you see. Well, actually Alfred 'ad it, only 'e didn't *know* 'e 'ad it. I've done some research and . . . that old lady, Ada Fauer, I've been tryin' to reach 'er. Do you know where she is?"

All at once something in my head clicked into place so abruptly, I thought I almost heard the sound. "Yes, I think I do, Elvira," I answered, knowing as I spoke that it was true. "What do you want to talk to her about?"

"About this idea. I'm thinkin' that if I could sit down with this Ada. Just 'er and me—two old ladies, like. I could explain it to 'er and we could settle the 'ole problem."

Barbara walked in just then with a tole tray of tea a peculiar reddish color, toast that looked and smelled like cooked shirt cardboard, and a pile of assorted big and little pills. There's a reason that at five seven a size eight is still roomy on her. I'm envious, but the price is too high. I mouthed thanks and she left.

"How, Elvira? How could you settle the problem?" I asked, half humoring her.

"The charitable foundation."

"The what?"

"You remember. When you met with Alfred the other day, he

'ollered out, what did you want 'im to do for those tenants, start a charitable foundation?"

"Uh-huh." I certainly did remember, he'd been so apoplectic that I'd thought his next words might be "And you're fired."

"Well, I 'eard 'im right through the door, and I thought, what a good idea! So I went to the library at lunchtime, and the next day I consulted a lawyer. It turns out it *is* a good idea."

I saw instantly how right she was. It was such a good idea that I felt ashamed for not having thought of it myself. If Alfie could subsidize his needy tenants and get tax breaks for it . . . and, my God, the PR possibilities. "Anybody ever tell you you were a genius?" I asked.

"Not 'ardly."

"What are you doing today," I asked. "Up for a drive?"

"You mean Ada's done a bunk? Left the city?"

"Depends what you mean by the city." God, we Manhattanites are provincial, even—or especially—those of us who come from someplace else. "How about I come pick you up at" —I looked at my watch—"one o'clock?"

"That should be fine. They say the snow's going to 'old off until tomorrow. Are we traveling far?"

"I don't think so. Where do you live, by the way?" She gave me an address in the East Thirties, and I told her I'd see her in a couple of hours.

I downed Barbara's pills with the cooling tea and gobbled a slice of the bread, which took an unenjoyably long time to chew. I eased myself off the bed and fetched my bag, from which I extracted my Filofax and a pen. The pain hadn't receded, but I was used to it now and moved accordingly.

Back on the bed, I reached for the phone and dialed 718 information. "In Brooklyn, Elie Halevi?" I spelled it. A second later a record provided a number. I'd lucked out. It had been a pretty good bet though. In New York, when you think Israelis, you think Brooklyn.

I punched in the number. One ring. Two. It was Saturday, he was probably driving. Three. Maybe it was the wrong Elie Halevi. Maybe the name was the John Smith of Israelis. Four. An answering machine, soft rock music preceding the voice.

"Hi, this is Elie. Give me the good news after the beep." At least I had the right guy.

"Elie, this is Liz Wareham. I—"

"Liz, Liz!" Ada's throaty croak. Thank you, God. "I don't know how to turn this damned machine off, honey."

"Ada! Just the person I was looking for. There's a button that says off. Push it."

"Where? I'm not wearing my specs."

"Oh, well, never mind. Leave it alone. It'll be okay."

"How'd you know I was here, Liz?"

"It took me a while, but then I remembered your neighbor, Weezie, saying that a cab was waiting for you when she saw you leave. You might've phoned for one, of course, but why? It wasn't rush hour and there would've been plenty of cabs to hail."

"That Elie! After he heard about Zeibach, he called me. Said, 'Bubby, you're coming to stay with me,' wouldn't take no for an answer."

"The police have been looking for you, Ada. Do you know that?"

"Uh, well . . ." She fumphed, her tone suddenly evasive.

"It's not about the needles, okay? O'Hanlon doesn't suspect you of killing Zeibach. I promise."

"Really?" Relief made her voice even throatier than usual.

"Really. Look, I need to talk with you about something very important. I want to come out there. What's the address?"

"I don't know if—"

"Ada, come on. This is *me!*" I snapped in a flash of impatient anger. She gave it to me—an address on Foster Avenue, which could've been somewhere north of Fairbanks for all it meant to me. I, after all, had grown up in Queens. I told her I'd see her sometime after two.

I broached another piece of the dreadful toast, which now tasted like cold cardboard, and tried to force myself to not get prematurely overexcited about Elvira's plan. Tough, because the prospect of winning the Westover war with honor was thrilling enough to have almost pushed the Rooney-Mentone nightmare out of my mind. Almost.

I decided to get John Gentle out of the way first. Mercifully, he wasn't home. I left a message saying I was out of the hospital and would see him Monday. With some reluctance, I left Barbara's number.

"Seth Frankel," Seth answered in an office voice that told me this was no leisurely Saturday for him.

"It's Liz."

"Great! Hang on, I'll get off the other phone." In a moment he was back. "You okay? Did you get home?"

"Yeah, to the first. No, to the second. I'm staying at my friend Barbara's for a couple of days. You must be going nuts with all this on your head. Inopportune moment for me to—uh—get food poisoning."

"If you say so."

"What do you mean?"

"Three separate reporters said that they'd heard you were rushed to the hospital half undressed, after you got hit by a cab you ran in front of." Shit! "I told them that what really happened is that the cabbie you were hailing, 'cause you were so eager to get yourself to the hospital with your food poisoning, was out to lunch and didn't see you dart out, and he nicked you. But I gotta tell you, Liz, what I said doesn't make any sense, even to me."

"Not much," I agreed, "but thanks. You continue to amaze me." I told him the true version. He'd certainly earned it.

"Wow!"

"Look, what I really need to know is what's up with Margaret. I left messages for her before . . . before this thing took me out of circulation, but she never called me and—"

"Not to worry. John took it over. She got in touch with him. I'm reporting to him on the media side and he's done some letters and memos for her himself. I mean *himself.*"

"Well, what did you think he was, illiterate?" I snapped, furious, for no reason that made any sense. I'd been unconscious in a hospital bed. I couldn't've done the work. But Margaret hadn't even *tried* to call me. She'd gone to my boss.

"Hey, don't bite my head off. You know, Liz, Herb at the *Times* dropped a couple of hints—some nasty old stuff about

Margaret, back ten years ago when she first went into business. Seems there was a fire in her grandmother's house. The cops thought it was arson, but no one could prove anything. The grandmother died, and a coupla months later Miss Margaret opens her own office with Mentone."

"Oh, I heard about that from another reporter," I tossed off.

"You did?" The surprise in his voice was clear.

"Yes. I can talk to reporters, just like John Gentle can write memos," I answered airily with perhaps just a pinch of childish spite. His call-waiting beeped. I gave him Barbara's number and told him I'd talk to him later.

I reached Norrie. "Hell, if you'd only let me stay with you that night, this wouldn't have happened to you! I'd've insisted we send out for pizza instead of Chinese food."

And Bobbie. "How'd you like New York Hospital? St. Luke's sucked. But I guess they did save my life—not that I deserved to have it saved, acting like an asshole drunk. I'm okay now—been to four meetings and I'm back on track. Art hardly lets me out of his sight though. Awful about Ray."

"What do you think you'll do, Bobbie? About work, I mean."

"Oh, I'm going to stay put. O'Hanlon said he didn't see any reason to tell Margaret about my . . . checkered past. He's really a decent guy. Maybe you ought to reconsider. Hey, everybody fights sometimes. Why, Art and I—"

"I'm glad you're better, Bobbie," I cut in quickly. "When I heard what'd happened, I kind of felt like I'd made it happen."

"You didn't! It's true, you really threw me a curve, suspecting me of . . . ex-con and all, I got so scared! But you didn't push me off the wagon. I jumped. Anyway, that's the past. All's well that et cetera." But it hadn't ended well. Not for Ray Mentone, it hadn't. But Bobbie was "back on track," and Ray Mentone was "the past."

"Take care," I said, "and give my love to Art."

Vi wasn't in, but Morley was. After we'd reviewed the dangers lurking in neighborhood Chinese restaurants, complete with the illustrative war stories of assorted friends, he ticked off my messages of yesterday. All except one had called me at home: Chris Maclos, who'd said that on reconsideration, she was ready to live dangerously and go with the Fiscal Fit brochure.

Score one for the home team!

Chapter 33

I called the Avis on Seventy-sixth Street, took a long, hot shower in Barbara's guest bathroom, and slipped on a pair of black leggings, boots, and a purple cable-knit sweater big and thick enough to camouflage my lack of a bra. After I'd toweled my hair dry and put on some makeup I peered into the mirror for an objective appraisal. Not great. Then again, I've looked worse. I dabbed on a tad more blusher, grabbed my bag, and walked out into the living room with the jauntiest hobble I could manage.

"I'll be back in a couple of hours, Barb."

"Are you nuts? Where do you think you're going? You're just out of the hospital! God," she added with a sheepish smile, "I sound like someone's mother."

"You are. Just not mine. I have to go somewhere with a client. It's really important, or I'd skip it today." Her angular face took on a worried look. She ran nervous fingers through her long, thick chestnut hair. I remembered that she knew the truth about what had put me in the hospital. "It's nothing dangerous," I said quickly, "I swear," I added, holding up my right hand. "This is a whole nother client. I'm meeting with two old ladies. Might even give us two a couple of role models for facing the A word."

"Your friend Ike's coming over tonight. He's going to be pretty damned upset if you're gone. He—"

"Is this *Barbara Garment* talking? My writer friend who's always telling me what a poor excuse I am for a feminist?"

"Okay, okay, point taken," she laughed.

"I'll be back way before he gets here."

One thing about me, I'm a terrible driver. I vacillate between too slow and too fast, and my attention tends to wander—just

when it shouldn't. Also, I have trouble about left and right. My
kids laughed uproariously at my efforts behind the wheel before
they were even old enough to talk. My friend Edna, who runs
an elementary school and knows about such things, claims that
I'm a low-level dyslexic. Two ex-husbands have used less techni-
cal terms, such as klutz.

I kept up a good front for the Avis staff, though, as I signed
numerous forms, nodded in earnest attention to instructions on
how to get to Foster Avenue, and finally drove the little blue
Ford something or other out onto Seventy-sixth Street.

Elvira was waiting in her lobby, and bustled out to meet me
as I entered the circular driveway in front of her building. She
hiked up her green tweed beaver-collared coat and slid into the
seat next to me.

"Right on schedule, aren't you, Liz?" She said it "shedule,"
the English way. "Where are we off to?"

"Brooklyn," I said.

"Ada is in Brooklyn? Does she 'ave family there?"

"No. Well, not exactly. Friends." I decided, perhaps a second
or two later than I should've, to take Second Avenue downtown
instead of the East River Drive, and made a right turn from the
wrong lane, drawing a chorus of angry honks.

"Do . . . do you know 'ow to get there?" Elvira asked, trying to paper over what I could tell was an instant distrust of her
chauffeur.

"Not exactly," I admitted, "but we'll manage. We're going
over the Manhattan Bridge," I volunteered, producing the single point of the Avis directions that I remembered as a confidence builder, adding for good measure, "the neighborhood is
called Flatbush."

"Where is the Manhattan Bridge?"

"Not to worry, we'll find it. Tell me more about the foundation and how it would work."

"Well, you see—oh, dear, I 'ope I 'ave this right—Alfred
would establish a foundation for the benefit of those tenants 'oo
couldn't afford their apartments at market value. P'raps Ada
will confirm this, but I reckon about sixteen of the twenty-four
fall into that category. In return, 'e gets tax advantages, which

will cover some of the money 'e'll lose by letting those people stay."

"Uh-huh. Oops!" I noticed an arrow directing me left for the Manhattan Bridge. "Sorry about that."

"But the *really* exciting part—the city has a new program where they're giving extra incentives for—oh, wot did they call it? Projects that demonstrate new ideas in urban living," she recited. "Now, I got that at the library—nice young man 'elped me, after I explained wot I wanted. And then the lawyer said it would wash!"

"Elvira, that is amazing! *You* are amazing. You haven't discussed any of this with Alfie?" I asked as I climbed the ramp of the bridge and sailed across.

"Not a word. Not yet. Some things make Alfred quite nervous. When we 'ave it all worked out, *you* can present it to him —along with all the PR advantages, of course."

"I'm speechless," I said, starting to turn toward her until I realized the car was veering too far to the right.

"Oooh," she squeaked, followed by a sharp intake of breath.

"It's okay. I . . . just got a little distracted." I followed the signs to Flatbush Avenue, an endless stretch of stores and apartment buildings, some going to seed, others already gone. "Now, let's see," I mused, having zero idea of where to go from there until an upcoming Sunoco station caught my eye. I made a beeline for it, even though it was on the other side of the avenue. More honking, but Elvira took it calmly this time.

"Three more traffic lights, okay?" instructed the pump jockey. "Then a right. Then—"

That's about as much in the way of directions as I can handle in one bite. I waited till he'd finished, thanked him, and figured I'd get the rest from the next gas station.

It took two more, as it turned out, but finally I turned a corner and we rolled up Foster Avenue, coming to rest in front of a comfortable-looking, frankly down-at-the heels yellow frame house with a deep front porch. "Here we are," I announced with some satisfaction as I unbuckled my seat belt and sidled out of the car as painlessly as I could.

"What's the matter?" Elvira asked as she watched me hobble to the curb.

"I—uh-fell last night. I was running to catch the phone and I . . . tripped over a cat." I managed a chuckle, and she joined me.

"Right there!" a voice from inside the house called in response to the laryngitic bell. After a few minutes the door was opened by a chunky young woman with exuberantly tumbled wavy black hair. The long, loose shirt she wore over her jeans said BABY in large letters, with an arrow pointing stomachward. This was, however, old news. The shirt was pulled up at the side to allow said baby, now in its mother's arms, access to its late lunch.

"Oooo, look at that!" Elvira cooed. "'Ow old is 'e?"

"He is two month," his mother replied with a smile. Her Israeli accent made the plural a challenge not worth pursuing.

"He's adorable," I said, not lying. Round red cheeks and hair as black and spirited as his mother's. "Is this the Halevi house?"

"I think you want my brother. Downstairs—but he's workin' today. I'm Shulamith. I can help you?"

"Actually, we were looking for a guest of his. Ada Fauer?"

"Oh, Bubby! Why you didn't say so?" She stepped out on the porch and pointed at a ground-level door around to the side of the house. "That's Elie's apartment. Bubby expectin' you?" I nodded. "Well, that's good. Lonesome for her out here. She comes up for some tea with me, but I'm sleepin' so much— Binyamin's up every three hours to eat. Great old lady," she said enthusiastically, "I mean—" she began to add hastily, with a guilty look at Elvira.

"I'm not offended," Elvira said crisply. "You're a young woman. I'm an old woman. No shame about it. Call a spade a spade, I say."

Ada opened the door just as my knuckles were about to rap.

"Hello, honey." The outfit of the day was shocking pink with silver-dollar-size polka dots in lime green—a two-piece crepe number from the sporty forties. The effect, with her orange hair, was, well, interesting. She gave my arm a squeeze and pecked my cheek. "This your ma?" she asked, holding out her hand to Elvira.

"Uh, no, Ada, actually—"

"I'm Elvira Treemor." Elvira gave Ada's hand a firm shake. "I work for Alfred Stover." I held my breath, fearing that Ada might turn mulish and blow the whole thing. Instead, she laughed.

"That's rich. So he replaced Zeibach with an old lady! What did he think, we'd get along?"

"That's right," Elvira answered calmly, "and I think we will. I'm a great admirer of yours—the way you're fighting to keep your 'ome."

Ada stepped back and regarded her with a skeptical eye. "You got that same fancy English accent as him, you his ma?"

I managed to suppress my chuckle. "No, Ada, Elvira's Mr. Stover's assistant, and she's so good at it that he brought her over from London."

"Uh-huh," Ada said noncommittally. "Come on in, sit down —take a load off." Her tone grew warmer as she continued. "You can hang your coats up there." She pointed to a carved oak wall rack which looked as though it had been, in its original incarnation, the headboard of a Victorian bed.

The square living room was furnished in early Salvation Army, Crayola colors providing brightness where the sun was unable to. Posters of Bogart and Cagney movies were taped to the wall. I eased myself into a square green armchair right under *Rocky Dies Yellow*. Elvira took a seat on the red sofa.

"Tea," asked Ada, "or brandy?"

"I wouldn't mind a tot o' brandy," Elvira said, "very nice on a cold day, don't you think, Liz?"

"Sounds fine to me."

Ada poured healthy dollops into three unmatched jelly glasses and sat perched forward in a curved blue plastic chair of a kind I remembered from the fifties, when it had been thought avant garde.

"Well," Ada said, "I'm all ears."

"Mmm, lovely," Elvira murmured as she sipped her brandy. Then she looked up, cocking her head like a purposeful robin.

"Ada," she began, "I don't mean to be too familiar, but *may* I call you Ada?"

"Sure, honey. I'm a familiar kinda person."

"I won't beat about the bush then, Ada. I've known Alfred a long time. 'E's very smart at some things, not so smart at others. But 'e's not a bad man. May fly off the 'andle sometimes, but 'e's not a *bad* man." She paused.

I sat back and enjoyed the brandy. Ada was doing just fine.

"Westover is—"

"There's no such *thing* as Westover," she cut in hotly, "and there won't be!"

Elvira held up her hand for silence, and continued calmly. "Westover is a project that will be good for Alfred and good for New York." Ada started to interrupt again, but Elvira was having none of it. "It can also be good for *you.*"

"Oh, I'm dying to hear how you figure *that,*" Ada brayed, the sarcasm dripping from each word.

"Well, that's wot I've come to tell you, 'aven't I?" And so she did—step by step.

Ada took it in, offering several nods, a couple of head shakes, and a few ambiguous grunts. "And he'd go along with this, Stover? He'd start a . . . a charity to let us stay in our apartments?"

"'E might."

"What about the eight who aren't poor? What are you saying, he should just be able to throw them outa their homes? That's not right! And what about the park views? I don't have 'em, but some others do. Stover'll just build a wall in front of 'em."

"Ada dear"—Elvira held out her glass—"might I 'ave just a bit more brandy?"

"My kinda girl," Ada said as she poured the refill, and one for herself.

"Thank you." Elvira accepted the drink and took a small sip. "About the views," she said gently, fastening Ada with bright bird eyes, "you know that's foolishness, don't you? Nobody's *entitled* to views. As far as the eight rich people, we'll 'ave to see about that, won't we? Some of them may *want* to move, especially the one's 'oo are losing their nice views. Others will want to stay. Maybe we can work that out somehow. Wot do you think, Liz?"

Now that I'd been invited, I spoke. "I think that if you buy the concept, Ada, and your neighbors do, there'll be a deal here —with some compromises on both sides."

"What if we don't?" Ada asked.

"Then your side will lose its credibility—and when you lose that, you lose everything. People care about the tenants like you, Ada—the ones that don't have lots of money and can't just go out and get another apartment just as good as the one they have. But nobody's going to cry about a few rich people who've been paying bargain-basement rents and are now losing their views. Forget about it!"

She took a second to answer. "I wanna go home. Elie's terrific, so's his sister and the cute baby, but Brooklyn's not for me." She leaned forward toward Elvira and grinned. "If we make a deal, will you come by and hoist a glass with me sometimes?"

"That would be very nice," Elvira answered as she rose from the sofa, "very nice indeed." She turned to me. "Come on, Liz, we've got to be going. The ride back may be a bit . . . strenuous." I could see a shadow of worry cross her face at the prospect of reentering a car with me.

"Ada," I said as we stood at the door, "are you sure you feel okay about going back to your apartment?"

"I feel fine about it now, honey—specially since you say the cops don't think it was me! After Elie heard about Zeibach, he kinda talked me into getting a little scared. You know, with the murder right next door, maybe the murderer would think I saw something I shouldn't and all that."

"And did you? See something you shouldn't?" I asked, my pulse suddenly racing with excitement.

"No. I mean, that apartment was where Zeibach took the girls. He had a regular bachelor pad set up there." Nobody'd mentioned that to me, but from the tidbits I'd picked up about Zeibach, it was hardly a surprise. "I'd hear them go in sometimes, a little laughing at the door. But otherwise, nothing. I told you—those walls are thick!"

Chapter 34

"No, I think that's a right turn you want, not a left," Elvira said mildly, adding a sense of direction to my growing list of her unsuspected talents.

"Thanks. Elvira, just curious—did you . . . have you helped Alfie in ways like this in the past?"

"From time to time, dear."

"Well, for God's sake, you should be a *partner* or something, not just a—" I bobbled as I realized I was about to demean the job she did have. "I mean—"

"I know what you mean," she said kindly, a smile in her voice. "The times were different when I went to work for Alfred, Ms. Liz. P'raps if . . . oh, there I go, don't I? If ifs and ands were pots and pans, there'd be no need of tinkers," she recited.

I mentally whacked myself for being an insensitive clod.

"You ring me Monday," she said matter-of-factly, "and I'll give you all my notes so that you can present the plan to Alfred. Ooh, mind where you're going. Bear to the right now."

"Elvira, I *can't* just take credit for your—"

"Yes, you can. And you must." Her tone said the discussion was closed.

"Elvira." I needed to change the subject before I screamed at the unfairness of it. "How close were Zeibach and Mentone, really? I mean, do you think Ray would've known where Zeibach's little love nest was?"

"Mmm. 'Ard to say. Wot *I* was wonderin' was whether that's where Zeibach and Doreen . . . You know, dear, some people 'ave no sense of fitness at all."

Or maybe "some people" might find it particularly thrilling to stick it to their husband by screwing his own employee smack in the middle of his own troubled property. "If Ray ever found out

about that, he'd've been pretty mad at Zeibach, wouldn't he?" I
asked, turning west on Thirty-fifth Street.

"Oh, yes, I should think so. It would've been the end of 'im
with Alfred. I'm afraid Alfred would've 'eld poor Ray responsible for Zeibach in this regard and—" I pulled up in front her
building, stopping the car with a bit more lurch than was desir-
able. "Liz, if you're suggestin' that Ray would have killed
Zeibach over it"—she shook her head emphatically—"that
would surprise me very much—very much indeed."

I got back to Barbara's a little after five, and by the time Ike
came an hour and a half later was settled demurely in a wing
chair before the fire, feet propped on an ottoman, browsing a
Vanity Fair article on Susan Sarandon.

Before his arrival I'd flipped on the TV and dialed around,
hoping the six o'clock news would provide fresh information on
Ray's murder, but all I got was rehash. During the evening I
made five different approaches to the subject, and Ike stonewalled each one of them.

Other than that, we all had a fine time. Barbara and Ike,
who'd spent almost no previous time together, seemed to get
along beautifully despite his official opinion that she was a
knee-jerk feminist spouter, and hers that he was a bad-news
dominant male. We ordered in from the very Chinese restau-
rant I'd slandered as the cause of my alleged food poisoning,
and pigged out on twice-cooked Szechuan pork, General
Ching's chicken, beef with orange flavor, eggplant with garlic
sauce, and dried string beans. Ike and I pigged out, that is.
Barbara, true to her conviction about meat of any kind, dipped
into only the last two dishes, but she did join us in polishing off
the two bottles of Grgich Hills chardonnay that Ike had
brought.

At ten-thirty or so she announced that she was fading and
said good night. About two minutes later Ike hoisted me gently
out of my chair and walked me to the guest room, where he
helped me off with my sweater and jeans, and tucked my
bruised, naked body between the flowered sheets.

As he knelt to kiss me, I grabbed his arm. "If you think you're leaving now, you're nuts," I said. So much for my vows to take the veil. I was probably ill suited to the life anyway.

"Aren't you a little on the battered side for—?" In the light of the bedside lamp, his blue eyes were neon bright.

"Aren't you a little unimaginative?" I invited him.

He wasn't, as it turned out. Not at all.

Chapter 35

I was standing in a bakery line, my ticket with a large L on it clutched in my sweaty hand. I was horribly nervous. I knew there would be trouble—knew it. The women standing in front of me all clutched their big letters too. I looked down and noticed that my legs needed shaving. It was only then that I realized I was naked— we all were. All naked. All women. One by one they handed in their letters and then abruptly floated off into space. My turn now. "No!" the baker in charge roared, waving his huge, floury hand. "Wrong. You're not L!" His face was Jerry Zeibach's.

I sat bolt upright and almost screamed with the pain of the sudden jerk of movement. Pitch dark. No Ike. I switched on the bedside lamp and sat, panting in the early morning darkness, until the beat of my heart slowed to normal. All at once Ann Marie Zeibach's tear-stained face popped into my head. L.W., she'd called me during her last heavy-breathing foray into telephone vengeance. L.W.

I lowered myself slowly back down onto the pillow, thought for a bit, and made a decision. I checked my watch. Six-twenty —too early to call Avis. I wondered what time they opened on Sundays. Maybe Ann Marie wouldn't even be home. Maybe she'd be staying with her mother in Brooklyn, grief-stricken over her brother's death. But she hadn't been too grief-stricken to continue her phone valentines to me. I decided to take the gamble. At least a trip to Ann Marie's place in Cedarhurst wouldn't be uncharted territory like Brooklyn had been. My mother lived there when she wasn't in Florida, and even with my lousy sense of direction, I knew the way. That settled, I shut my eyes and drifted off, dreamlessly this time, for another couple of hours.

As I drove the little red car east on the Long Island Expressway, the sun flooded my windshield, making it hard to see even through sunglasses. The cloudless sky had that hard blue enameled look—rare in February. A good omen, maybe.

The way I figured it, Ann Marie had seen my name in her husband's book the night I'd met him, and jumped to the conclusion that I was the L.W. whose initials were all over his book, slotted in for fun and games in the vacant apartment next door to Ada. It was logical. I couldn't even blame her. In her place I probably would've thought the same thing.

Now, all I had to do was explain to her that she'd fastened onto the wrong L.W. Maybe she could even provide a clue to the right one.

I parked in front of a luncheonette called Zooky's, and found a tattered telephone book. I'd called 516 information from Barbara's and gotten the Zeibach number, but I hadn't been able to wheedle the address. I ran my finger down the column. There it was—Jerry Zeibach. Not Gerald or Jerome. Just plain Jerry. 17 Debra Drive. My mother lived on Andrew Lane. Developers out here in the forties and fifties had tended to name the streets they created after their kids.

The man behind the counter energetically provided directions, which even I could follow, since the Zeibach house was no more than seven blocks from where I stood. A few minutes later I pulled up in front of a large raised ranch, fifties vintage, with a white brick front. Four Tara-type columns, which looked as though they belonged to some other house, surrounded the Chinese-red front door.

I advanced on it, shoulders squared in resolution, and pushed the bell. The ding-dong chimes conjured up scenes from the lost world of Beaver and Wally. I could almost picture Mrs. Cleaver, just having pulled a batch of sugar cookies from the oven, wiping her hands on a spotless white apron as she ran gracefully to the door on spike heels to greet her visitor.

The reverie shattered instantly when the door opened. Ann Marie Zeibach's face was the color of vanilla pudding, punctuated by blue and red echoes of yesterday's eye and lip makeup, which she hadn't gotten around to removing. It took her a beat to register that I was really standing there.

"You're not coming into—" she yelped as she started to shut the door.

"Yes, I *am!*" I battered it back and marched in ahead of her. Ribs be damned, I'd shlepped myself out here and we were going to talk. She stared at me for a second, caught off base by my vehemence. *She* was the rightful attacker—the wronged party, not me. What was going on here? She tightened the belt on her fuzzy yellow bathrobe and closed the door.

"You gotta hell of a nerve is all I can say. Bustin' into my house after—" Her nose started to redden, signaling that she was about to cry. Mine does that too. We had something in common after all.

"Ann Marie," I said, "I'm sorry to bust into your house. I'm sorry about your brother. And your husband too," I added quickly, "but I have to talk to you. It's important to both of us. You're getting yourself sick obsessing about me and making these phone calls. And frankly, you're driving me nuts."

"Too goddamn bad!" Her voice quavered.

"Look," I said, feeling freshly sorry for her, "I understand how you'd be furious." I looked down at the flagstone floor of the vestibule as I forced myself not to say what I really thought —that the fury should've been directed at her late scumbag of a husband. "But you've got the wrong woman."

"Oh, sure!"

"And I'm going to prove it to you. Could we maybe sit down?"

She thought about that for a moment, curiosity battling outrage. "Okay," she mumbled, and walked down the two steps to the living room, her pom-pommed mules clattering on the stone steps. I followed her. It was a large square room with a fluffy white rug and three overly massive tweed sofas arranged, conversation-pit style around a huge coffee table that looked to have been hacked from a plastic redwood tree.

I eased into the sofa directly across from her. "You don't have your husband's appointment book, right?"

"No. Hey, I told the cops that. Somebody musta stolen it. You said you were gonna prove." She folded her arms across her chest in challenge. "So prove."

"How many times did you actually see my name—my name, now, not initials—in his book? Think about it before you answer," I added.

She rolled her eyes upward in concentration. "Once," she admitted finally.

"And I *met* him exactly once, at a building he was handling. There was a problem there. The police came and took everybody's name and address. Your husband"—I couldn't make myself refer to the bastard as Jerry—it seemed such a friendly kind of name—"must have jotted down mine so he could report it to Alfie Stover and Ray."

"Yeah, but all over the resta the book—I'd take a peek when he was in the shower or sleeping—L.W. all over the damn place!" The tears came and she rubbed them away with her fists.

"Ann Marie"—I leaned forward—"were there other initials too, like A.B., maybe, or V.R.?" Zeibach was such a prodigious screw-around. What if he'd met Arlyne or Vi up at the Stover office and . . . ?

"Ye—es," she managed to get out through a sob, "there were others, but I don't remember them. They didn't come up often. Not like that goddamn L.W." she finished on a wail.

"Shhh, now, shhh, it's okay." I continued making those noises, and after a while she stopped. "Let me ask you a question. Didn't all those initials come *before* he wrote down my name?" She looked at me and then nodded. "Don't you think if we were having such a hot affair, he'd have gone out of his way to *not* write down my whole name, after he'd been so careful just using initials?"

She bit her lower lip, which made her look touchingly young. "I wish I'd of had a kid," she said softly. "I wish he'd of let me have a kid. It wouldna been so bad then, his running around, you know? I said that to Ray, and he thought it was stupid. He didn't say so, but I could tell."

"*I* don't think it's stupid at all," I said, meaning it. "Sometimes men don't understand . . . things." A question hit me and I asked it. "Ann Marie, did your husband have an appointment with L.W. the day he was . . . the day he died?"

"Cops asked me that. I don't know. I got so bent outa shape when I saw your name there that I didn't look at the next page. Like a whole real *name* seemed so much worse than just the initials, you know?"

"Funny thing, those aren't even the initials of my whole real name."

"Huh?"

"Elizabeth. That's my *real* name. E.W."

Then my jaw dropped, literally, as something jumped into my head and almost exploded it. I sat there, reeling, and felt the sweat break out on my face.

"Hey, are . . . are you awright?"

"Yeah." It came out a whisper. I stood up. I didn't have to bother putting my coat back on. I'd never taken it off. "Ann Marie, I—I have to go now."

Chapter 36

I managed to get back to the city, but I have no idea how. My mind seemed to have gone on hold. I was operating on pure instinct. I parked the car. Sunday—no problem finding a space. Lucky thing. The way I was, I'd've left the damn car standing in the middle of the street and not given it a second thought.

I rang the outside bell and waited, heart pounding, a peculiar reddish haze clouding my eyes. No answer. I rang again—longer this time. After what felt like hours, I heard a responding buzz and pushed the door open. I bounded up the flights of stairs, unaware of any pain in my ribs or shortness of breath.

I reached the top, and then we were face-to-face at the open door, my eyes locked into hers.

"How could you?" My voice sounded small and faraway to my own ears. "How could you do it to me?" It made no sense. Three people had died, and all I could focus on was what Norrie had done to *me.*

"Come on in," she said buoyantly, reaching out a hand, from which I flinched reflexively. I did walk in, though, without even considering what a dumb thing that was to do. But none of this felt real and my usual thought processes seemed to be jammed.

"I understand that you don't want to touch me just now—that you're upset," Norrie said with a chuckle. "I don't blame you a bit. Here, sit down." I did, gingerly on the far end of the white sofa and let my eyes scan the chaste white room, which looked as charming as ever. "Want some tea? A drink?" she asked. The good hostess.

I shook my head. "No," I said quietly.

"You don't need to be afraid. I mean, I wouldn't . . . you know, slip anything in." She sat on the rocker and stretched her long legs out in front of her. She was wearing the new red turtleneck she'd bought the night she killed Ray Mentone. "I wondered who'd figure it out first, you or Ike."

"I knew after the rats that the tricks and Zeibach were connected. It would have been too big a coincidence," I said, eyes fixed on the twisting hands in my lap, as though I were talking to myself. "I thought it was Arlyne, or maybe Vi, or Bobbie. Up till an hour ago I thought so. I knew it couldn't be you."

"I'm curious, what tipped you?"

"Initials."

"Initials?"

"In Zeibach's appointment book. His wife was fixated on the idea that I was having an affair with him, because she found appointments with L.W. every time she sneaked a peek, and then, last Sunday night she saw my name."

"Ah-ha," she said, nodding.

"I went out there to persuade her finally that I wasn't the L.W. she wanted so that she'd stop calling and hissing at me on the phone at all hours. It suddenly hit me while I was telling her that my real initials would be E.W., that *yours* would be L.W. Lenore Wachsman. Then it all fell into place."

"Now, if we were reading a thriller, the next thing you'd say was 'what a little fool I've been,' " she said, a smile teasing at her lips.

"Fool is certainly the right word," I said bitterly. "Why, Norrie?"

"Why for which?" she asked, eyes wide.

"For all of them, I guess."

"Well, let's see." She held up a finger on her right hand as though she were counting "one." "Jerry Zeibach was a sleaze. I finally got so I couldn't stand him. He was a lot like Arnold, you know. Even insisted on calling me Lenore—same as Arnold did. Of course, he was a bit cruder."

As far as I was concerned, you'd have to go a long way to find someone cruder than Attila the Dentist, but Zeibach certainly qualified. "They even fucked the same way," she said, her eyes suddenly brighter—wet and shining. "They liked to hurt. We'd go to the edge with pain. Exciting." She saw me look away in distaste.

"Not your thing, Innocent Liz," she laughed, "not your thing at all. But it's mine. Testing the limits—pain and pleasure, pleasure and pain, till you can't tell which is which. Screaming with excitement when the wave breaks and you go over the top." The rapturous look on her face vanished abruptly. "But then they overstepped their bounds—started to put me down. Nobody puts me down," she said slowly, "so of course they had to go."

"Why . . . why didn't you just leave Zeibach the way you did Attila . . . I mean, Arnold?"

"Oh, I tried to finish Arnold off too. Several times, in fact. I remember once, he'd fallen asleep, and I was just sitting there in bed, hating him. So I took this heavy statue off the night table, an Aztec god that we'd gotten in Mexico, and I was going to let him have it, bash his skull in. I raised it up"—she pantomimed as she spoke—"and just stayed like that for, I don't know, two minutes or so. Then I put it back on the table and went to sleep."

"What stopped you?"

"Who'd have been the prime suspect?" She laughed merrily. She was having a good time. "Then I played some tricks on him. The same kind I pulled on those apartment owners—the ipecac, the lye. But not the paint. I invented that one specially for Kevin Craigie, the preening little shit. Wasn't that one funny?" She studied my face. "You don't think so? Well, no accounting for taste. Anyway, my last effort with Arnold was the bees. You remember, I told you about that."

"Yes, I remember." I felt like throwing up. "You told me Arnold had accused you of planting bees in the room when you knew he was allergic. You also told me that it wasn't true," I added.

"What a Girl Scout you are, Liz. I told you he tried to put me in the bin shortly after that. *That* was true. But I was too smart for him. I won. I made him let me go." A small, triumphant smile played on her lips.

One peripheral mystery cleared up—why Norrie'd come away from her marriage with no money. Under the circumstances, she could hardly have risked going to court. "But you weren't married to Zeibach. Couldn't you just stop seeing him? Why'd you have to kill him?"

"You don't understand, do you? The power. I had to get the *power.* He had it and I needed it. Just leaving wouldn't have given it to me. It was so easy with the needle. Bigger needle than I was used to when I worked in Arnold's office, but not hard to do. Medical book told me how—worked just like it was supposed to. I just fed him some extra booze with a couple of Valium in it and waited till he fell asleep after we fucked. Then, zap!"

Zap! Like Wonder Woman. Was that how she saw herself—the avenging heroine? "What about the tricks? Steed Leonaides, you didn't even *know* him."

"He wasn't supposed to die," she replied indignantly, "that was an accident. But I *did* know him—as well as I needed to. He looked right through me when I was there showing the apartment. Brushed me off, right in front of my customer, when I asked him about the maintenance rise."

"He probably didn't *know* about the maintenance," I cut in, my voice clogging with the threat of tears. "His wife was handling all the details of selling the apartment. He was such a nice—"

"Stop whining!" she snapped, her mouth twisting with a fury I'd never seen. "What do you know about it? They weren't 'nice.'" She mimicked my voice perfectly on the word, clicking another cylinder in my mind—which seemed to be back in some kind of working order. "Nobody's *nice* when you're a broker." Her words grated through clenched teeth. "They don't return your calls. They lie. They break appointments. They try to chisel every last dollar. Can't stand to see you make your full commission. No matter how rich they are, they try. And you're nothing to them—nothing. You don't have the power. You're just the little real estate agent. That's what Bebe Nordenheim called me once, 'the little real estate agent.'" She took a deep breath and ran her hand over her mouth, as if to forcibly relax it. "Bebe Nordenheim was a snobbish bitch; Fred Shepperton was an ass-pinching slob, and Kevin Craigie was a depraved little shit!"

"And what about me, Norrie? You played tricks on me, too—

and damn near killed me with that LSD trip!" My own anger took over with no warning.

She leaned way back in her rocker, and then swung forward to face me directly. "So we get back to what *really* bugs you. 'How could you do this to me?' " The mimicry again—and perfect. "You, my friend, are a hypocrite. Kind enough, but a condescending hypocrite."

I told myself that I was listening to the rantings of a crazy woman, but her words found their mark and stung. I bit my lip and told my lurching gut to calm down.

"Ah, I've hurt her feelings," she crooned mockingly. " 'Norrie, you can sell real estate. You'll be *great* at it! I've got this client. I'll talk her into giving you a job.' " I winced at hearing her throw my words back at me in my own voice. " 'Sorry, Norrie, I've had a fight with Ike and changed my mind about selling my apartment. Too bad you worked your buns off to make a deal on it. Oh, if you could use a couple of bucks, I'd be glad to—' "

"Stop it," I screamed, *"stop it!"* I took a shuddering breath. "It wasn't like that," I said in an almost whisper. "I didn't mean it to be."

"I know you didn't, Liz." Her voice was conversational. Normal. Warm, even. "You barrel along from success to success. Big job. Million-dollar apartment. Rich, handsome guy hot to have you live with him. Two great kids." She stood up and executed a pirouette—and not a bad one. "And when it occurs to you, you scatter largesse here and there." She came around behind the sofa and leaned over my shoulder. "A little informal social work among the less fortunate?"

I stood up and faced her. "Could we shovel out some of the self-pity here? Just *some* of it? Hell, you had so much talent. Your club act—your impressions. You're still pretty damned good. That was you, of course, on the phone telling me to get right over to Margaret's office that night."

"Uh-huh. I also got my friend Margaret out of the way," she said proudly. "Now, *that* was a little tricky, but I figured a heart attack for dear Selma would do the trick. I called right from the salesroom." She laughed, savoring the memory. "Oh, my God!

I'll be right over." Her Margaret imitation was as effective as when she'd pulled it on me.

"Ray?"

"Why did he have to go?" she asked. I nodded. "Come on, Liz, you must've figured that out. Ray was going to *tell*—about Jerry."

"He knew?"

"He knew we were seeing each other." I almost smiled at the decorous euphemism. "And where we met for our little parties. I think Ray was just as glad that I got Jerry out of the way. Jerry was starting to embarrass him with Stover. He'd've kept his mouth shut. But Ike questioned Ray about your rats, and then you accused him of playing the tricks. He put two and two together and came up with me. He threatened me he was going to tell Margaret." Her jaw worked in a little knot. "I don't like threats."

"Wait a minute. How do you know so much about what was going on with Ray?"

"Because I was fucking him too," she said as though explaining the obvious to a child. "Pretty tame stuff, actually. Ray was kind of gentle in bed."

"Why didn't you just kill him in bed—like you did Zeibach?"

"Oh, Liz, I *am* disappointed in you! I saw a much better way, a way to get rid of Ray and zap Margaret too. She dismissed me, that woman. She had the power to dismiss *me*—like sending back a side of spinach she hadn't ordered. I couldn't let that be. What could be better? Kill Ray in her own office. Maybe she'd even be blamed. She could've made up the phone call about Selma and sneaked back and done it. Even if she never got charged with it, there'd be that cloud over her and her precious business."

"So you made a Margaret call to Ray to set up a meeting before he had a chance to call her."

"Now you're getting it!"

"And when he arrived, there you were, waiting."

"Right. With my little gun—a gift from the late Jerry. We used to play with it sometimes." A lewd grin stretched her mouth. "You wouldn't know anything about that, would you?"

"I'm afraid my sexual repertoire is what you'd call limited," I said, sounding prissy and stiff. "Ray was already dead when you called me?"

"Yes. Nice touch to call you first as myself, don't you think? It amused me. I told you the truth about that night—almost. I *did* go to the office to clean up some things. I stuck around till Selma was gone. She usually left about six, and she did that night. I wanted to get Margaret out before six-thirty, to be on the safe side, because Ray was coming at seven."

"Why all that stuff about the light under the door at a quarter of?"

"That was for Bobbie. I wanted to make sure he wasn't suspected. He left in a rush just after six-thirty to meet Art downstairs. Bobbie and I are friends," she added, a warm glow in her doe eyes.

"I thought we were too," I said softly. "So while I was finding Ray's body, my dear friend was in my apartment, drinking my booze and putting acid in my aspirin bottle."

"You deserved it. You snatched your apartment away just when I had a buyer. And you offered me money for my time! What? Two thousand, maybe? Like a *tip.*" Her eyes blazed at the indignity. "That buyer came to me directly, from an ad. Know what I'd've made? Thirty thousand dollars. Full commission!"

I walked to the window and gazed out at the perfect winter sky. "Full commission," I said almost to myself. I turned back to her. "What about the rats? That was before you knew I was taking the place off the market."

"Well"—she smiled, the fury of a moment before vanished—"that was an impulse. Just for *fun.*"

"How did you happen to have all that stuff with you? Rats, pills—do you carry those things around just in case someone hurts your feelings? Or when you need a little fun?"

She giggled at my sarcasm. "Recently, yes. I'd planned the acid for you, specially. I knew you'd enjoy it. But I didn't know exactly when I'd deliver it. And then when you phoned to invite me for the very evening of Ray's death, well, that was as good as an omen! I'd have you find the body, and I'd plant the pills." A frown furrowed her brow. "But it turned out to be kind of a disappointment. You took them so soon! You see, I replaced about half your aspirin and then shook the bottle up. I'd've enjoyed the waiting—days going by, wondering *when.*"

She walked around the sofa and flipped up the lid of the small trunk that stood in front of it. "My box of tricks," she said, leaning over and reaching into it. "Don't get scared—no more rats. But what have we here? Some gunpowder. I hollowed out a very special log for Leonaides—a real light one—and filled it up. Boy, was I surprised when I heard it pierced his eye and killed him! Oh, here's Kevin's paint." She held up the can and looked at it lovingly.

Suddenly the reality of what I was hearing hit me full force, and I was, belatedly, scared to death. I started to back toward the door.

"Wait a minute," Norrie called. "I said wait a minute!" The force of the command, along with the gun now in her hand, stopped me cold. "You're staying right here," she said softly, "I'm almost finished."

"You must hate me very much," I said, my eyes hypnotically fixed on hers.

"No, no," she said tenderly, pointing the little gun at me. "I don't hate you at all. I love you. Your energy. Your spirit. You're too dumb to know that life is shit. So you make it work out." She bent over the box again and drew out a large syringe. "Now, let me show you something." She walked toward me, gun in one hand, syringe in the other.

Oh, my God, I thought, she's going to kill me. My mind raced around itself and came back to square one. If I tried to take the gun, it could go off. Maybe it wasn't even loaded. But could I take that chance? No, I couldn't. And the syringe . . . "Norrie, Norrie, please—"

"This is how it's done." With a smile she quickly put the gun down on the sofa, made a fist, and drove the needle into the crook of her arm, pushing the plunger down firmly. I stood there and watched, unable to move, or even speak. "Now," she said cheerfully, "we have somewhere between three and four minutes left. Let's put them to good use."

"Norrie!" I unfroze and started for the phone, but instantly the little gun was back in her hand.

"Sit down." She motioned toward the sofa. "Come on, hurry. I don't want to take you with me, but I will if I have to. Now, sit." I sat. "It's show time!" she said with a flourish of her gun hand.

Norrie began with First Ladies—Barbara Bush, followed by Nancy Reagan and Jackie Kennedy. She shifted to old movie queens—a great Bette Davis gave way to Marlene Dietrich. "I cahn't heelp eet." Suddenly the delightfully musky bray broke off and her knees buckled.

I ran over and caught her before she hit the floor. But it didn't matter. She was dead.

"Norrie, I am so sorry," I said to nobody.

Epilogue

I twist in bed as I wake. My room is semi-dark. It could be six in the evening or six in the morning. I don't know which, and I don't much care. It's Tuesday, or maybe Wednesday—well over a week since Norrie died.

Ike had gotten to her apartment no more than five minutes after my call—well ahead of the rest of the police team. He'd walked in, mouth white-rimmed with anger, and skewered me with eyes that looked bleached.

"You couldn't let it alone, could you?" He spoke with a quiet fury that was scalpel-sharp. "Jesus, why couldn't you just let it alone!"

I switched into automatic pilot then. Gave my statement, drove the car back to Avis, collected my stuff at Barbara's, and, over her energetic objections, insisted on going home.

The next morning I dressed, arrived at the office not one minute late for the Monday morning meeting, and responded tersely to my colleagues' quest for fuller information on the suicide/murders than was carried in the papers and on TV.

Even if I'd felt like it, there'd've been little to add. The *Post* even carried an interview with Arnold Wachsman, DDS, about how he'd always suspected that his ex-wife was crazy, but, being the warm, compassionate humanitarian he was, had not dealt with the situation decisively enough. "Call me soft-headed, but I loved her," his last quote read. I'd've lost my breakfast if I'd eaten any.

It was the call from Margaret Rooney that pushed me over the edge.

"Liz, I'm so relieved this is all over. I know you lost your objectivity there for a while," she said warmly, "that's why I thought it might be best for me to work directly with John Gentle—just until it was all over. And now it is, thank God, so we can go back to the way it's always been. You know how terrific I think you are!" The old Margaret pat on the shoulder, but it wasn't working. "And Arlyne thinks so too," she continued. "You know, I've decided to take her on as a partner. Maybe down the line we'll even change the name to Rooney and Berg. What do you think of that?"

You wouldn't want to know. "Sounds fine, Margaret," I said, and hung up.

I told Morley I was going away and might be back sometime.

"When?" he asked.

"You never know," I said, meaning to smile but not making it.

I walked into John's office and made his day with Elvira's solution to the Westover war.

"Hey, kid, you've come out of this riding high! You're a real trouper."

"No, I'm not, John," I said quietly. "I'm not a trouper at all. You're going to have to see this through. I'm going away."

"This some kind of joke?" he asked. "Hey, I know you were there when Wachsman . . . Well, you're upset. I understand, but—"

"No, John, you *don't* understand. You don't understand at all."

I went home then and locked myself in. I called my mother, kids, sister, Barbara, and told them I was going to London and from there up to the Cotswolds to cool out for a couple of weeks. They wished me bon voyage, though Barbara sounded a bit suspicious and so did my daughter, Sarah. But maybe that was my imagination.

So here I've been for the last nine days—or is it ten? I don't move out of bed much, except to feed the cats. I watch old movies on television, but nothing else. Especially no news. I do not answer the phone. I ate my last can of Progresso minestrone yesterday, didn't finish it. I got sidetracked by a bottle of wine, instead. Down near the bottom, I was able to forget that if I'd only let things alone, Norrie might be alive—under arrest, facing a trial, but at least alive!

I still don't know where it went wrong. Where it broke down

for her, or why. But I *should've* known. Should've noticed. Should've been there. Otherwise, what does friend mean? We do throw that word around, and . . .

I drift back to sleep. I'm standing on the stage, back at NYU, where we did the rep plays. We're rehearsing a play, but no one will tell me which one. I can't remember my lines. The other actors glare at me, not speaking. "I can't help it," I cry out, "I didn't know which play to learn!" Then I see Norrie enter from stage left, the long hair streaming down her back, her velvet doe eyes full of laughter. She walks over to me and touches my cheek. "I'm sorry, Norrie," I cry, hardly able to get the words out through my tears. "I am so sorry."

I feel again a stroke on my cheek and a soft sound. "Shhh." I open my eyes and look into Ike's blue ones.

He continues stroking my cheek. "It's okay. It's okay, my Lizzie."

"How . . . ?" My voice gives out. It's grown rusty with disuse.

"If you mean how did I get in, I had your key—from when you were in the hospital. If you mean how did I know you were here, I don't know, I just did."

I turn my face away. "You were right. If I'd just let it *alone*—"

"She'd've killed herself anyway. If not that day, the next. Or the one after that. You're not omnipotent, Liz. You couldn't've stopped her." He puts both hands on my shoulders and turns me to face him. "And I'm not omnipotent either," he says quietly. "I couldn't've stopped *you.*"

He sits down on the bed and takes my hand. I don't pull it away.